Issued

Issued

A NAVY SEALS OF LITTLE CREEK ROMANCE

PARIS WYNTERS

TULE
PUBLISHING

DEDICATION

For my father.

I miss you every day.

Your memory will live on and forever be celebrated.

ACKNOWLEDGMENTS

First and foremost, thank you to my Heavenly Father for blessing me beyond all measure.

Thank you to my family for your support and encouragement. For picking up the slack and adjusting your lives so that I could get this manuscript done. Thank you for the laughs we shared about how I was writing a romance book, yet how you pushed me to finish it.

Thank you my amazing agent, Tricia Skinner, for believing in me. Thank you to Jane Porter and Meghan Farrell for believing in this book. Thank you to Sinclair Sawhney for pushing me with the edits and guidance to make this story the best it could possibly be.

A huge, HUGE, thank you to Liz Hess at Pearl Edits. I don't think I would have ever gotten the first draft of this book to where it needed to be without you. And thank you for all the lessons on blocking and for making me sketch out rooms. It was destined for me to find you.

Thank you to all my amazing CPs (especially Britney, Emily, Debra, and Despina), my readers, and author friends who make me strive to become a better and more daring writer.

And lastly, THANK YOU with all my heart to those men and women, their families and friends, who voluntarily sacrifice their lives, well-being, and time to defend this great country we live in. Your sacrifices and memories will never be forgotten.

CHAPTER ONE

Jim

WHAT I WOULDN'T give to be lugging around a sixty-pound rucksack and coating my boots and fatigues with dust instead of standing in front of my commanding officer as he thumbs through a file about me. Hell, I think I'd even take one of those grueling two-mile Atlantic Ocean swims through ball-shriveling, sub-seventy-degree water over this. My teeth grind as Commander Redding shuffles through the thick pile of papers, scanning the reports from the Navy doctors and shrinks before he delivers the verdict. I only hope it's not too bad. Not much worse for a SEAL than being injured while on duty. Unless we're talking being pulled from my men and getting stuck stateside.

I clear my throat and straighten to my full height. "Sir?"

Commander Redding grunts but doesn't look up from the papers fanned out across his desk. So I wait in his compact office on the Little Creek base, watching the top of his silver-streaked head while my ears focus on the faint ticking of a clock. Even within the secure walls of this office, the briny scent of the Chesapeake Bay reaches my nose. My muscles are stiff and sore and in desperate need of a hot shower, but for now, my aching body and throbbing head would be thrilled to collapse into the empty chair to my left. Still, I keep standing the way years of training dictate. Shoulders back. Chest out. Eyes straight ahead.

"Take a seat, Jim."

Thank fuck. I bite back a sigh of relief, walk over to the chair, and sit.

Redding compiles the papers into a neat stack and then places them back into the manila folder with my name on the tab before arranging the file in the middle of his spotless desk. Not surprising, given how even his camos are always immaculately pressed. He sits back in his chair and every flicker of relief evaporates when I get the first good look at my C.O.'s expression since I walked into his office. His furrowed forehead and tight lips are noticeable even within the creases of his sun-weathered face, a sight that ratchets up the anxious energy bubbling in my chest. Redding is known for being tough, but fair. Which means the doctors' reports must be worse than I thought.

Fuck.

I clench my hands together in my lap until my bones grind. Bracing myself for the worst.

"Can't return you to the field right now and, based on these reports, I'm not sure when—or if—that will ever happen." As expected, my C.O. pulls no punches when delivering this information. Even as prepared as I am, his words still hit like a series of iron fists to the chest.

Fuck. Fuck. Fuck.

I sit there in a daze with my mind spinning. I can't be kicked out over some stupid head injury. I'm meant to be a SEAL. This is my entire life. If I'm not a SEAL, who am I? What the hell do I even do with myself?

I lift my chin. No, this isn't fucking going to happen. I won't let it. "Sir, you can't discharge me. Not yet."

"Only so much I can do." Redding drums his fingers against his desk. "But—" He pauses, pinning me with his sharp, blue eyes.

I lean forward, my muscles urged into action by a flicker of hope. "Anything. I'll do anything to return to the field."

Redding nods. "Remember the discussion we had about a new program the military was considering? The one where you did all of those extra evaluations and signed papers, allowing us access to your files?"

"Yes." I frown at the abrupt change of topic. I don't see how those touchy-feely tests I volunteered to take have anything to do with my current predicament.

"Well, the military has decided to move forward with the project. And I recommended you as one of the first to participate." Redding straightens in his chair and studies me. "Of course that means your participation—your performance—also reflects on me."

A light goes off in my head. Now it's all starting to make sense. The program must be some kind of a new treatment for brain injuries. Hell, Redding doesn't have to ask me twice—I'm in. I'll even start taking the damn medications the doctors have been prescribing me, *and* I'll cave and agree to *talk about my feelings.* Which will undoubtedly be just as terrible as it sounds but, hey, I'm good for a little group therapy, so long as all of that talking gets me back together with my men.

For the first time since I entered the sterile, immaculate office, my shoulders don't feel compressed by an invisible weight. I meet Redding's gaze. "I'm in."

My commanding officer offers up one of his rare chuckles. "You don't even know what the program is yet."

My nerves start rattling again. Redding could be a tough old goat who'd just as soon swim naked through shark-infested waters as dole out too many compliments, but up until this moment, he'd never laughed at my resolve. My shoulders stiffen. I'm a SEAL through and through. *All in, all the time.* That SEAL motto has always been a perfect fit. In my years of service, I've protected my men and excelled at every mission they've thrown at me.

An image of the anger etched across Lux's face during our last assignment flashes through my mind and my throat tightens at the memory. *Almost* every mission.

I clear my throat and shake my head to chase the image away. "What is the program then?" Not that I'm worried. After all, I survived the grueling SEAL training and countless life-threatening missions. How tough can some woo-woo program with entrance exam questions like *"what do you enjoy doing in your free time?"* and *"if someone hurts your feelings in an argument, how are you likely to react?"* be?

Maybe the faint smile lingering on Commander Redding's typically humorless lips should have clued me in, but nothing could have fully prepared me for his response. "A spouse-matching program."

What. The. Fuck.

I cough when the saliva goes down the wrong pipe and the sound is harsh in the otherwise quiet room. It takes me a moment of hacking to recover. I blink rapidly as I try to find the words to respond.

"Is this some kind of a joke?" I blurt, before I have time to think.

"What do you think, Stephens?" All traces of amusement vanish from Redding's face, and his voice is stern. Right. Of course it's not a joke. Redding is a good guy, but he wouldn't know a joke if one walked up and punched him in the balls. No way he'd ever pull a prank like this.

"Sorry, sir."

I swipe a hand across my damp forehead. Is it hot in here? Because I'm suddenly sweating. A spouse-matching program? Seriously? When the hell did the military get involved in our domestic lives? Motherfucking grunts. This has to be related to all the stupid shit that's been in the media lately, about soldiers entering into fake marriages to help nab better insurance and housing.

"Look, I realize this all comes as a surprise, but frankly, it's a great opportunity for you. You're lucky that the committee liked what they saw, and I know you're the right man for the job. And according to this," Redding taps the file with one tanned finger, "they've already found the ideal candidate to be your wife. A civilian."

My mouth opens and closes a couple of times, but no words come out. I run my hand through my hair and stand up because there's so much nervous energy pulsing through my muscles, I can't possibly sit still. While I pace back and forth, my head spins, not just from the headaches, but the implications. The one rule I had for myself was to never get married again.

No wife. No children. No family.

Not after everything I went through with Raychel.

The reminder of that rule makes everything clear. I stop pacing and face my commanding officer. "Sir, I'm sorry, but I can't."

I'm not even sure how they can ask this of me. Marry a complete stranger? Come on. Why don't we jump back in time a century or two while we're at it? Churn some butter by cranking a handle, use a chamber pot whenever we need to piss?

Redding cracks his pinky knuckle, which is a sure sign that he's displeased with my response. "If you want to stay in the military, there is no other choice." Redding pulls a new folder from his desk, opens it, and taps on a page. "This woman that they're assigning you is the only option you have."

Shit. I swallow hard but hold my ground. "No."

Redding's frosty eyes narrow to slits, making ice trail along the back of my neck. "I suggest you think hard before giving me your final answer. Lux filed a report about your behavior, you know. Along with the most recent medical reports, you'd be smart to reconsider." He sighs and rubs his jaw. "Jim, you're a great SEAL, and you know the last thing I ever want to do is see a good man like you sidelined. But there is only so much I can control."

He slides the folder across the desk toward me and I thumb through the contents. At first, I'm so wound up that the words don't penetrate, but after a few seconds, I settle in to skim. According to the description, the military is testing out a program to lower the divorce rate and cut back on the dumb shit some assholes are doing to play the system. Just like I fucking thought.

"Second page lays out the details of the program," Redding says.

I grunt and flip to the second page. Blah, blah, just a bunch of garbage about how military personnel can be matched with other active-duty personnel or civilians, and how the committee screens us all for behavioral, mental, and personality traits. How all civilians in the program are thoroughly background checked. Like no shit. Nothing earth-shattering about that.

I flip to the third page and my heel starts bouncing against the floor. Fuck, agreeing to this program means an honest-to-God marriage contract. My eyes land on the middle paragraph and for the first time since I started reading, something like hope kindles in my chest. Interesting. So after a year, either party can ask for an annulment and, once filed, both parties will go their separate ways. No alimony, no court battles, no lawyer fees. Just a nice and simple split.

Must be the proverbial silver lining in what's otherwise a complete shit storm.

Still. Even with the one-year expiration date, every cell in my body is screaming, *hell no*! Run away! Especially when I spot the every-other-month, couples-counseling requirement. I'm trapped, though. I've reached that point in a mission where there's only one play. Only one way out that won't result in complete failure.

Redding knows it too. I can tell by the way he's watching me with that expectant lift of his bushy eyebrows. My gaze drops to the empty line at the bottom of the contract and my gut gives a sick little twist.

"Remember what we say, Jim—the only easy day was yesterday."

The SEAL saying registers, giving me that last push I need. My fingers tighten around the pen and my hand shakes as the tip touches the paper. I scribble my signature in a swirl of blue ink, drop the Bic as if it were a heated branding iron, and step away from the desk. Hardly the first time I've put my name on an important piece of paper and yet, somehow, I feel like I've signed away my entire life.

That's it, then. Guess I'll be shacking up with a new Mrs. Stephens any day now.

That thought only turns my stomach even more.

Air. I need fresh air and the roar of the ocean to soothe

the chaos churning away inside me. I turn and head toward the door, my head spinning.

A wife.

I'm being assigned a wife. Playing guinea pig for some shitty new government matchmaking program and being strong-armed into marrying a woman I've never met. By the military.

Redding calls out from behind me, interrupting my retreat. "Jim, remember, you need to make this work. For my sake, and for yours."

I glance over my shoulder and nod at my C.O. before hurrying toward the door, eager to escape Redding and his cell-like office and the shaky blue signature I'd left on the paper on his desk, like I'd sold my soul to the devil. As I open the door and burst outside into a sun-drenched day, one question continues to cycle through my head. Over and over again.

What the fuck did I just agree to?

CHAPTER TWO

Taya

I N LESS THAN a minute, I'll be meeting James A. Stephens, the man who's assigned to be my husband, for the first time. A groan rumbles past my lips, my breath fogging the shield in front of my eyes. I clutch my left fist and downshift to third gear, and the loud whoosh of the wind against the bike drops a little in volume. The GPS alerts me through my earbuds that his house is three hundred feet away. What the hell am I thinking marrying a perfect stranger?

Oh, yeah. I'm homeless. My father was murdered. And the people responsible are walking free because there wasn't enough evidence to convict the bastards. So, what better way for a fresh start on life than to volunteer to be assigned as a spouse to a member of the military? Didn't sound so bad after everything I'd lost. Everything that was taken from me.

My heart hammers against my rib cage as my right thumb, ring finger and pinky reduce the throttle on my bike, two of my fingers always on the front brake. Some days, I wish I had a sibling, someone to grieve with over the loss of my father. After five months, the painful ache hurts as much as the day they lowered my dad's coffin into the ground. I sigh and dip my shoulder as I lean into the unfamiliar turn of this street.

Virginia Beach, with its salty ocean air and the constant lull of crashing waves, is a fresh start. Complete with a roof over my head, medical benefits, and a built-in bodyguard. Not that I can't protect myself, but when the person who killed the man I loved most is my former best friend that I've known since childhood, I'm at a loss. Marco knows me too well. And disappearing is the only way I can truly be safe.

When I overheard one of my former search and rescue teammates talking about the program at last year's conference, I choked on my water laughing. An arranged marriage? Not my idea of happily ever after. But the sly veteran quirked his eyebrow in my direction and threw a five-hundred-dollar dare out, so I picked up my phone and made a quick buck. What were the chances my shoddy application would be picked?

I snort. I should've known better than to trust fate. But I had to go through the screening process. God only knows what the repercussions would've been if the military found out I wasn't serious when I filled out the application. But since finding a match could've taken a while, I did have the option later to withdraw my application.

Except my circumstances changed in a terrible way. This new program is now about to become my saving grace . . . with a man whose name and address are on the piece of paper in my pocket. But who in their right mind signs up to be "issued" a husband, even with a rigorous screening process? At least I won't have to look over my shoulder here. Or be reminded of everything that I lost at every corner.

My heart twists sharply at the memory of all that's vanished forever, before kicking up to a rhythm of stampeding wild horses the closer I get to the two-story, cobalt-blue Colonial house where my future husband and the officiant are waiting. Holy hell, I'm going to be someone's wife by the end of the day.

I pull up to the curb, kill the engine and push out the kickstand. Dismounting, I take a moment to look around while my ears adjust to the quiet after hours on the road. The landscaping is immaculate. The Ford F-250 looks brand new, or at least it's washed and shined to reflect even the dimly lit morning. The rocks lining the walkway to the front door are perfectly spaced, like someone had laid them in rows by hand.

Everything is just . . . too perfect.

I close my eyes and mutter a prayer this man isn't one of those people who has to line up his cereal boxes in size order. Or worse—alphabetically. Because I'm anything but organized. And I can't cook for shit.

I shake my head and pull off my helmet and roll my shoulders before reaching back to rub along the crease between my neck and trapezius muscles. Upper body muscle kinks are the one thing I hate about long rides.

I take a deep breath and make my way up the stone walkway. Time to rip the Band-Aid off. This marriage is my choice. My chance at a new life in a new place. No sense in stalling now. Each step is slow and methodical until the heel of my boot strikes the first stair of the porch, while my fingers grip the white railing like a lifeline. My feet stall at the mat in front of the storm door, eyes unblinking and focused on the small eggshell button to the right. My finger stops merely a hair from the bell.

Somehow, my situation hasn't felt real until this moment. The call from the Issued Partner Program committee the day after my house burned down was a miracle. I'd nearly forgotten about the application. The final interview had been three months prior and then radio silence. Perhaps fate does have something in store for me. I try again to press the doorbell but my hand freezes midair.

I shake myself. *Get your shit together, Taya. You can do this.* My finger crashes into the ivory button. *Crap.* Bending over and mumbling a string of curses, I yank at my finger joint to unjam it. The door clicks, and I recoil. A behemoth of a man stands in the entryway, tightlipped and unblinking. My earlobes burn from embarrassment. Every time I do something stupid, my earlobes decide they'd like to change colors. I hate it.

"Um, hi. I'm Taya." I extend my hand.

The red-bearded giant stands there, arms folded across his chest. Staring.

I stare back, blinking. "I'm . . . uh . . . your soon-to-be wife. I guess. Sort of."

"Not mine." The gatekeeper smiles wide and steps aside,

his arm holding open the door. "He's inside."

I curse myself. Perfect. I've already managed to misidentify the groom-to-be. And here I thought the most awkward part was over. Would've been helpful if the military sent me a color photo instead of a black-and-white, clean-shaven image. At least then I wouldn't have made such a stupid mistake. I suck in a deep breath and squeeze between the meaty body in front of me and the doorframe, finally entering the foyer.

"Jim, your future wife's here," the giant bellows behind me, causing me to jump.

Inside, a low, smoky growl rumbles from the man leaning against the archway between the hallway and living room, thumbs tucked into the waistband of blue jeans, his frame seeming to take up the entire entryway. The bill of his green, tattered baseball cap dips down and casts a shadow over his eyes. His mouth twists into a scowl while the sunlight seeping through bay windows spotlights the hard angles of his jaw.

Pushing off his shoulder, the man stands tall, his head almost touching the top of the archway. The fingers of my left hand curl and the padding of my helmet squishes beneath the pressure as my mouth goes dry. His charcoal-gray T-shirt stretches when he folds his arms across his chest, the sleeves tightening around flexed biceps. His lips press into a thin line while his fingers drum against taut forearms. "You're late."

The corner of my eye twitches, and I bite hard into the

wet flesh of my inner cheek, trying to contain the angry words threatening to erupt. While I'd like to blame it on being distantly related to the Huns, Mongolians are generally a calm race, contrary to popular belief. But he sounds just like my stepmother, who blew a gasket when we first met because I ran ten minutes behind for lunch. And growing up with the emotionally abusive bitch for a primary caregiver had been a special kind of hell, always having to defend myself and my actions to her. Maybe I should've looked for a program to be a mail-order bride to a yogi. Serenity would do me some good.

The redwood tree behind me glides past. For such a large guy, he's not only graceful but makes no sound when he walks. Like a freakin' ninja. He stops and his gaze bounces between me and my future husband, then smirks. "Officiant's waiting. Let's get this show on the road."

My soon-to-be husband glares at the other man. "Glad you're enjoying this, Bear."

Bear—awesome name, by the way—continues to the kitchen and I follow with Jim taking up the rear. The tension in my body eases a small degree. Being between two large men, two SEALS, offers a level of safety I haven't had in a long time. If only it could last forever.

I peek around Bear when we get to the archway. Holy shit. The kitchen is amazing and spacious. Everything is white, including the tiles of the backsplash, the gray granite countertops contrasting nicely. And the ceramic jars in size order. Countertop appliances lined up. Not a utensil out of place.

Just great.

My eyes drift from the stainless steel appliances over to the corner to the nook and my knees practically buckle. I can't wait to sit there and read in the sunlight. Especially with the oversized windows.

Bear steps forward and my gaze bounces back to the center of the room to the huge island where Jim is standing next to a man, who must be the officiant, while he glares at me as if I just ran my key across his pristine truck. Why the hell did he volunteer to have a wife assigned to him since he seems pissed as hell I'm here? Or maybe it's just me that rubs him the wrong way.

I focus my attention to my feet when my heart begins to bang against its boney prison. During the final interview, the member of the committee assigned to me explained how the military hopes the program will reduce the divorce rates among special ops personnel by pairing them with compatible spouses. I'm starting to think they have a few kinks to work out of their system, though. How else could they think *I'm* a good fit for him?

When I look up, everyone is staring at me. Guess this is it. Time to get married. I force a smile onto my face and walk over to stand next to Jim, placing my helmet on the countertop once I'm beside him. Bear stands across from us, arms folded, and the corners of his lips twitch as if he's fighting a smile. Glad someone finds this amusing.

The man looks up from the paperwork splayed out in

front of him. "Now that everyone is here, I just need both of you to look over the marriage license. Make sure your information is accurate. Once that is complete, I'll have your witness sign it."

"Witness? I didn't bring one." My voice cracks at the end.

"Senior Chief Stephens requested Lieutenant Commander Donaghue be present. But there's no statutory requirement that witnesses be present at the marriage ceremony in Virginia," the officiant says as he hands me the license.

I take it and glance over my information. Everything is perfect. Well, except for the fact that my former street address is now a vacant lot since the fire. My throat tightens and my palms start to sweat. Fire? That was far too kind. Arson. A monster, formerly one of my best friends, had burned my house to the ground, and that knowledge has haunted me every day since.

I can't think about this now. I swallow past the lump in my throat and hand the license over to Jim to peruse. When he is done, he hands it back to the officiant.

Once he completes his section of the license and everyone signs off, Jim walks the men out. I follow behind but stop in the foyer as the rest of the group heads outside. My shoulders sag as I sigh, not sure if I am relieved or sad. This is my new life, complete with a new home and a new husband. If only it were under different circumstances. At least for me.

The Eldorado stone fireplace in the living room to my right captures my attention. Since I was a young girl, I've dreamed of a home where I could cozy up in a room warmed and illuminated by the flickering light of a fire, breathing in the scent of pine as it burns. I walk over, running my fingers along the richly carved mantel lined with various pictures of Jim, the largest frame showing him in uniform.

Navy.

My hand involuntarily lifts and I'm tempted to touch the thin gold line that trails down the cobalt-black picture frame. I hold back. Jim might not appreciate me touching his things.

Instead, I examine his face.

His expression is neutral, but his eyes are intense. I take a step back and his gaze burrows straight through me. I squint and lean in to examine the picture. Rows of service ribbons and medals adorn his uniform. The purple service ribbon and navy-blue service ribbon with a white center stripe grab my attention.

Purple Heart and Navy Cross.

Not every person shows extraordinary acts of heroism when the shit hits the fan.

"You can sleep in the guest room. I've moved most of my stuff out of there." Jim's baritone voice vibrates through the room.

I spin around and find him standing in the foyer, his gaze bouncing between the picture and me. Without saying another word, he pivots and begins to head up the stairs, pausing after a few steps to crane his neck over his shoulder, his large hand wrapping around the wooden banister. "You coming?"

My cheeks heat as I nod and make my way over to the staircase then climb up behind him. My gaze roams over Jim's jeans, boot-cut and frayed at the seams. They're worked in and worn, sitting on narrow hips. I swallow hard when my eyes travel lower. But then his smooth gait from moments ago falters and his cadence worsens with every step.

We're halfway up when he pauses. His shoulders slump and he drops his head. His stance is achingly familiar. How often had I struggled to take one more step forward only for life to suck the energy out of me?

My gut twists and I remove my hands from my pockets in case I need to catch Jim should he falter. Who am I kidding? He's such a goliath. Both of us would go crashing down to the first-floor landing. When Jim continues up the stairs, I follow without hesitation.

He leads me down the hall. His steps are smoother now, though he's noticeably slower than he had been downstairs. I'm so intent on studying his gait to make sure he's alright that the rooms we pass do so in a blur.

"This is it." He opens the door midway down the hall and steps aside so I can walk in.

The curtains are white lace and look more like the doilies my *emee* used to knit than actual window coverings. I chuckle. Maybe Jim's own grandmother helped him decorate. A giant stuffed bear is stationed in the corner to my right and a garish pink lamp, glass crystals dripping from the lightshade, adorns the bedside table. I've never been much for interior design, but the inside of my bedroom looks like the crew of HGTV uses the space for ritual sacrifices once a month.

I blink rapidly, trying to take in the sight before me. "Dear God." Millions of flowers and decorative designs compete for dominance on the quilted blanket covering the bed, but nothing can distract from that bold neon pink.

"I have the receipt. If you want to exchange it for something else, you can." He's still standing by the door, but he slouches and runs his thumbs across his fingertips, dipping his chin.

I want to laugh at the absurdity of the room but the vulnerability in his stance stops me mid-smile. Crap. This is unfair.

He crosses his arms again and tilts his head to the side, and I can't help the small smile that spreads across my lips. God, my father used to cock his head like that whenever I took too long to answer.

Pain stabs at my heart at the memory. To hide my reaction, I step farther into the room and make a big production of placing my helmet on the desk over by the window. The quilt and all of its flowery glory is certainly an eyesore, but in the scheme of things, what difference does it make? I'd wear nothing but pink and flowers for the rest of my days if it meant bringing my dad back. Besides, I don't want to hurt his feelings. The guy did make an effort to set up my room even if he was way off the mark. "No. I love it. Thank you."

He nods and shifts from one foot to the other. He reaches up to rub the back of his neck. "Gotta get to work. My number is on the island in the kitchen if you need anything."

Jim turns, and I step forward. "My stuff is still outside. Mind if I park my bike in the driveway?"

Hand on the doorframe, Jim's head cranes around and for the first time, his piercing green eyes are completely visible. His gaze lingers, traveling up and over the length of me, and my body clenches.

"I'll meet you outside. I, um, need to use the restroom." My fingers drum against my outer thighs as I wait for a response.

He nods then walks away, leaving me standing in the room struck by a pink tornado. So, after inhaling a long breath, I head toward the bathroom. Why the hell is there only one bathroom in this freakin' huge house?

A minute or so later, I dry my hands and head downstairs. The sun kisses my cheeks when I step out the front door, and I welcome the warmth. While the air is crisp and refreshing, I miss the blare of sirens and the backfire of passing buses. Virginia Beach is too quiet. It's not home.

I don't know if I'll ever have a real home again.

Jim is standing by his pickup, staring up at the sky. When the door closes behind me, he turns my way, then walks over to the driver's side door and climbs up into his truck. So much for a goodbye. With a shrug, I head over to my bike. A moment later, a grinding noise fills the air and I look over my shoulder to see the garage door lifting. When Jim pulls out, he stops next to me and rolls down his window. "Park in the garage. Looks like it may rain."

I glance up at the blue sky with hardly a cloud in the sky. A smile finds its way to my lips. I appreciate his show of kindness, even if the concern for my bike seems misplaced. Guess he knows something about the weather I don't. Can he be any more like my dad?

My smile turns bittersweet as I look back at him and nod. Once he drives off, I pull my bike up the driveway and into the garage, fling the two duffel bags over my shoulder and press the button to close the garage door before heading back inside.

No sooner do I make it back up the stairs and into the guest room when the annoying chimes of my phone go off. I really need to change that ringtone. But the sound is loud enough to be heard over the roar of my bike's engine. Dropping the bags onto the floor, I pull the phone out of my back pocket.

A blocked number.

Crap. Did Marco find my new number? My hand trembles as my finger hovers over the green answer button, but on the third ring I answer. No sooner do I put the phone to my ear than an annoying recording starts about ways I can make money working from home.

Seriously? I've had this number less than two weeks and I'm getting telemarketing calls already? What the hell? I groan, end the call, and plop down on the bed. Oh my God,

I've landed in a pile of marshmallows. Or maybe after the eight-hour ride on a motorcycle from New York, any mattress would feel like heaven.

The house emanates pure masculinity, with testosterone practically seeping out of the walls, except in my room. A burst of laughter escapes the depths of my throat as I glance around the room once more. I can't even imagine Jim going shopping for all those items. He put a lot of thought into setting up the room, although he might as well have been shopping for his grandmother's arrival.

I snicker. If he thinks all women are uber-feminine and love nothing more than pink and flowers and hearts, I must have given him a heart attack when I drove up on my bike.

Lifting my phone, I open up my photo gallery. Thumbing through the pictures, I select a bunch of Marco and hit delete. My chest tightens and my pulse thunders in my ears with each image of my former best friend that loads onto the screen while my free hand clenches the blanket, strangling the puffy cloth beneath me. Maybe I should've just gotten a new phone.

But then I'd lose the pictures of my dad and Lyons.

I pause on a photo of Lyons, Marco, and me. For years, we'd been the closest of friends. Lyons is the jokester while I'm the risk taker of our crew. Marco was the grounded one, the one I would count on to tell me the truth, no matter how blunt. Like the time I asked for his opinion on my prom dress, and he told me I looked like a poorly wrapped, silver Christmas present. They were like the big brothers I never had.

My throat spasms. Somewhere along the way, Marco had changed, had gone to work for Santoro, and used his family's bakery for illegal activities. He started lying and then one day he used me to get to my father. My fists clench and unclench. No way some random guy robbing a convenience store got one up on Dad. Especially for a head shot. Dad's death was a hit and it was my fault. I'm the reason Santoro found out about the investigation.

My jaw clamps tight against the tears blurring my eyes, and the force hurts my ears. Dad was a great cop and he would've been able to collect enough information on Santoro to have the bastard locked away for good. My stomach roils. If only I would've kept my mouth shut, he would still be alive.

After the funeral, I found a box full of evidence hidden amongst my deceased mother's belongings in Dad's storage unit. And after I turned it over to Lyons, who worked in the 104th Precinct just like my father, I packed up whatever belongings survived the fire, changed my number, and disappeared to Virginia.

Pain rips through my heart, so strong that I can barely suck in a breath. I turn on my side and tuck my knees to my chest. Tears flow down my cheeks. Marco and Santoro are still free to walk the streets while the only family I had left in the world lays under six feet of dirt. My chest heaves as I force air into my lungs to try to gain control, but it's no use. A strained cry escapes my clogged throat and I let the tears stream freely until all that's left within me is the coldness of the city I'd left behind.

CHAPTER THREE

Jim

THE SHARP, METALLIC bang snaps my attention to the rear of the truck. My hands ball into fists as air forcefully exits my nose. Why can't people respect my stuff? Like gently closing the tailgate, not flinging it shut with all the herculean force one can muster. My blood pressure skyrockets, and I strangle the steering wheel. "You're kiddin' me, right?"

Bear tilts his head forward as he climbs into the passenger seat, his eyes barely visible behind Oakley frames. "Check yourself, brotha."

I turn the key and my truck roars to life. My pulse pounds against my temples and I take a deep breath. I want to vent, let out how this whole situation, being stuck stateside and being treated by my superiors like I'm broken—useless—is bullshit, but I don't want to say words I don't mean.

The sight of the manila envelope resting on the dashboard, its contents a prickling reminder of my current circumstances, jacks up my heart rate, and I think I might explode. So, I shift the truck into drive and head toward Little Creek's base gate, barely able to keep driving under the speed limit. I slam my foot on the gas the moment we're off base, and the truck's exhaust thunders. The sound of freedom. But who am I kidding? No matter how fast I drive, there's no escaping.

Bear grips the grab handle as I whip the steering wheel to the left and skid onto Shore Drive. "Figured you'd take your sweet-ass time getting home."

"You know leaving a stranger—Taya—in my house unsupervised for the past twenty-four hours is driving me nuts. God only knows what she's doing. If she's moving things around. Or not putting things away in their proper places."

Bear curses under his breath when the tires squeal as we round another turn. "Marge's gonna kill you if you flip us. And God help the new Mrs. Stephens. Hope he created her with enough tolerance to deal with your level of OCD."

Easing onto the brake, I inhale and count to ten, hoping to banish the tension from my body. Maybe focusing on something other than my current situation will work. "How are things with Hayden?"

Bear groans at the mention of his oldest daughter's name. "She's still a stubborn pain in the ass."

"So, basically, a chip off the old block?"

His nostrils flare as he draws in a deep breath. "Shut the hell up."

I fight back a grin. "Don't snap at me. I'm not the one you're mad at."

"You're sure about that?"

"Cut the kid some slack. She's just trying to find herself." Hayden's the only one, besides Marge, who can rattle the big guy.

Bear's knuckles pound against the center console. "That 'kid' is almost twenty years old. How much is there to find?"

"So, you're saying you had it together at that age?"

Bear snorts. "I'd been deployed by her age and had been in my first gunfight in a country whose people were looking to kill me. Wasn't much room after that for weird hair and dumb facial piercings."

Hayden is like a niece to me, and this whole situation between her and her father over her appearance doesn't sit well. My own father would've used his fists, his belt, and even his words to remedy the situation—definitely not the controlled patience Bear exhibits. My best friend should be happy. His daughter is on the dean's list. Who cares if she has gauges?

But she's not my kid. I doubt I would be a good father. Bile claws its way up my throat. Kids won't ever be a part of my future.

My fingers run along my jawline. I should shave tonight; my stubble is getting long, and I don't need my commanding officer riding my ass about breaking regulations. Not after he appears to have *saved* my career. According to my C.O., being the first and only SEAL to participate—hell, pioneer—the military-wide Issued Partner Program is the only way to stay in the Navy. Taya's the only way. The five-foot-seven firecracker who made my dick jump for joy the moment she pulled up on the Kawasaki green Ninja.

I suck in a sharp breath at the memory of how she'd looked climbing off that bike and pulling the helmet off of her head, sweeping back her hair like the star of some teenage wet dream. I'm not supposed to be attracted to her, but the glimmer of compassion I witnessed in the way she tried to protect my feelings about the god-awful room decor only stoked the already burning embers of interest.

"So, is the fact that you're attracted to your temporary wife going to be a problem?" Bear waggles his brows, which remind me of flaming caterpillars. My best friend never holds back. Not during BUD/S. Not when he thought I was making the wrong decision marrying Raychel or when I fucked up in the Sandbox that one time, which ended with him taking a bullet in the ass.

"I can keep my dick in my pants." After six months overseas, in the middle of the desert, I'm accustomed to jerking off. Would it have been nice to get one last no-strings-attached, sinful night with a random woman before officially signing documents to be matched with Taya? Of course. Not that I'm a man-whore. But it'd be a mistake to have sex with my new wife since she's only temporary. Sex would only complicate our time together, and complications are the last thing I need.

My job depends on making this sham work for the next year. The job I've dedicated the last eighteen years of my life to. The one I've taken bullets for and buried friends because of. Which means, for the next 365 days—the time I promised my boss I would give toward this ridiculous program—my dick will have to continue being satisfied with the calloused skin of my left hand. Because cheating's not an option. Never was and never will be. And having sex with Taya might cause her to have feelings, and as much as I don't want to be married, I won't intentionally play with someone's emotions.

I press on the brakes and stop at a red light just as another unwelcome image assails me. Raychel, dark eyes narrowed, as she packs her bags to leave me forever. *What did you expect? You're never home. You have no aspirations to move up in rank. And with the injuries, Christ, you'll never make admiral. Did you think I planned on being just some SEAL's wife forever?*

A brick sits in my stomach. The truck lurches forward and my hands clench the steering wheel. I'm barely a shattered version of my former self, plagued by headaches, dizziness, and a damn injured body.

We pull up to the light blue Colonial, and Bear unbuckles his seat belt. "Taya's not Raychel. Give her a chance."

"I don't have to listen to your relationship advice. Contrary to what you believe, women see you as just an overgrown teddy bear. Your wife is the one we're all afraid of." I wave at Marge, who's standing at the door.

Bear's caterpillar brows pinch together as he exits the truck, then swings the door shut. I drive off, smiling for the first time after spending almost twenty hours yelling at a bunch of turd nuggets in the NUG program, and goddamn, more than half of them are nowhere near ready to apply for BUD/S. And, of course, the other trainers had to ask me questions about my issued spouse or give me shit for my participation in the program. I might as well have been one of the *new guys*.

Pulling into my driveway, I take a couple of minutes for myself and attempt to fend off the incoming headache, even though I know it's no use. They're a part of my current medical condition, and since I refuse to take medication, I'll just have to deal with the pain-in-the-ass cranial throbbing.

After rubbing my temples for a minute, I grab the manila envelope off the dash, flip open the tab, and pull out the larger of the two gold bands. Lead by example. I kick my fluttering heart into place as I roll the ring between my fingers. Slipping it on, I exit the car and head toward the house. A small rumble forms in my throat midway up the gravel walk path. Damn gardeners. Using the toe of my boot, I adjust one of the rocks back to where it belongs.

The fresh air does little to chase away the dull throb intensifying in my skull. Maybe I'll take Taya to the store to return that admittedly god-awful blanket for a distraction, and she can pick out something she likes. I shake my head and close my eyes. Christ on a cracker, I should've opened the encasing before buying it.

I walk into the house and head into the kitchen. The windows are open and a thin haze of smoke lingers. Taya stands in front of the microwave, hair in a frazzled ponytail.

The curve of her ass peeks out from beneath the edge of powder-blue shorts, and I clear my throat, focusing instead on the steady rise of smoke pluming around her and the acrid bite of charred bread. "What happened?"

Taya spins around and stumbles, almost dropping the plate of pancakes in her hand. Her eyes are wide, like a doe's. "I didn't hear you come in."

"Again, what happened?" My fingers tap the tabletop as I await her answer.

Her lean frame shrinks. Placing her breakfast on the island next to a glass of milk, she pulls out a chair. "I forgot about the first batch of pancakes in the microwave. And had set it too high."

With a fork, she piles too large of a helping of food into her mouth. Who the hell manages to burn pancakes in the microwave? And why did she use the microwave? I have all the ingredients needed to make them homemade.

Dear God, please don't tell me you sent a woman who can't cook.

She shovels another massive pile of food past her full lips. Lips that had my attention the moment she walked through the door. Her gaze bounces between the envelope and my finger. "What's that?"

"Copies of the paperwork." I gently toss the envelope onto the marble countertop. "And your ring."

She chokes. I can't blame her. Rings are a detail that had evaded me as well. Ours aren't anything spectacular. Just plain gold wedding bands. Something I never wanted on my finger again.

The cords in my neck twinge.

Maybe a drink of water will help me relax. Halfway to the cupboard, my body goes rigid, throat tightening. Burnt crumbs, a plate with charred pancake stuck to the ceramic center, and a couple of utensils sit in the sink. A deep growl rumbles in my chest. This woman invades my home, makes it smell like crap, and leaves a mess. I try to bite back the words that want to spill forth, but each filthy utensil and crumb is equivalent to nails on a chalkboard, and the pain in my injured brain ratchets up in intensity, causing flashing spots to dance in my field of vision. "Is cleaning up after yourself a problem?"

Every sinewy muscle in her body tenses up. "I'm going to clean it up. Figured soaking the dish would help the stuff come off quicker."

I turn too fast and the world spins. There's a ringing in my ears and for one gut-wrenching moment, everything goes dark. My knees buckle and I sway sideways until a small, cool hand slinks under my arm while another lies delicately against the heat of my chest before I can hit the ground.

Taya leads me over to the chair she just vacated, one palm a reassuring pressure against my chest while the other is now wrapped around my waist. "You should sit down."

The urge to sink into her is strong but I straighten and weave my hand between my waist and her arm to remove her grip on me.

My stomach sours and churns when hurt and confusion

flash across her features. But I didn't ask for help. I don't need it. I hate that she's seeing me like this, all weak and shaky. Taya reaches out as I walk toward the kitchen island on unsteady legs and my jaw clenches. I turn to face her, intent on taking the focus off my weaknesses. "What was so important that you got distracted enough to burn microwavable pancakes? And where did you get them from?"

Taya's ears turn red, the color crawling down to her throat and chest. "It was an accident. And I went to the small market down the street. How the hell else do you think I got them? Do I look like some magical genie who can blink and *poof* pancakes here?" She snaps her fingers in front of my face and my mouth contorts in annoyance.

The glass of milk rattles when my palm connects with the granite, and Taya's hand recoils. "Just because you're some lucky *dependa* who got into the program doesn't mean you own this house. It's mine. And I don't care what some contract says."

Placing her hands on her hips, she fires right back. "I'm not some child you need to yell at because I made a mistake. And what the hell is a *dependa*?"

"A woman who tricks some weak sap in the military into marrying them." The words hiss through my clenched teeth.

Raychel was the ultimate dependa.

I wince. Thinking of her name is like summoning Voldemort.

Taya's fingers ball into fists at her side. "*Trick* into marrying you? I was assigned to you. I'm not sure who I'm being compared to, but you don't know a thing about me. I'm not some *dependa*. I don't need you. Or any *poor sap in the military*."

I stare unblinking, lips pressed tight.

Her lips curl back in a sneer. "And why did you volunteer? Was it because your muscular six-foot-whatever physique isn't enough to keep a woman once you start overreacting to simple mistakes?"

"Six foot *four*. And I didn't volunteer. I was forced into joining the program." My heart hammers like it belongs to a rabbit running for its life, every nerve firing, causing an electrical hurricane to rampage through my body.

Her mouth opens but nothing comes out. Her chest heaves and she blinks rapidly for a moment before she takes a deep breath. She grabs the plate of half-eaten pancakes and scoops them into the garbage. "I didn't mean to be disrespectful. I'll be more careful in the future."

A wave of nausea sweeps through me as the magnitude of what I've just done hits home. This woman—my *wife*—lost her appetite because of me. My breaths come so damn frantic, so shallow, I have to look down at my feet and try to center myself. Feel the ground below my boots. When she heads over to the sink, I cut her off, gently taking the plate from her. "I'll clean up."

"It's fine. It's my mess." But she lets me take the plate, her eyes cast down.

"Taya, I'm sorry. You're right, I overreacted." My voice quivers and I reach out my hand, brushing a lone, dark brown strand of hair from her face with trembling fingers. I don't want to be the kind of person who makes a woman afraid. I don't want Taya to be scared of me. But my head—the injury—maybe it's more than I can control.

Taya looks up, her eyes glistening, a tear slipping free. She wipes away the salty droplet with the back of her thumb and raises her chin, no longer shying away from my gaze. "We both have our reasons for being here. So, how about you treat me as a roommate until we figure this out? I'll follow whatever rules you want since it's your house. And when the time for the annulment comes, I'll leave."

The look on her face halts me. Strange how tears can spike a woman's lashes and make her eyes seem so much brighter. I want nothing more than to dry those lingering trails away. How would she react if I gave into my impulse and leaned over to brush wet, trailing lips down her cheek and across her ripe lips? Would it ease the strain and sadness that wilted her mouth into a frown?

Freak out. That's what she'd do. Impulsivity is just another gift, courtesy of my brain injury.

Instead, I fight off the urge and look her directly in the eye to show her I mean my next words. "I'm sorry. I'm a little OCD. Never officially diagnosed, but I definitely have a few of the quirks."

She huffs and her lips twitch at the corners.

The tension in the room eases, only to be replaced by something different but no less devastating. After placing the dish in the sink, I turn back to her. "Having you here is going to take some getting used to, but it's your home too. I'll try and remember that."

My gut twists when she tenses at the word *home*. The same way I used to react when I was a kid and afraid to go home. Before my mind can continue coming up with reasons for her familiar reaction, she places a hand on my forearm, pulling my attention back to the conversation.

"Living with you is new to me too." She bites her lower lip, fingers tapping against her thigh. "Do you have a spare key? I had to leave the back door unlocked when I went to the market."

Fuck.

"Yeah, I'll get it for you."

We need to talk about precautions, especially since we live off base. She needs to be more careful. But the conversation will have to wait until tomorrow. She'll have questions, some I won't be able to answer.

I reach past Taya and grab the envelope from the island. Her brow furrows and she shifts from one foot to the other, placing a lock of hair behind one ear. Pulling the small gold band from the confines of the envelope and tucking the yellow packet beneath one arm, I capture her hand before she can lower it fully.

Her touch is like an iron brand, and I'm not sure if I want to let go or pull her close enough to burn us both. I compromise by slipping the ring onto her finger. Taya's eyes widen and the atmosphere grows solemn.

My thumb moves in slow, soothing circles across the

back of her hand and I enjoy the sensation a little too much. The skin is soft and delicate compared to the calluses on her palms. When she pulls her hand gently from mine, I offer her the envelope. "Your copy of the contract."

"Thank you." Taya slips past me and climbs up the stairs, retreating to her room.

I stare at the empty stairway for several long moments after the click of her door closing, lost in my own thoughts. What are her reasons for being here?

CHAPTER FOUR

Taya

NOTHING LIKE TOSSING and turning the entire night. Again. What I wouldn't give for the wail of ambulance sirens or the high-pitched squeal of a train. I never thought loud, obnoxious sounds would be comforting. What I wouldn't give to be back in my own bed, or look out my window at the city alive with lights, like someone had taken a handful of glitter and thrown it as far as the eye could see. I even miss the fearless pigeons who beg worse than dogs. Never in a million years did I ever think I'd miss those flying rats.

My heart sinks. Lingering on the thought of home only reminds me of the fact I no longer have one of my own. Or a family. And returning to Maspeth is not an option. I'm not sure if it will ever be. The parks, the handball courts, the bodega . . . they all remind me of my father. And they will all remind me that I am alone.

Maybe I should've gone away to college instead of staying local, not to mention living in my childhood home. Maybe if I had, leaving New York wouldn't be so hard.

Maybe I wouldn't be seeking the comfort familiarity brings—and the safety net it offers.

I stare at the ceiling and dig my fingers into the blanket. I'm here now, in Virginia Beach. To start a new life. Build a new family. Wallowing in the past won't help me achieve either of those things.

My gaze drifts to the bed and I wince. Neither will hiding in my room all day with this god-awful eyesore. I kick off my blanket, my lips twisting in a wry grin. God, this blanket is seriously awful looking, but man, is it soft. And warm. It gets the job done. Basically, I just have to refrain from looking at it for too long.

I run my fingers through my hair. My scalp is greasy and this humidity is causing my roots to gunk up quicker than normal. Guess Jim isn't the only thing I have to get used to, living here. My stomach knots in confusion at the thought of him. He's guarded and rigid, yet seemingly caring enough to decorate this room for me—he failed, obviously, but the fact that he tried makes me wonder what other layers he has.

I roll off the mattress and stretch when I stand. Might as well shower and start my day. The stillness of the empty house is almost haunting, but at least Jim's out. There's nothing like having a grown man snarl so loud when he needs the bathroom that the door rattles. Maybe he only has one layer: intense.

I step into the bathroom, toes flinching as they touch the chilled ceramic floor. I turn the polished chrome shower handle, releasing thousands of lukewarm drops. Steam fills the room and fogs the mirror as I strip out of my pajamas, anxious to let the hot water soak my skin. But I freeze as soon as my foot lands inside the ceramic tub.

No shampoo.

Or conditioner.

I backtrack and open the cabinet under the sink. Nothing. Wrapping a towel around my body, I step into the hall and make my way over to the linen closet. Empty. What the hell does this man wash his hair with?

Groaning, I stomp back into the bathroom and flick off the shower. So much for the luxury of clean hair. Ugh, I should've grabbed shampoo when I bought the pancakes the other day. But who doesn't have shampoo? Like deodorant and lotion, I get. But shampoo?

Returning to my room, I throw on a pair of yoga pants and top. I might as well go to the supermarket now. I grab the ever-growing shopping list off my desk and head downstairs.

Grabbing a pen from the counter, I quickly scribble shampoo and conditioner on the list. How the hell am I going to get everything back on my bike? At least New York has an extensive subway system, making grocery shopping easy.

I bring the pen to my mouth, but stop before it reaches my lips. I'm a chewer. All of my pens and pencils back home had jagged tips. But this is not my pen. And it isn't my house.

I put the pen down with a *clang* and grab my helmet off

the side counter. Now to find the spare key. Of course, Jim didn't leave it on the counter like he said. Did he even remember to leave it?

The front door creaks open just as I round the corner into the foyer. Jim doesn't notice me right away. His head hangs, his shoulders heavy, as he takes off his shoes, keys dangling in his hand. He slowly lifts his eyes to me.

I point to the keys. "Can I borrow those?"

He looks at them and then back to me. "Left the spare next to the coffeepot."

The one morning I didn't bother drinking coffee. Figures. I must look like such an ass. Clearing my throat, I tuck the shopping list into the side pocket of my yoga pants. "I'm going to the store to pick up some stuff. You need anything?"

"Yeah, a few things. I'll take you." His voice is soft, a whisper almost, as he starts putting his shoes back on.

"You don't have to." My eyes dance over his slumping body. Something isn't right. "You okay?"

He looks up and searches my face a bit. "Just a headache."

From the looks of it, more like another migraine. And while I understand how bad the sharp head pain sucks, the grouchiness side effect is one I can do without. Especially after two days of not sleeping.

He opens the front door and once I'm out of the house and the door is locked, we head down the walkway to the truck. Jim's feet drag along the asphalt driveway and he reaches out, grabbing the tailgate when he stumbles.

"I know how to handle a larger vehicle. My father used to own a truck similar to yours." I rest my hand gently on his shoulder, letting him know I'm close by if he needs me. "I can drive."

"Fine." He sighs as he hands me the keys, his hand clammy.

My mouth falls open. That was easy. Too easy. I expected some resistance or maybe a little rebellion from the man. My brows knit together as I watch him make his way to the passenger door. Being married to a SEAL was supposed to be safe, but after our conversation that threats do exist—even to me as his wife—I'm beginning to wonder what I've gotten myself into. And worse—what I might have gotten *him* into.

We should be okay. My dad is dead. Any lingering evidence was turned over to the police department. No reason for me to be on Marco's or Santoro's radar any longer. Hell, even if Marco wanted to find me—which, why would he?— he'd have a tough time since the military is very protective of their members' information.

My teeth sink into the flesh of my cheek when the truck shakes as Jim gets in and falls heavily on the passenger seat. Despite all of my logic, the back of my neck prickles. What if instead of moving forward I just sidestepped to being in a different kind of danger with a man who currently doesn't seem to be able to even protect himself, let alone protect me? Should I tell Jim about Santoro and Marco?

My mouth goes dry at the thought. I hadn't updated my IPP application about the change in my circumstances. What if my dad's death were grounds for disqualification? I shiver. Things with my new husband might be a little awkward so far, but at least I had a place to live. A chance at a new life.

Before I even consider saying anything to Jim, I need to be sure I'm safe in the program. The thought of yet another major life upheaval makes me want to crawl in a hole and never come out.

Ugh. I'm making a mountain out of a molehill. Jim's injuries are probably temporary and I'm probably safe. Yeah, I'm just overreacting. I take a deep breath and hop in myself, the truck barely budging, and settle into the seat.

"Jesus, you're a freaking giraffe," I say, pulling the driver seat forward.

His lips quirk up as he fastens his seat belt. "Not my fault you got wiener-dog legs."

"Wiener dog? Really?" I turn the key and the engine roars to life. "I'll have you know I'm five foot seven."

"You sure about that?"

I turn my head over my shoulder as I back out, hiding my smile.

The road stretches out in front of us, the white lines beaming in the sun. Jim's eyes are fixated straight ahead. He's pale, his hands limp on his thighs. Is it because of the headache? Or because of me? My heart thumps painfully in my chest.

He inhales, leaning back in his seat and closing his eyes,

and I turn my attention back to the road.

"Blinker." His sharp tone startles me as it cuts through the silent cabin. Jim points to the turn up ahead, which isn't for another half a mile. He shifts in his seat, spine snapping straight. "Left blinker."

Of course, he's a back-seat driver. I comply and harshly grab the steering wheel again. As much as his comments grate on my nerves, this is his truck and he's looking so vulnerable, so I take a deep breath and keep any snarky rebuttal to myself.

"Careful of that black sedan." He nods to the right of the fork we're about to reach.

"I saw him." Stopping at the red, I wipe my sweaty right palm on my pants before moving it to the gear shift.

I reach for the radio. Maybe some music will distract him from pointing out things as if I'm a new driver. I push the black button and the harsh, high-pitched sound of pedal steel fills the car. I sway my head to the rhythm and mouth the words to "She's Actin' Single." I love this song.

"You know Gary Steward?" The renewed interest in his voice makes the blood rush hot through my veins.

I smile, but don't turn to look at him.

"Never figured you listened to country."

"You'd be surprised." I let out a little puff of air and try to suppress the smile that tugs on the corners of my mouth when his knee begins jerking up and down in time with the base drums of the song. Good. He's feeling better.

Pressing on the break, I turn the truck into the parking

lot. Yes, front-row parking. I jump out of the truck and straighten my clothes a little. Jim heads off and grabs a cart, leaning over it to support some of his weight. He follows as I run around picking fruits and grains. He occasionally grabs something off the shelves and throws it into the cart. I stop in front of the hygiene section and my cheeks heat instantly.

This is awkward.

My ears burn as I reach for the tampons with shaky hands and bury it deep into the cart, under the pack of toilet paper. I swiftly turn around and make my way down the aisle. I peek at him over my shoulder, pretending to look for stuff. He doesn't seem too frazzled. More like bored, as he absentmindedly scans the rows of products.

"Jim." A tall man wearing a baseball cap with a bone-frog symbol on it nods at him in passing.

"Mike." Jim matches his tone and throws him a smile. I know that smile—tight lipped, brows furrowed, head tilted slightly to the right. He has given me a few of those. It's his fake smile.

Jim heads down the cleaning supply aisle, grabbing a gallon of floor cleaner. He spins the bottle around, reading the label. Ingredients lists are worse than procedure lists for science class experiments.

I'd love to blame Jim's apparent label dissection on his OCD, but my father did the same thing. Ugh, how many shopping trips took hours because Dad and I had to argue over the quality of name brand versus generic? Not to mention most of those items have the same exact ingredients but because one carries a particular name, the product costs more.

I'd do anything to have him here right now. Arguing with me over Charmin versus store-label toilet paper.

The pain catches me off guard, stealing my breath and making me lean over the cart and squeeze the handle until my knuckles go white.

I wait a few seconds for the sensation to pass before I turn down the next row and force myself to focus on shopping. I grab a family-sized box of Lucky Charms off the shelf. Nothing like empty calorie marshmallows to satisfy my sweet tooth. Jim pulls up with the cart, running his hand through his hair and down his neck. I go to add my box of cereal to the cart and pause. "Holy crap."

He shrugs. "I like Oreos."

Like is an understatement. Five packages of double-stuffed cookies are crammed into the cart.

"Though, I shouldn't really be judging because . . ." I shake my box of Lucky Charms a couple of times and then pose with it. "Magically delicious."

"You sing along to Willie Nelson with that mouth?"

"Right after I take a hit of that marshmallow goodness." I sniff at the box. He shakes his head and his mouth creases as he tries to hold back a smile. I place the cereal box on top of the other shopping with theatrical caution and we walk to the register side by side.

Jim pulls his wallet out from his back pocket and I grab his forearm. "I'll pay. You only got a couple of things."

"No, I got it." He hands his credit card to the cashier and I squeeze past him to start bagging the groceries.

After loading everything into the back seat of the truck, Jim walks to the passenger side again. I chew the inside of my cheek. His headache should've dissipated by now. Maybe he's got a concussion.

By the time I climb into the truck, Jim has the glove compartment open and takes an envelope out. He fishes out a debit card and hands it to me. My name is etched across the bottom.

"This isn't necessary. I'm no *dependa*." I throw the card onto the armrest console and start the car. I may have lost everything, may have quit my job to get away from New York, but I still want to keep my dignity. The same way Dad worked extra shifts to pay bills insurance wouldn't cover when Mom got sick. "I lived at home to pay off my college loans and still paid my dad rent. I'm not here to try to fleece you." My shoulders stiffen. Our family paid our own way, even if we had to eat ramen for dinner for a month.

"Listen, I'm sorry about that." He faces straight ahead as he takes the card and flips it around in his hands. "This is different. The military has some strict guidelines when it comes to finances. It's a bit difficult to understand. Hell, it's difficult to explain too. Having a . . . *someone* . . . depending on me—"

"A dependent." I shift to face him. Might as well call a spade a spade.

"Yes, for lack of a better term. Having a dependent

means my pay increases so that I'm able to support you. Financially. As my wife."

"Right . . ." My voice trails off as I get stuck on that one word.

Wife.

He meets my gaze. "Brass is really anal about it, but to be fair, they have to be. They're just trying to protect the families. Give them benefits. In case something happens, you know?" He looks down at his lap and massages his legs with his hands.

Something already happened to him. Something that is causing the dizziness and migraines. But what? Do I even want to know? And what if it's . . . permanent? I take a moment to collect myself before speaking. "Makes sense."

He rolls his eyes, then smiles. A genuine smile, none of that snarky, fake stuff. It's nice. Sweet even. "You didn't finish reading through the contract."

I quirk a brow at him. How the hell did he know that?

"Don't give me that look. The acronym-laden lingo in the finances section made my head spin. So if it makes sense to you, either you're a fucking genius with a military past I don't know about or you haven't gotten to that section yet."

I giggle as I reach into my bag and get my wallet out. I gently take the debit card from Jim's hand, our fingers brushing. His skin is rough, yet warm. I want to linger in the soft touch, but don't. I place the card in my wallet and put my bag on the floor. Our ride home is quiet, but this time a comfortable quiet. A peaceful quiet that brings a calmness long forgotten. Maybe this marriage might actually work.

CHAPTER FIVE

Jim

AFTER SPENDING THE entire afternoon training a new batch of rancid-smelling guys hoping to become SEALs, I welcome the soft sugary aroma teasing my nose as I twirl the inviting treat between my fingers one last time before popping it into my mouth. A satisfactory crunch lingers in my ears, rich chocolate overwhelming my taste buds. Damn, I've never tasted a better Oreo.

Shoving another cookie into my mouth, I return to my laptop. What is the military's obsession with PowerPoint? If I knew part of my job would entail inserting audio files into slides I would've paid more attention in high school computer class. But the slideshow isn't the worst part. I have to give a presentation to a bunch of dumbasses who aren't even gonna make it through Hell Week.

My fingers hover over the keyboard, but the white of the screen starts drowning out the letters that blink in and out of focus. I straighten my spine, close my eyes and breathe in deep. A stinging pressure behind my forehead and left eye makes itself known.

There goes my evening. My brain obviously has other plans for me tonight.

The headaches have been coming more frequently lately. I lock my fingers behind my neck and start massaging the base of my skull, breathing deep to force oxygen into my lungs, but it doesn't help. My head gets heavier by the second. Maybe I should finally fill my prescription since ibuprofen doesn't cause a dent in the pain on those very rare occasions I resorted to needing some extra help to get through the day.

No.

No prescription pills.

Hate taking meds. Always have, even over-the-counter stuff like ibuprofen or cold medicine. And with the prescription migraine drugs, I'd be walking around in a fog all day. Or look like a drooling fucking zombie.

Fucking pills are just a crutch, a Band-Aid. Ones that could lead to addiction. Not going down that road. I've got this.

The headaches will go away. I'm okay.

But maybe . . .

I push myself off the couch and take a few steps toward the center of the room. I can't believe I'm about to do this. My teammate, Lucas Craiger, swears yoga will help. Granted, his mother is a yogi. But desperate times call for desperate measures.

Leaning over with my palms splayed on the cool wood floor, I plant the soles of my feet firmly and lift the rest of my body to create an inverted "V." Downward dog, I think Craiger called it. More like 'ass in the air like you just don't care' pose. Can this be any more awkward?

Twisting my neck from side to side to chase away the ever-present crick, my gaze falls to the floor. Maybe this pose wasn't the best idea. Nothing like noticing how the wood is more cinnamon to my right and paler in the region under my hands. Time to call Bear's cousin again and get the floors refinished. Guy did a decent-enough job when I hired him six years ago. Well, decent by my standards. Maybe he can come the next time we are sent to training.

My stomach hardens. Wishful thinking. If the migraines don't get better, I'm not going anywhere. Scrunching up my face, I try to remain calm, but too many things are crammed in my head, which feels like it's stuffed with cotton. Memories from my time in Afghanistan, issues at work, my assigned wife.

I close my eyes and try to quiet my mind. Concentrating on my breathing, I inhale slowly through my nose and exhale through my mouth. Inhale. Exhale. Inhale. Exhale. With each breath, my muscles relax, the throbbing in my skull lessening.

"Never would have taken you for the yoga type."

My eyelids snap open only to find Taya standing in the archway staring at me. Her eyes are scrunched together as if she is concentrating to make sense of something, and the left side of her bottom lip rests between her teeth.

I recognize that look. Hell, I'm sure I've had the same

expression on my face at one time. She's checking me out. I shoot upright and spin around, banging my shin into the coffee table. The blood that pooled in my head during the pose, rushes to my cheeks.

Taya stifles a laugh but doesn't blush or glance away. Instead, she runs her gaze over me, a distinct spark of interest lighting her eyes.

I walk back to my previous spot on the couch and sit, willing the heat to drain out of my face. When was the last time I blushed? Fucking hell. "Thought you'd gone to bed."

She huffs. "I couldn't fall asleep. Guess I'm too used to the noise of the city. Here, I've just been tossing and turning almost every night. Never thought silence could be quite this loud."

"Too much silence can be overwhelming."

"It's just not home." She rocks on her heel a little, toes wiggling to keep her balance. She tilts her head back, running a hand over the archway before scratching at the paint with her fingernail.

Massaging my temples, I take a second before responding. "Had the same issue when I first got deployed. Changing environments is always a struggle in the beginning."

She hums in agreement and turns toward the hallway. "You want anything from the kitchen?"

My eyes follow her. "A glass of water."

The clangs coming from the kitchen cause my heel to bounce against the floor a mile a minute. Getting used to living with someone again isn't coming as easy as I thought it would. Hell, I've lived with my bunch of morons in tight quarters overseas. But my house is my safe space. Especially during recovery. But now someone else is here, and the privacy I crave—the privacy I need—is nonexistent. Rubbing my brows, I release an exasperated sigh.

Taya walks back into the living room, holding a bowl in one hand and my glass of water in the other. She puts the glass down in front of me—and she actually uses a coaster—before she takes a seat on the other couch. I mutter "Thanks," then pick the glass up to take a couple of small sips.

I gaze over to Taya, who is now curled up with the bowl of cereal balancing on her knees. Her hair is pulled into a high ponytail, which sways forward as she leans in to bring a spoonful of cereal and milk up to her mouth. When she goes to scoop up more cereal, she moves the spoon around in the bowl, pushing the marshmallows out of the way and only allowing grains floating in the milk to glide on the spoon.

I stifle a laugh as I return my half-empty glass of water to the table.

Taya's head jerks up and she swallows hard. "I'm just trying to get the boring stuff out of the way first. Not my fault they refuse to make marshmallows-only boxes. It's what the people want. Even Cap'n Crunch offers the 'All Berries' cereal. But Lucky Charms? Nope."

She scrunches her small nose up, eyes focused on the bowl, searching around and then the left side of her mouth stretches into a crooked smile and her eyebrow raises. She leans back into the couch and takes a big, confident spoonful of marshmallows. She chews them slowly, with her eyes closed, the inside corners of her eyebrows lifted up.

"How was your day?" she asks, in between bites.

"Fine." I tap my fingers on my knee.

"The humidity was out of control today." She sighs and shakes her head. "The weather report shows it's only going to get worse in the coming days."

I nod in acknowledgment and reach down to wipe some dust off my computer keys.

"Were you working on something?" She takes the spoon out of her mouth and points to my laptop with it.

"Yes."

She brings the bowl to her lips and gulps down the remaining milk before reaching across the table to grab a magazine. She places it in front of her and puts her empty bowl on top. "So, yoga?"

"A team member suggested I try it. Said it helps with the headaches. Between being in the sun all day, not sleeping much, and the computer screen poking at my brain, I'd figured, why not give it a try." I close my laptop.

Taya pushes a strand of hair not in her ponytail behind her ear. "Computers certainly put a strain on the eyes. Did it help?"

"A little."

She nibbles her lip while she watches me, like she's trying to make a decision. Then, she rises from the couch and walks toward me. "Here, let me try something for your headache."

Alarmed by her approach, I rear back in my chair. "What? No! I'm fine. I don't need any help."

She glares at me before taking another determined step. "Learned a technique when I had to go to physical therapy once. I used to do this for my dad all the time when he came home stressed from work."

Her voice wavers at the end and sorrow fills her eyes. My protest dies in my throat. I might not want this marriage, but that doesn't mean I have to be a total asshole. "Fine. But hurry up. I've got work to do."

Not the most gracious of acceptances, but she'll have to take what she can get.

Her expression brightens, and she walks until she's standing behind me. She's standing so close, the sweet floral scent of her shampoo tickles my nose, and then her soft, warm hands gently land on the back of my neck. My body responds by sending blood rushing below my waistband. My hands clench the armrests. *Please, just get this over with already.*

Her fingers slide up my neck, until they nestle on either side of the muscled columns and just beneath my skull. "Take a deep breath."

I comply, hoping that focusing on my breathing will distract my dick.

"Now, exhale."

When I do, her fingers exert an upward pressure, deep into my neck. I flinch. It's uncomfortable as hell. At least for the first second or two. But as time passes, the pressure that fills my head like helium in a balloon eases and I inhale a ragged breath.

"That's it," she says, adjusting her positioning. She waits until I breathe a few more times before applying the pressure again, in a slightly different spot.

She repeats this cycle one more time. Before I know it, she's stepped away. I immediately miss the warmth of her hands.

"So? Any better?"

I blink. Holy shit. My headache is still there, but it's more bearable now. I roll my shoulders and groan. "Yes. Better." I turn to look at her and offer a faint smile. "Thank you. You must have magic hands."

She grins back and wiggles her fingers at me. "Wouldn't you like to know?"

She freezes the moment the words come out of her mouth. Her eyes go wide with shock. Meanwhile, my gaze wanders to her hands while my dick throbs once more at the lurid fantasies her teasing words conjured. I clear my throat.

No. Not awkward at all.

When she darts for the safety of the couch, I grab the remote to turn the TV on. Anything to kill the mood. *Law & Order* is on, one of those late-night marathons they do every weekday. The perfect antidote to lust.

"Oh good, it's one of the older episodes." Without looking at me, she settles herself more and moves the bowl out of the way with her hand to get a better view of the screen. It slides on the shiny cover of the magazine and tilts, one side of it touching the table. "Mike Logan is my all-time favorite character on this show."

I grunt and stand from the couch, snap up the bowl and wipe the table with the back of my hand before carrying it into the kitchen. I don't care about the show. I just want some peace while I'm doing my work and my body's reaction to her touch offered me anything but. I tighten my grip around the sponge, the foam spilling from between my fingers. I clean up her dish, and run my wet hands over my face, pressing on my temples with my thumbs before remembering that my head feels better. I use the little kitchen towel to dry my hands, and walk back to the living room, hoping that by some miracle, she will have puffed up to her room. But sure enough, she is still there. Right where I left her.

I drop down on the couch and turn my laptop back on to continue my work. I turn the TV volume down a bit and look over at her. The blue light of the TV reflects on the wet surface of her eyes and her eyelids droop until they are fully closed. She remains unflinching, even when loud gunshots and sirens wail through the speakers.

The back of my neck prickles. Are these the kind of sounds she fell asleep to back home? I count at least three different explosions, four shootings and a handful of screaming matches coming from the TV. She manages to sleep through all of them. I mean, I know her dad is a police officer and that she's from New York City. I've never been there and don't want to draw conclusions, but maybe it is as noisy and busy as television makes it out to be.

The background noise of the TV isn't as annoying as I'd thought it'd be. The act of blocking it out allows me to focus on the task at hand. Compartmentalizing is something I am used to. Had to do lots of it when deployed. *And* after I got back. It's the only way to get through stuff. Cutting them into sections, shoving the bad ones deep into a dark corner of my mind, and placing all my attention at what needs to be done.

My fingers move swiftly over the keyboard, and I'm done with the presentation in record time. The show is still going. I sneak a peek at Taya. She is fast asleep, shoulders rising and falling rhythmically. Peacefulness on her pretty face.

Pretty?

Yeah, with those large doe eyes, the hint of olive in her skin tone, and thick brown hair, she is very pretty. Stunning, actually, even in a plain, threadbare, gray T-shirt and not a trace of makeup. Her cheekbones are particularly impressive. Perfectly rounded and high on her face. My gaze falls to her lips. They are thin and rosy and delicate. I swallow hard when my mind drifts to wondering what they would feel like against my own lips.

I stand and physically shake myself to chase away the thought, before walking over to grab the throw blanket that her feet have already found their way under and covering her with it. It's hot as hell during the day, but the temperature has been dropping quite a bit at night. She'll get cold like this. Last thing I want is having her sniffling and leaving her germ-infested tissues everywhere.

I pick up the remote control, and the tip of my finger hovers over the plastic of the red power button. But I don't push it. This ridiculous show is the closest she can get to home. I won't take it away from her, as much as leaving the TV on will eat up at my insides. And my electric bill.

I clutch the glass tight in my hand and shuffle to the kitchen. Taya is getting under my skin, and I don't like it one bit.

CHAPTER SIX

Taya

I GRASP THE thick blue mug, three fingers poking through the stubby handle, and inch it toward my face. I squint my eyes, contemplating whether or not to drink the inky-black liquid. I can smell the stale bitterness as I bring it closer to my lips. It's tasteless, as expected, but the smoothness calms my soul with every horrible sip. The smoldering Colombian brew swirls around my tongue. I finally decide to swallow and warm vapors ooze down my throat.

Tossing the throw blanket over my legs, I lean against the side of the bay window, inhaling the steam rising from the mug like mist off a lake. A chill crawls up my spine as a cold dampness seeps into every crack of the house. Virginia Beach weather lacks any sort of consistency in March. While yesterday, I could ride in a tank top, today is in the low fifties and overcast. As gray clouds pass above an even grayer sky, I just want to curl up and read a book.

Taking another sip of coffee, I admire the scene outside. The meticulously manicured grass of the backyard, the perfectly aligned PVC fence, the hedges trimmed at impeccable angles. The sun pokes through a pocket in the clouds, and a ray of light comes to focus on the ground. *Come here, come here.* As if it heard my plea, the sunshine travels toward the nook, warming me through the window. I lean my head back and soak up the temporary heat.

Dust motes float across my eyes, the light refracting off each particle. The warmth on my skin brings me back to the other day in the kitchen. There had been an unexpected electricity in Jim's touch the other day. I can't quite put a name to it.

"Ouch." I look down to see I've managed to rub my wedding ring, pinching the sensitive skin between my fingers. Stupid hands. I lean my head back and groan. Why am I thinking about this? Jim was forced into the program. No way does he plan on staying past the annulment deadline. If only he'd volunteered, then I wouldn't have to worry about where I'll be in a year. And if I'll be back in Maspeth, constantly looking over my shoulder.

I inhale deeply, then exhale. Inhale. Exhale.

Most of the week, Jim's hardly been home, working long hours, so when I woke up this morning, the house was empty. Quiet. Again.

Before he left to go to work three nights ago, he gave me a crash course about his life and what that means for me now that we're married. He informed me he isn't just in the Navy, which his application already told me, but that he is a SEAL. He explained how his schedule is inconsistent, he could vanish for work at any minute, and he ran through all the security and secrecy aspects of what that meant for me. He called it OPSEC. Pretty much, keep my mouth shut.

I set my coffee aside when another chill consumes me, and I yank my blanket up to my chest. I'll never have a family again and every time a sliver of annoyance glints in Jim's eyes, the knife twists a little deeper, reminding me this marriage has an expiration date.

My stomach somersaults and the bitter black coffee creeps its way up my throat. Oh my God, was Jim dating someone when I was assigned to him? Was he forced to give someone up? How much of his life did the program—did I—really upset?

And what if Jim finds out I barely have clothes and a minimal amount of cash? I sit up and remove the blanket from my legs, the temperature in the room seeming to get warmer with every passing second. Nope. He's already so obviously put out by my intrusion into his perfectly orga-nized little world. He doesn't need to know about the fire, or what led me to accept the offer to join the program. That knowledge would only add more stress to our fragile rela-tionship, and we definitely don't need that. *He* didn't need that. Especially since the knowledge of my past might get us both kicked out of the program.

I reach past my coffee for the laptop sitting on the kitch-en table. Inhaling, I click open the web browser, and my fingertips punch at the keys. It's time to stop analyzing my husband and find work. While it's entirely possible Jim might be a kind man and help me out if I tell him about the fire, I don't need his charity. Or pity, for that matter.

After punching in my username and password on the job search site, I scroll through the newest postings. If only I could have continued working for UBM Technologies. I miss my former job. My former clients. I spent five years working for and managing most of their computer securities companies. I loved when my projects succeeded. And it wasn't about the money. Of course, that was a great bonus. But watching something I worked hard on come together? Priceless.

But I didn't want to leave any tracks for Marco or Santoro to find. So I quit. Then I used whatever money I had to pay off any bills lingering, pulled out the remaining cash, and closed my bank account before disappearing down to Virginia Beach.

My index finger slides effortlessly over the touchpad, scrolling through openings. Long minutes seem to pass—at least that's what the second hand on the clock adjacent to me says. "This is pointless."

I wish my dad had never joined the task force to take down Santoro. I'd still be living at home and he'd still be alive. I shiver and my chest tightens. Sour bile sears my tongue. My heart is beating too fast, as if I'm being chased, and my throat closes. If only I had known then Marco was involved. Things might be different. My father might still be alive.

I remembered that day all too vividly. I'd been cooking when the doorbell rang. That should have been my first clue that something was wrong. Lyons never used the bell. He always walked in because he had a key to my place. And so did Marco. Those were my last moments of blissful ignorance. Right up until I'd opened the door to reveal Lyons standing there, shoulders hunched, eyes downcast in a way that wasn't at all like my friend. The smile on my face had died the instant he refused to look me in the eye.

Lifting my hands as if I could ward off the news, I knew, before the words left his mouth. *Your dad was shot during a random robbery. He didn't make it.* Then the world went silent, as if I'd been dropped into a sensory deprivation tank.

Keys jingle in the lock and I jump, nearly spilling my coffee all over my laptop while my heart pounds against my ribs. The momentary fear abates when Jim's cough echoes through the foyer. I hurry to compose myself before my *husband* steps into the kitchen. I suck in a deep breath and exhale slowly, flashing a smile in his direction when he comes into the room.

Jim prowls toward me. His shirt is in his hand and his bare chest is coated in a fine sheen of sweat. My fake smile vanishes and lips part at the sight of all his naked skin. His movements are slow and deliberate. Lean, corded arms swing back and forth as he comes closer.

My pulse picks up and my breath shortens. All of the oxygen has been stripped from the room. For Christ's sake, someone would think I was having a panic attack, except there's a hot, wet weight between my thighs that seems to pulsate every time he moves.

I exhale sharply, shifting uncomfortably in my seat, and I practically groan out loud when my legs clench together.

Placing his keys into the wooden decorator bowl on the countertop, he stares at me from beneath his hat. His gaze drops from my eyes and rakes over the rest of me, falling lower and lower. Of all the times not to wear a bra. My cheeks heat up as I pull my coffee mug to my lips, faking a sip. I swear I'm going to burn that stupid hat so I can see exactly what he looks at. Jim holds a take-out bag from the sandwich shop down the street in his free hand. The aroma of the sweet cheese and bacon fills the kitchen and my stomach rumbles.

He lifts a brow. "Hungry?"

My cup, still at my lips, tilts forward. Lukewarm coffee dribbles down my chin. Just great. A string of snorts and choking sounds erupt from Jim as he poorly attempts to stifle his amusement. The back of my hand swipes over my chin to clean the liquid, and my eyes narrow.

His mouth crimps and faint pink colors his cheeks.

I pull myself together. Barely. "Yes. Thank you."

He lifts his shoulder in a shrug, using his shirt to wipe some of the sweat from his face as he sets the bag down on the kitchen table. "Don't get too excited. They're just leftovers."

This must be divine payback for the other day when I took my sweet ass time in the shower. Jim knocked so hard the wooden door almost splintered. When I finished, I scurried past him, head down, so he couldn't notice the barely contained Cheshire cat grin plastered on my face.

Jim turns and heads toward the fridge and I get distracted by the beauty that is Jim in motion. Good God, his backside is just as glorious as his front, and a beautiful dragon adorns his shoulder blades. He reaches in to take out the juice, the edge of his shorts riding low on his ass. An ass that's just as distracting as the tattoo, if not more so. I dart my eyes away and wipe my chin again—just for good measure, in case I'm drooling.

I catch a glimpse of him from my peripheral, and his muscular thighs flex as he reaches deeper into the fridge. A tiny groan erupts from my lips.

When he stands, I refocus on the dragon rather than his delectable ass and study the way the blue lines intricately swirl with black-and-gray ones. Strategic white accents give the tattoo dimension. The artwork is amazing. My stomach clenches as I rescan the tattoo.

Four.

Four times he's been shot in the back. Is that what happened to him? God, what damage did those bullets actually do? My heart thumps so hard I can feel the beat in my throat. Jim might not be all peaches and cream, but someone felt it necessary to make him a target. Like Santoro made my father a target. If steam could escape out of my pores right now, I'd be a toxic cloud.

"Problem?"

I jerk and nearly spill my coffee again. "What? Uh, no. Sorry, just thinking. Were you dating anyone?" The words spurt from my mouth like water from an open fire hydrant.

Crap. Why did I go there?

"No, wasn't with anyone." Jim's jaw clenches when his gaze returns to me, his head tilting sideways.

I follow his unblinking gaze to fingers where I've been twirling my ring again. I tuck my hand under the laptop, biting my lower lip. A low growl rumbles from his chest and the bulging vein in his neck pulses like a racehorse's hooves thundering down the final stretch. He lifts his glass to his lips, taking a swig, his gaze still glued to mine.

"I'm looking for a job." I smile and turn my laptop in his direction. The tension in the room hangs like a dense fog in a valley. My palms are sweaty. They're *never* sweaty.

"Oh." There's a slight crack in his voice and the inflection makes my thighs clench. I can't get myself to look him in the eyes until Jim takes a final gulp and sets the glass down with a decisive *thunk*. He drops his head and spins the glass around on the counter. "What kind of job you lookin' for?"

"Anything, at this point. I worked in marketing before, but no opportunities are listed in the field down here."

Jim lifts his head to meet my gaze and his neck cords as he continues to fidget with the empty glass. Something's up. By now, the glass would've been put in the dishwasher. The man never leaves a thing out of place.

His gaze moves to my laptop, which still faces him, and his lips turn into a frown. "Wheelie much?"

My fingers clamp down onto the ceramic mug. Ugh, my

background picture. Please don't tell me he's siding with Lyons. "Um, yeah. I used to stunt ride."

His gaze locks with mine.

I tilt my head sideways. "Don't get your panties in a bunch. I don't stunt anymore."

A deep rattling sound startles both of us. Jim reaches across the island, grabbing his phone like a lifeline—a saving grace from the awkwardness in the room. His fingers peck at the screen and when he returns the device to the counter, the front door clicks open.

Visitors.

"Hey, fucker." A husky voice echoes across the room a couple of seconds later. A bald man, dressed in athletic shorts and a sleeveless shirt, saunters in. Bear, right behind him, and a third guy. Bear turns toward me and grunts, dipping his chin, and I can't help but smile at his wordless greeting.

I nod in his direction. "Hi, Bear."

The other two snap their heads my way, ogling me. You'd think I was a celebrity, and not the good kind. The bald one quirks an eyebrow and his pupils dilate as his eyes scan over me. I swallow hard, uncomfortable by the attention.

"Martinez." Jim's voice is deep and threatening.

Martinez bows his head and walks away.

"Taya." My name escapes Jim's mouth in a deep and direct tone. "We need the room."

My head shoots up in surprise, brows knitted together.

Bear places his hands wide on the counter, leaning his

weight forward toward Jim.

Closing his eyes, Jim takes in a deep breath. His tone is much softer now. "You can't be here. Work stuff." He looks as though he's about to combust, his body still tense.

"Oh, ok. No problem." I swing my legs to the floor to leave the comfort of the nook, relieved I don't need to reveal my past to anyone.

But there is a problem. A big, big problem.

The house was empty when I woke up. And relaxing in the kitchen's bay window nook with a warm cup of coffee and a small throw blanket seemed like a great way to start my morning. In the T-shirt I slept in. Without a bra. And in my underwear.

Why didn't I put on a pair of shorts? I'll tell you why. Because I'm an idiot. An idiot who didn't think maybe my *husband* might bring his friends over.

I spring up, grab my laptop and the sandwich bag, and head to the sink. I keep my eyes focused forward, avoiding all four men, and place my mug in the sink. There's no need to bend over to place it in the dishwasher. My feet scurry across the cool tile until I reach the landing of the stairs. I race up to my room.

Although I do my best to avoid looking at Jim, the heat of his eyes on the back of my thighs will not go away anytime soon.

CHAPTER SEVEN

Jim

I PUSH MY hips into the lower cabinets, hiding my hard-on. When Taya stood up, muscular legs bare, with a royal-blue T-shirt barely covering her solid round ass, heat sizzled up my spine. And then she pranced past all of us in purple underwear. My heart jackhammered and sent a shitload of blood rushing to my already semi-hard dick, thanks to her ogling me earlier.

"That's your new *wife*. Mind telling us how you got so lucky?" A few inches shorter than both Bear and me, Anthony Martinez is built like a linebacker. Wide shouldered and heavily muscled, he's a man who's used to getting his way. The bald, brown-eyed bastard is a ladies' man at heart and a constant pain in my ass.

"The assholes who make up the committee thought we'd be a good fit. Something about her application must have stood out." I spin the empty glass on the countertop, willing my erection to go down before these fuckers catch wind of it and harass me about it.

Martinez shakes his head. "Let me guess. You didn't

bother asking what that 'something' was, did you?"

Lucas Craiger unscrews the cap to his water bottle and takes a swig. He swallows and sets the plastic container down on the counter. "Dang. I thought you'd be able to put in a good word for me. I want a hottie with a body, too."

My fists ball tight as I glare in his direction. If he thinks he can talk about Taya like that in front of me, he has another thing coming.

Craiger puts his hands up in defeat. "Hey, I'm just saying!"

Martinez grunts in agreement. "Jim's just being selfish."

"Shut up before I break your nose again." I unclench my fists a little at a time, surprised by the lingering urge to plow them into my teammates' faces. It isn't that Martinez and Craiger are wrong. Taya's ass *is* amazing. And the beauty of her curled up in my kitchen nook didn't evade me. The way strands of brown hair cascaded around her face from the loose bun was so relaxed and comfortable. So natural. But their comments irritate me. Even though I was forced into this marriage, Taya isn't some swipe-right booty call and I'll put them on the ground before I allow them to treat her as such.

I point a warning finger at Craiger and the younger man goes very still, a rabbit caught in the crosshairs of a rifle. "Say another word about her ass and I'm coming after you next."

Footsteps thud down the steps. Taya grabs her keys and helmet. "Heading to the library." She turns on her heels and heads toward the front door, her ass sashaying in tight blue denim.

My balls pull tight and my dick salutes her. Groaning, I take a moment to collect myself. "Hey, Taya. I, um . . . I'm making burgers for dinner."

Christ on a cracker, I sound like a moron.

Taya turns, eyes darting around the room as she fidgets with her helmet, saying nothing for a handful of heartbeats. "I think I'll grab something while I'm out." She takes a couple of steps toward the door, then stops. "But thank you for offering to cook."

Taya leaves, the loud growl of her bike zooming through the mostly quiet neighborhood. My head dips, shaking side to side. God, that girl rides too fast.

My attention turns back toward my friends, only to find white teeth appearing from behind Bear's red beard, his lips turned upward into a wide smile. "How long before you two end up in bed?"

Great, now my best friend has to push my buttons. My molars grind together, my blood pressure rising. "Not happening."

Bear kicks out a foot. "So, you've been standing in the same spot for the past twenty minutes why?"

The three bust out laughing.

I sigh and close my eyes, my head pounding. But the pain in my head distracts from the throbbing in my dick, and a moment later, I'm finally able to step away from the kitchen counter without causing myself any undue embarrassment.

Bear sits by the window. In her spot. I bite back the urge to tell him to get up. "Not many are lucky enough to have Redding pull a favor like that."

"A favor?" I pace around my kitchen, my hands on the back of my head. Searing pain shoots through my temples and causes a wave of nausea to sweep through me.

"Why are you complaining? I wouldn't mind someone prancing around my place in her underwear." Martinez just won't shut up.

My forearm shoots out and swipes across the counter, sending a slew of cooking utensils crashing to the ground. The metal clanking reverberates through the room. The noise matches the pounding that echoes inside my skull and for a second, I feel good.

But only for a second.

That's how long it takes for me to realize I've done it again. I've lashed out without stopping to think first. I relax my hands and focus on the deep breathing the doctor suggested. Once I think I've regained control, I address Martinez. "It's temporary, and once the required time has passed, I'll file for the annulment and she'll be gone and I'll be back in the field."

Martinez leans closer, perfectly composed except for the pulsing vein in his neck. "I ain't Lux. Not gonna run and tattle. You take your shit out on me—direct it at me—one more time, and I'll put you into the ground."

"Don't you ever mention his name in this house again." The rage ignites for a second time. I inhale another deep breath, close to throwing a right hook at Martinez's jaw. Lux can go fuck himself. He should have kept his mouth shut. We take care of one another, not snitch to brass. The team came home safe instead of being blown to bits by a bomb, and that's all that matters.

"You two shitheads, knock it off." Bear crosses his arms over his chest. "Don't make me come over there."

I pinch the bridge of my nose. I'm becoming more and more like my father. I shake my head and my shoulders slump. "Sorry."

I turn to rinse out the mug in the sink. It doesn't ease the pressure in my head, but it gives me something to do to combat the restless energy coursing through my body.

"You fill that prescription yet?" I must be in more pain than I thought if I missed Bear's approach from the other side of the kitchen, though the big bastard can be eerily silent when he wants to be.

I tense, the muscles in my shoulders growing tight as I dry the glass and replace it in the cabinet. "I don't need any damn pills."

"Do you even know where the prescription is?"

I turn, outraged. "Of course I do."

"So, you're ignoring doctor's orders for shits and giggles?" He quirks an eyebrow and I rankle at the challenge of it.

Leaning back against the kitchen sink, I cross my arms over my chest as my teeth grind together. We've had this conversation more than once since my return home. Bear's the only other person who knows about the headaches. "I don't need them."

Bear is the picture of calm, his fingers tapping a rhythm against the top of the island. "You want to be stuck doing NUG training for good? Or be discharged?"

My eyes narrow at his words. "What are you getting at?"

"Forget the program and Taya, you think Redding is going to let you anywhere near action again if you aren't cleared by the doctor?"

I squeeze my eyelids close together. "Because of a few migraines?"

"You willing to bet the rest of your career on it?" Bear straightens to his full height, his expression implacable and one brow raised high in challenge. "Cause that's exactly what you're doing."

I let out a breath and close my eyes, consciously releasing the tension which worked its way through every muscle in my body. It doesn't help. If the results from my physicals don't come back squeaky-fucking clean, I would've joined the program for nothing.

"Fine." My concession isn't graceful, but Bear grins. "I'll fill the damn prescription."

"Awesome. I don't have shit to do today. I'll go with you. Where is it?"

My eye twitches. *Asshole.*

"It's . . . in the guest room." Before Taya moved in, I'd used the closet in the spare room for extra storage. While I'd cleared out most of my things, the prescription remained in the closet, filed with the rest of my medical information. Out of sight is out of mind, and I didn't want to lay eyes on it again. It's a literal sign of weakness.

"Sweet. House tour." Martinez sidles closer, Craiger following behind.

"You're not wandering through my house. This isn't a fourth-grade field trip."

Craiger grins. "So, you're going to leave me and Martinez here? In your messy-ass kitchen? We're not cleaning up after your temper tantrum."

The two are pranksters, and by the time Bear and I get back, they may have tea bagged all my dishes. They've done worse over the years and I don't have the patience to deal with their bullshit. Granted, the kitchen is already a mess thanks to my outburst, but there are worse things to come back to than a few spilled utensils. I might be their superior out in the field, but when it comes to civilian life, they are all too willing to prove just how big of a pain in the ass they can be. I frown at Bear. "Can't you babysit?"

"Sorry." He doesn't sound like it. "You might need help finding the thing." He knows me well enough to keep the topic of our little disagreement to himself. I don't plan on going back on my word, but I can't blame Bear for being cautious since I have a reputation for being uncooperative when it comes to my health.

"What thing?" Martinez, ever the nosy bastard, tosses an arm over my shoulders, and I shrug him loose almost immediately.

"Let's go." I'd rather have them trail along than leave them to their own devices. Plus, Bear isn't going to back down, and with Taya gone, this may be my only chance to get the prescription. So, I hurry and scoop up the utensils and place them back in the metal holder on the counter before we leave the kitchen.

"Now, if you'll look to your right you'll see the master/guest/only fucking bathroom." Bear points to the door midway down the hall, giving an impromptu tour as we head up the stairs toward Taya's bedroom as if he's a guide on a shuttlebus full of tourists.

Craiger's index finger taps his lips. "Whole lotta house for just one bathroom. Is there one hidden in the master bedroom?"

Bear turns and barks a short laugh. "A two-bedroom, two-bath house in this neighborhood is much more expensive."

Martinez claps his palm on my shoulder. "Cheap bastard."

My fingernails dig into my thighs and I struggle not to blow out a frustrated breath of air. Patience has left the building. Sometimes their teasing just goes too far. "Was only me and Raychel. No need for an extra bathroom. It's impractical, especially being gone eighty percent of the year."

Bear stops at the painting hanging on the wall a few meters from Taya's bedroom and runs his fingers along his beard. "Here's a shining example of the shitty representation of expressionist art Stephens likes to decorate with."

Martinez and Craiger *ooh* and *awe* politely, and I turn just enough to glare at the lot of them. I made that 'shitty representation' after a mandatory psych eval when I'd first returned to the States. I liked the way it turned out and since I was the only one living here, I hung it up, something that was purely mine and not something I shared with Raychel. But if Bear's words are any indication, my one foray into drawing something other than stick figures and geometric shapes had fallen short with the general public.

The three men look at me, their expressions matching embodiments of innocence, and I try to speak as if my teeth aren't practically glued together. "Are you going to critique every inch of my house?"

They all look at each other and after a silent exchange, nod.

My eye twitches again. "You realize this is why you never get past the living room when you come over?"

Bear grins, and Martinez shrugs, the epitome of disregard.

Craiger smiles. "That you know of."

Too bad religion isn't my thing anymore. I could really use a blessing from the Virgin Mother for patience. "If I knew of a foolproof way to get blood out of carpet, I swear to God—"

"You gotta learn how to relax." Martinez squeezes the top of my trapezius as he steps around me to grip the doorknob. "This it? The little cutie's domain?"

I scowl, reaching out to grip his wrist. A surge of pressure keeps him from opening it and stepping into the room but the action drains the expression from Martinez's face.

The man can be dangerous when he wants to be. It's why I enjoy working with him. He's dependable in a fire fight and good company when he isn't busy being an annoying asshole. You don't lay hands on a brother unless there's a reason for it, and Martinez likes physical contact less than most. I let him go with a slight dip of my head. "Her name is *Taya*."

"Taya." The word rumbles low in his throat as he enters her bedroom.

I step forward, a snarl on my lips. If they keep poking at me, I'm going to lose it. Bear grips me by the shoulder, pulling me up short. "Deep breaths. You know they don't mean anything by it."

I nod, but he waits a few extra seconds before releasing me.

Bear nudges me with his shoulder. "Get in, get out. No harm done."

I walk inside without responding. I can justify it any way I like, but being inside of the guest bedroom feels strange now. The room smells like Taya. It reminds me of sandalwood and apples, the scent underscored with something musky and wholly female. It's enough to make my mouth water. I try to fight it, but Craiger's words make me wonder.

Does she taste as earthy and full-bodied as she smells? I turn away before the others notice how rigid the thought of tasting her makes me. I glance around. My guest room, a room that has always seemed unremarkable and cold, now radiates "Taya." She's everywhere from the books against one wall to the makeup and hair products cluttering the surface of my old desk. My fingers twitch at my sides, and I fight the urge to walk over and organize the area.

Martinez is scanning Taya's things. "She has more of these *Halo* books than you do." He walks toward the bookshelves.

I close my eyes and shake my head. They really are going to critique every corner of the place.

"It's a strange squad. The best ones always are." Craiger points at a T-shirt tossed across the chair in the corner.

I glance at the shirt and my eyes widen. "Admiral Parangosky. Nice."

All three men look at me as if I've sprouted a second head and my eyes narrow.

"The *Kilo-Five* trilogy?" I ask, trying not to sound as horrified by their ignorance as I feel, and making a mental note *not* to talk to Taya about cleaning up her room.

"You are seriously the biggest geek." Bear's hand connects with my shoulder. "And it looks like you found your geek queen."

Craiger picks up an eight-by-ten frame from one of the bookshelves and studies it for a moment before angling it in my direction. "Who do you think this is?"

The photo is of an elderly Asian woman standing on an outcropping, nothing but snow and clouds behind her. Her hair is a long black braid hanging over one shoulder and her furred hood and mittens.

"We're not here to poke around her things. Put the picture back."

Martinez walks up behind Craiger. "Looks Mongolian. See all the iron pendants—about two hundred—and the textile snakes attached to the leather coat. Plus, the equine details on the flat drum fit the shaman culture of the region."

Both Bear and I turn to stare at him.

He throws up his hands, palms facing upward. "What? Some of us like to travel in between deployments. Excuse me for being three-dimensional."

Bear angles his chin sideways, one eyebrow cocked.

Martinez acquiesces. "Fine. Two-dimensional."

Craiger places the frame back, the tip of his tongue poking out from the corner of his mouth and his brow furrows. "You think they're related? They sort of look alike."

I stride over to the closet, and Bear whistles when I open the doors. "Is this all she owns? This is barely the essentials, even by military standards."

Her lack of clothes makes the closet painfully bare. Simple tees and a couple of pairs of jeans rest on hangers. A black sweatshirt with neon pink lettering stating "Ridin' Dirty" hangs in the corner. Even her shoe collection is pitiful, consisting of four pairs of sneakers. A complete contrast to Raychel, who loved nice things and being the center of attention.

I reach for the shoebox on the top shelf and wonder if Taya's lack of clothes is by choice or if she simply has nothing to her name. If she's down on her luck, it would explain her decision to join the program. I grab the box from its perch on the top shelf and step back, hating the idea of any person having so little.

A thump grabs my attention and I turn my head over my shoulder. Bear bends down to grab a scrapbook off the floor. He runs the tips of his fingers over the open pages with a couple of newspaper clippings taped to the pages. "Jim, check this out."

The scrapbook is obviously Taya's, as I made sure everything that belonged to Raychel was either thrown into a box for her to pick up or tossed in the trash. I take a couple of steps, but hesitate at first to take the book. Invading Taya's privacy isn't why I came into the room. Then I notice some of the headlines:

Officer Shot Down
Santoro Still At Large
Community Shaken by Grief

A fourth article is accompanied by a picture, a grainy black and white of a weeping woman dressed in all black. An older gentleman stands beside her, the arm across her shoulders. There's something about the way the woman holds herself that's familiar.

"Think that's Taya?" Bear asks.

Taya's father is a cop. Wouldn't be out of the norm for her to have attended a funeral for a fallen officer. I step closer and scan the small lettering under the photograph, but no names are given. Quickly, I glance over the rest of the article. The officer, Thomas Byrne, was killed in the line of duty. "Article states the guy had a daughter, Irene. Must be her."

The articles unsettle my stomach. Why would she be keeping this kind of stuff? I mean, I read the news. I'm aware about the rise in danger police officers face these days, stuck between criminals and communities that hate cops. Just the other day at work, the news broadcast was covering a story about two officers killed in the Bronx, shot to death in their squad car in broad daylight. And the boys in blue are just as tight as our brotherhood. But still doesn't explain why Taya is collecting articles on these deaths.

I fight the urge to flip through more pages and grab the book to close it and replace it on a shelf, hoping I put it back in the right place before Taya thinks I'm snooping. After the book is in place, I reach up and grab a shoebox from the top shelf and tuck it under one arm, then shut the closet door.

Craiger knocks into the side table next to the bed, causing a bottle of skin cream to fall to the ground and spill onto the floor. "Why do you need to vandalize my house?"

"*Vandalize* is a strong word," Bear says, though there's a smile on his face.

"What can I say? I'm a strong-language kind of guy."

"Rated E for everyone?" Martinez asks as Craiger puts the bottle back in place and wipes up cream off the floor with a tissue.

I let out a huff of barely repressed humor. "Please. I get a

T for 'teen' at least."

"Throw in a few more F-bombs and a nipple and you could work yourself up to an M for mature," Martinez pipes in, picking up a discarded pair of panties with a raised brow and aims them at me.

"I live for the day." I snatch the impromptu slingshot from him and he winks. Unrepentant. I ball the silk in my fist and glare a hole in the back of Martinez's head as he saunters out of the room.

When Bear comes closer, he shoves one of Taya's comic books at me. "For the road. I figured it's a better souvenir than her panties."

Cursing, I toss the underwear back in the general direction Martinez found it. Bear's booming laugh bounces down the hallway as he catches up with the other two.

She's only been here for a short while, but already there's a warmth to the room that was lacking before. The casual messiness is almost comforting even though the clutter gives me the chills. I shut the door and take a deep breath of apples and sandalwood lingering in the air.

A part of me wants it to disappear while the rest of me can't seem to get enough.

CHAPTER EIGHT

Taya

I BLINK MY tired eyes rapidly, trying to chase away the dryness. Nightmares about the fire and Marco wake me up, causing my mind to race, especially after the news about the latest killing in the Bronx. I recognized one of the officers. He worked with my father on the task force put together to take down Santoro.

Shortly after I moved back in with my dad, he told me he volunteered to join the task force put together to take down the crime boss. My apartment building was being turned into condos and while I hated the idea of returning home, it made financial sense since I was still paying off my college loans. I felt the universe brought me home for a reason, and I believed if I was by his side, nothing would happen to him. I was naïve and idealistic until reality spit in my face.

My lips press tight together. How could Marco betray him? Betray a man who was like a father to him? And for what . . . money, power? Lyons and I never found out the reason, not that I would ever accept it.

The rising sun teases warmth through the blinds' thin barrier and I swing my legs out of the bed in a spill of blankets. God, I haven't been running down here yet, which is a shame, considering my new proximity to the ocean. The fresh air should help clear my head, calm me down.

I strip down before putting on a pair of azure-blue compression shorts and a white running tank with a patriotic rabbit in the middle. Tossing my hair up into a quick ponytail, I make my way downstairs and grab my keys before heading out the door.

Instinct sends me into a smooth canting trot. Riding is freedom itself, but running pushes me like my bike can't. It leaves me sore in a way that's reminiscent of good, hard sex. Satisfaction that can only be garnered from pushing myself past my limits. Pleasure that comes from a hard climb and an implosion of endorphins and sweat-slick skin.

I run until everything that keeps me awake and hurting in the early hours of the morning washes away under a heavy fog of exhaustion. My feet pound the concrete of the boardwalk with all the elegance of a sack of wet cement. The graceful steps of ten miles earlier have long since disappeared. My rasping throat is parched. I should have brought a bottle of water, but the thought had been negligible compared to the need to get out of the house.

My head bobbles loosely from side to side with each footfall, and my run takes on a sway that threatens collapse.

I slow to a walk as the warm humidity wraps around me like a blanket, oppressive and oddly sticky. Thick, salty droplets flow down my face, dripping onto the concrete when I stop and lean my forearms against the aluminum railing. My head throbs with every heartbeat, my legs struggling to hold my weight. I close my eyes and focus on the ocean's lullaby, breathing in its poignant, salty breath. Why haven't I come out this way sooner? Five miles isn't too far of a run—or a drive—to come and relax by the water.

As my breathing returns to normal, the pounding in my head subsides. I stand straight and fill my lungs full of the fresh, cool air blowing off the ocean. My legs are stiff, so I raise my right foot and clasp my ankle as my fingertips trail over the patch of numb, bumpy skin.

I remove my hand from my scar. I close my eyes tightly and try to drown out the images of Marco pulling me out of my burning house. The bastard started the fire, claimed it was to destroy some evidence my father had. Then had the balls to tell me he was trying to keep me safe.

My fingers curl into fists. He was so fucking good at covering up the start of the fire that the arson investigator couldn't find any foul play. And my claims as to what he said, while taken seriously by the precinct, weren't enough to arrest him, especially once the arson report came back claiming it was an electrical fire.

So much for taking a mental break from the past. I walk to a nearby ledge to stretch my quads and gaze out into the waves, watching the surfers, to keep my balance. I've always been in awe of the way people can ride waves the way I ride pavement.

I switch legs, and the river of sweat free flowing down the center of my back like rain on a window pane shifts its course. I drop my foot back down to the ground and clasp my hands together behind my back. While the stretch feels wonderful, the skin around my shoulders is tight. And my face. A slight stinging is present. It's my fault for not wearing sunscreen. I walk to a bench overlooking the beach and sit, my body still needing time to recover before making the trek back home.

A red-and-blue surfboard in the water catches my attention. Its rider attacks the steep slope, projecting half of the board off the wave's lip, and then drives it down toward the bottom of the wave without losing momentum. *Awesome.* The wind brings about a shiver as it cools my overly warm skin, but all of my attention is focused on the surfer. There's grace in the way he arcs through the crescent-shaped waves. I can't pick up much detail from where I stand, but his gray-and-blue shorts contrast sharply against the churning blue of the ocean.

Water clings to the muscular length of his arms and chest, and when the sunlight hits it just right, the droplets sparkle. Briefly, Mother Nature transforms him into a dancing Adonis sprinkled in starlight, and my insides clench hungrily while my mouth goes dry.

I don't know how long I stand there watching him. Long enough for the sweat to cool. When Mr. Gray-and-Blue Board Shorts rides the wave in before jumping off the board into the water, I can't help but feel as if the show ended far too soon. The surfer turns his board around and hops back on to paddle out to the next set of waves.

Shitballs.

Even from this distance, the gray-washed details of the dragon tattoo stand out. *Jim.* My pulse rate starts to jackhammer, and my legs clamp together as that wild ache for him returns. Seeing him, muscles bunching and body in confident motion leaves my knees weak. I roll my eyes and sigh.

Jim paddles harder as a large wave reaches him. Popping up to his feet, he carves through the water. He performs a bottom turn and when he reaches the crest of the wave, he gets the fins free just long enough to let the tail of the surfboard slide down the face of the wall of water.

My jaw drops, and the corners of my mouth turn up. The way he controls the board, the precision of each trick, the flex of each muscle. Breathtaking. I could sit here and watch him all day. I gulp, my throat dry from both the run and the sight of my—err—husband.

With the board tucked under his arm, he jogs through the shallows of the water. He drives the blue-and-red board, the colors swirling to create a tribal design, into the sand. His head shakes, drops of water flying in all directions as they leave his dark brown hair. His palms run over his face and come to rest at the back of his head. His chest expands, and then every muscle goes rigid when he faces my direction.

The expression on his face is like those on marble statues. Vacant. Cold. Faintly superior. A low groan rumbles in the back of my throat when he tucks the surfboard under one arm and propels himself closer. Each step deliberate, hitting the sand with a domineering *thunk*.

My fingers snake around the railing as a throaty moan escapes my lips. I'm a hot mess. And now I'm practically dripping with need.

"Need something?" He stares into my eyes, unblinking, as if locked onto a target. Or fighting to keep from looking elsewhere. Like my traitorous nipples. I can feel the fuckers jutting out.

Hell, what do I say? Um, yeah, I need you between my legs. Uh, nope.

"Did you . . . lock yourself out?" He drops his board to the ground and steps forward, closing the distance between us until only the metal railing separates us, and my lungs halt midbreath.

"No. I went for a run. And I took a breather. You know how it is." My gaze skates from his sinful mouth down the curves and ripples of his abs to—

Crap.

Unable to look away, I take in the bulge straining at the seam of his shorts and swallow tightly. God, could I fit that thing in my mouth?

"Yes." He turns toward the ocean, away from me.

Did I just say that that out loud? "Um. I'm sorry, what?"

"I said, yes . . . I know how that is. Do you surf?" A wicked grin is plastered on his face. He's already OCD, and I don't need him to tell me he's a mind reader too.

"No. It's not a big thing in New York. Neither are the waves for that matter. Unless you head east to Montauk. But the traffic is killer, even on a bike." I tuck a loose strand of hair behind my ear, trying to compose myself.

Jim chuckles, but then his knees buckle and a hand flies out to grab a bar of the railing to keep from falling. Heat rushes over my skin as my fingers touch his—a small gesture to let him know I'm there if he needs me. "Are you okay? Can I do anything to help?"

When he tilts his head up to face me, his eyes narrow and a vein in his neck bulges out. "Nothing I can't handle."

My teeth sink into the skin of my cheek. Jim's knees have buckled several times now, and though I don't know what is going on, the signs of something bad—something he is too stubborn to admit to—are present. God, the man deserves a good spanking. Before I can stop it, the corners of my mouth curl up into a smile at the thought. I shake my head, chasing the thought away, and refocus on the seriousness of the situation. "My mother died when I was a child. Car accident. My father didn't handle it well. There were signs he was suffering from depression, but I was too young to know what they were. Otherwise, I would've stepped in when he was too stubborn to get help."

Jim's lips press into a thin line. "I'm not depressed."

"I know. But I'm not blind, either. I know something is going on. And when you're ready to tell me, I'm here." I rest my hand on his forearm and offer a weak smile. Do I feel a little bit like a hypocrite, asking him to open up to me while

I keep my past hidden from him? Maybe. But my problems aren't physical. And I can't help but think we're both safer with him not knowing. At least for now.

"I'll be fine. No need to worry."

I nod, not wanting to push the situation further. "By the way, just wanted to let you know I found a job. I'm the new waitress at Shaken & Stirred."

"Taya." He lowers his voice and reaches for my wrist. "You don't have to take the job. Not when you have a degree. I can help you find something better."

I pull my hand back and narrow my eyes as I glare at him. "There's nothing wrong with being a waitress."

He crosses his thick arms and puffs out his chest, one eyebrow raising.

"Fine, it's not ideal."

Jim snorts.

"You have no idea what it's like looking for a job in the real world," I say, kicking myself at those last two words. "I mean, in the world outside of the military. It's hard. And everything here is new. Being married to you is new. I'm just trying to pull my own weight financially."

I *need* to pull my own weight financially. Unless he's reconsidered making an honest attempt at this marriage. That would be my first choice, but unfortunately, that's not a solo decision. Without Jim onboard, I'll be completely on my own a year from now. Everything happened so fast with Dad, that up until this point, I'd only been able to react as my life imploded. I'd have to take advantage of the relative security of the next three hundred-plus days here in Virginia Beach with Jim to form a backup game plan for my life.

Jim's posture relaxes and his shoulders slump down a bit, his gaze falling to the sand. "The SEALs are my life. Don't know what I'd do if I couldn't be one anymore." He takes a step closer, his finger lifting my chin so my gaze meets his. "And I mean it. If you want to find something else, something you might enjoy more, I'll help."

Truth is, there is something I would enjoy doing more. I'd already reached out to the team leader of one of the Virginia Search and Rescue groups I know. It's something I miss, and I'm ecstatic about the opportunity. The teams down here are the gold standard.

But most SAR personnel are volunteers so I need a paying job, one that has some flexibility so I can train. But I'm not exactly ready to share this with Jim, not after spending years being ridiculed by my stepmother for being involved. And not when I've witnessed other SAR team members dealing with resistance from their families.

His eyes roam over my face as he awaits my answer, our lips mere inches from each other. His breath kisses my skin as my own becomes shallow and my eyes begin to close. But he clears his throat, pulls his hand away, and steps back.

I reach down and pick up his surfboard, running my fingers over the waxed surface before handing it over to him. "I appreciate your offer. But I do need to get going. My first shift starts in two hours."

"Have to run to base myself." Jim's brows furrow as his

fingers scratch at his scalp and his gaze bounces all over the place. "One of my teammates is having a birthday party tomorrow. We need to go . . . together. Especially since we are part of the program. Not sure who will be there, but my commanding officer wants us to show we are putting one hundred-and-ten percent into the program. Will that interfere with your schedule?"

Shit.

I force a smile. "I'll see what I can do."

He nods and tucks his board under his arm. "Have a good first day."

I head toward home, my heart galloping in my chest. Forget first-day-of-work jitters. Tomorrow will be our first outing as a couple. Why didn't I think that we'd be under scrutiny? This is a new program and of course everyone will be watching us, especially as one of the first matches.

A wave of anxiety washes over my body.

What if participation in this program doesn't just shove us under the microscope but also thrusts us into the limelight? What if this program puts me on display? Even tagging me in an online photo for promotion purposes would be enough for Marco to easily find me, if he was looking. Or worse, Santoro.

I pick up my speed, allowing the steady pumping of my legs and the breeze in my face to soothe away my fears. Marco and Santoro haven't come looking for me yet. What reason would they have to track me down now?

CHAPTER NINE

Jim

SOME DAYS I kick myself for the choices I make. Like today. Not only did I almost kiss her, breaking my own damn rule about no sexual contact, but I faltered in front of her again. The sympathy in her eyes was just like that of the medical staff at base. And I don't need sympathy. I need to be cleared for duty. I need to get back out into the field. Why can't the damn doctors understand it's just a minor TBI? And what the hell are all the over-reactive claims that a little rattling affected my judgement? Unless my superiors are just using the whole traumatic brain injury excuse to keep me here longer while they figure out how to make our Afghani counterparts happy.

But Taya also opened up to me, and in a way I didn't expect. My own childhood was fucked up. Not that I lost a parent the way she did. In some way, I wish I had, since it might have been better than what I actually went through.

I lay my things, one by one, along the length of the workbench in my garage, careful to set them each so they line up. Keys, phone, wallet. The walls are lined with shelves filled with labeled bins, and the epoxy floor is sparkling clean. Everything neatly arranged, so that I can relax when I come in here to work.

Surfing is my escape. A place to get lost among the waves of deep royal blue, floating in a void, free of gravity. To become one with the ocean's power, synchronizing my board to ride each crest. And to silently sit and stare as smudges of coral, lavender, turquoise and a fiery orange blend together to create a sight so astounding it sweeps me away from my worries.

But seeing Taya on the boardwalk, lithe body coated in sweat and chest heaving, I wanted nothing more than to bend her over the nearest bench and peel those tight little pants down her hips. Reveal every inch of her skin to the sunlight and bathe it clean with my tongue until she whimpered beneath me.

And the scent of apples and sandalwood she left behind was like silken fingers around my cock bringing me to throbbing, frustrated attention, like a pornographic magic trick.

"Fuck."

I toss my baseball cap across my worktable and stab impatient hands through my hair. Then she tells me she'd taken a job as a waitress. As if I can't provide for her. I'm still getting paid. I haven't been discharged yet. And my bank account has enough to support us both.

Pulling out my supplies, I lay the board across the bench and begin to wax the surface of it. Bringing the board back to its usual gleaming perfection relaxes me, the motion of righting my board and cleaning the marks of the day away comforting. Especially after dealing with the trainees. One month down, twenty more weeks to go before I don't have to look at their damn faces anymore. Nothing like being an instructor for SEAL school.

On the other end of the workbench, my phone vibrates. I want to ignore it and enjoy my solitude for a little while longer, but I catch sight of the name on the caller ID.

Bear.

Setting the wax aside, I pick up and press the phone to my ear. "What's up?"

"Got bored waiting for Marge. How's the wife?"

Pressing the speaker button, I set the phone aside to free my hands. I grab the bar of wax and get back to work. "Got a job."

"Good for her. Less time she's gotta spend around your surly ass."

I snort.

"Ya tell Taya 'bout the injury yet? She's not a dumb girl and I can't see her cutting you down. Not after she kept that ugly-ass comforter you purchased. Still don't understand why ya didn't ask for Marge's help."

"Don't need her reporting my health." My chest tightens like I'm having a heart attack when I recall how wide Taya's eyes went and how the color drained from her face when I lost my balance. I pause, rubbing my face as if I can wash the stain of weakness away. "Taya can't find out I'm taking medication or about what happened."

"Jim, any of us would've made the same call. Can't beat yourself up over it." Bear exhales loudly. "And listen, I'm proud of you. I know you think you're invincible, but there's nothing wrong with needing help."

"Because I really had a choice," I mutter under my breath, barely loud enough for him to hear. Bear went with me to the pharmacy and has been texting me when it was time to take the pills like a damn reminder alarm.

A searing pain grows in the back of my head and works its way forward in between my eyebrows. I rub there firmly with the pad of my thumb. On most days, my new meds work great for the migraines. This headache isn't nearly as bad as it has been in the past, but my body doesn't seem to want to break its habit of being a pain in my ass. If only the balance issue and the dizzy spells would lighten up as well.

I sigh and remember what the doctor told me. At my last checkup, he said to be patient and that my body needs rest and time to heal. And that I'm lucky there's no permanent damage, at least none they can see yet.

I glare down at my dick. So much for decreased-sex-drive side effects. If anything, my dick has been out of control lately. And the more Taya supports me, the more my resolve to keep her away dwindles. I just have to remember this is only temporary, just need to keep reminding myself what marriage was like the first time around, and what my being away so much pushed Raychel to do.

"Why not trust Taya a bit?"

"I trusted my first wife and it blew up in my face." My ears heat with old shame, taking some of the starch from my sails. My eyes squeeze shut and, when I reach up to massage the ache forming at my temples, my fingers run over the haggard lines of my own features.

"Raychel betrayed you, humiliated you, cut you down for not wanting to become an officer and ultimately, broke your heart." Bear grumbles as if he'd spent hours punching through a concrete wall only to get nowhere. "But you need to stop accusing every woman you meet of being another Raychel. Especially when it comes to Taya. She cares, and you're being bullheaded."

The muscles between my shoulder blades clench. I'd thought my ex-wife cared at first too, and look how that turned out. Raychel's dream was to be an admiral's wife. Not that I knew it when we dated. She always pushed me, but I thought it was because she saw potential. But I wanted to be out in the field, be with my brothers. And when I expressed that, I saw who she truly was. The affairs started shortly after. Or maybe they were even happening before. My neck cords at the thought.

But I close my eyes and breathe in through my nose and out through my mouth. In and out. In and out. Just like my *therapist* taught me.

Think happy thoughts.

Something.

Anything.

The only thing that comes to mind is Taya's smile today.

Laying my wax comb aside, I spray the surface of my board with a nearby spray bottle. Even filled with restless, destructive energy, I can't bring myself to leave my board half-finished. It isn't in me. Sometimes, I chomp at the bit of my self-imposed control. I want to do something, something wild and thoughtless, without caring about any consequences, but lately, that always seems to backfire. For now, I'm like a dog caught short by the end of its leash.

"This is probably just as weird for Taya as it is for you. The woman moved to another state. Left her life to start over with you. Yeah, fine, Redding pushed you into the program. But can't be easy for her. Wasn't easy for Marge at first being married to a SEAL and we knew each other since high school." A raspy sound comes through the speaker, one I'm familiar with. The big oaf is clearing his throat, about to make some stupid dig. "And if you're planning on buying her something, send Marge a picture first."

I thrive on perfection, and Taya makes me feel imperfect. Like everything I do is wrong. Setting up her room, wrong. Offering to help her find a better job, wrong. Getting angry . . . okay, she's justified there. I groan, rubbing my temple.

Maybe this time, I'll succeed. A glint of metal winks at me from the other side of the garage. "I could change the oil in her bike? It sounded like shit the last time she went out."

"Would've gone with flowers or something, but whatever. Wait, how'd she get to work?"

Good question. Shaken & Stirred isn't too far from the

house, but certainly not walking distance. "Maybe Uber?"

"Ah crap, Marge is here. Gotta go."

"You guys shopping for the barbecue?" Bear and Marge's annual get-together is often the highlight of the spring for me.

"You know it. The woman spends thirty minutes chatting it up with some Stepford Wife in the produce section, but I'm the monster if I so much as look at my cell."

"Give her a break. She likes spending time with you. God knows why."

Bear laughs. "Fuck you," he says fondly, and I grin as the call disconnects.

My chest squeezes. I love my best friend, but at times, his relationship with his wife is too much to handle. It leaves me longing for a relationship I'll never have. If my own parents didn't enjoy spending time with me, how could I expect anyone else to?

But I'm better off without someone caring for me. God only knows, one day I might not come home. Or, come home completely destroyed and unable to provide for them. No way would I want to burden someone with that.

I take a step forward and raise a brow in appreciation. "Hello, beautiful." The moniker fits perfectly. Taya's Ninja 650 truly is a beauty, and I eye the clean lines.

I reach beneath the bench for an empty canister and new jug of oil. Taya's engine sounded a little loud when she'd first arrived, and the rumbling had only become more cantankerous each day. So, I stopped at the auto store the other day and picked up oil.

I pull out the funnel, oil tray, and wrench, setting them down in the center of the garage before pulling the bike out to fiddle with it. Listening to the dirty oil filling the tray beneath the bike, I flex my jaw. God, her ass looked good in her compression shorts, the material so snug it was if they'd been poured over her skin, cupping the rounded globes of her ass with such a firm, steady pressure that I was legitimately envious. The blue had brought out the olive tones in her skin, and I'd been mesmerized by the play of delicate muscle in her thighs and calves.

My skin is on fire, arousal like a razor's edge along my nerve endings. Keeping busy should've been enough to distract me, but damn if every move I make doesn't feel like her fingernails stroking down the length of my cock. Rubbing one out in my board shorts isn't usually my definition of a grand ole time, but I'm so horny, almost any sensation is like angel hair on my nut sac.

I squeeze my eyes shut, trying to resist because I can't go there. I can't jerk off to her. I won't do it.

The throbbing is incessant, bordering on painful. I've been so hard for so long, my erection has become my own version of hell. With a gruff sound in the back of my throat, I grab my phone from the work bench and peck at the screen.

I know just what I need because I refuse to spill my load over a cutie with a booty and pretty brown hair. Down that path leads to destruction. In a few seconds, my go-to porn site pops up. Porn has always seemed a little empty, but it gets the job done. I don't bother searching out anything specific. As soon as I spot the thumbnail of a minxy little blonde, tits exposed and mouth gaping, I click on it.

The blonde on screen spreads herself across a king-sized, four-poster bed. I groan as I hook my board shorts below my throbbing balls, which are taut and drawn up. Another voluptuous blonde joins the first and my palm cups my dick, lightly moving up and down my shaft, my thumb skimming the delicate skin.

I tighten my grip on my shaft and pump a little faster, watching two women devour each other's mouths, my skin growing hotter. Both women are softer, large breasted, and most importantly, neither looks like Taya.

I grunt, my eyes locked on the screen. My balls are heavy, tingling with the need for release. I keep watching, keep stroking. The moans and whimpers of the girls are musical. But when my eyes unwillingly close, it's Taya I find. Gripping me. Wet for me. Aching for me.

Pleasure bursts through my whole groin and I groan.

Loudly.

My dick pulses uncontrollably, and I jerk harder and faster, up and down, up and down. When she drops to her knees and those rosy lips part, the moans of the women on my screen now her own, I'm done. My balls tighten, spine arching, a shudder wracking through me. My cock twitches, and with an epic roar, cum jets between my fingers so hard it splatters onto the garage floor.

I grab a roll of nearby paper towels and wipe a sheet across my stomach to clean up. I'm glad I hadn't hopped into the shower as soon as I got home. Now I can enjoy the afterglow under a spray of hot water. I'm straightening to do just that when the loud metallic clank of keys hitting granite catches my attention. When had she gotten home? The door leading to inside the house is wide open. I hadn't thought to close it since I'd only planned on waxing my board before getting ready for work.

Had she seen me? Heard me?

My dick twitches at the thrill of her watching. I'm surprised at how much I like the idea. How much I want it to be the case.

No. This can't happen again. No slippery slopes. They only lead to bigger mistakes. Taya's temporary. She's my ticket to getting back into the field and nothing more. And I won't do anything to make her feel otherwise. I won't intentionally hurt her.

CHAPTER TEN

Taya

I 'M SUPPOSED TO be getting ready for this birthday party, but of course Jim continues to be the only thing on my mind since yesterday evening. God, catching Jim masturbating, thick hand fisted around his equally thick dick, nearly brought me to my knees. Why'd he have to leave the freakin' door open yesterday?

Leaning over, I grab my vibrator from the nightstand drawer and switch it on. The purple, textured sex toy buzzes to life and I lower it between my thighs, touching it gently to my needy sex. The fingers of my free hand curl into the comforter beneath me as the pleasure coursing through my body becomes an urgent stab of desire and I moan as the image of Jim stroking himself raced through my mind.

I'm teetering on the brink of heaven, every nerve ending on fire. My muscles tighten as I press the vibrator hard against my clit, pushing myself closer to tumbling over the edge. Everything is about to go blissfully white when there's a knock at my door.

Oh. My. God.

Turning off the vibrator, I launch out of bed and mumble a silent prayer that Jim didn't hear anything. "Just a minute."

I throw on a pair of black jeans and one of the few nice shirts that survived the fire, a loose tank top with sequins, before scurrying over to the door. I take a deep breath and adjust my ponytail. When I pull the door open, no one is there, so I take a step into the hallway. Halfway down the stairs is Jim. His ears and neck are beet red.

Oh. My. God.

He stops when the floor beneath me creaks but doesn't turn around. "Ready to leave?"

"Just need five minutes."

He nods and continues on, and I step back into my room and close the door. He heard. Oh my God. How am I going to sit the rest of the night next to this man? Not that I'm embarrassed about pleasuring myself. But it was to him. And I wish it wasn't a vibrator actually getting me off, but my husband.

My streak of terrible luck continues. I won the jackpot when it comes to husbands in terms of hotness, yet the man wants nothing to do with me.

Even if he does make an overture, I'm not sure what I'd do. My body has one thought—hell, yes!—but my mind isn't convinced. I'm not in the market to be a booty call.

Not even if the caller is my husband.

I take a deep breath and head over to the desk with my makeup case and apply some lipstick and mascara before fixing my hair into a low ponytail because the humidity today killed any chance of doing something fancy. Once I put on some pearl studs, I race down the stairs and out the door to the driveway where Jim is waiting in his truck.

The ride is uncomfortably silent but at least it only lasts twenty minutes. Twenty long minutes. I sit straight in my seat when we arrive at Shaken & Stirred. "I didn't know we were going here."

Jim shifts the truck into park and turns to me. "Didn't find out until an hour ago. Should've mentioned it. Is it a problem?"

I shake my head and try not to grimace. Having my brand-new coworkers wait on me doesn't make for the most fun evening—it's quite awkward actually—but I'll live. The whiskey bar is relatively new, but unlike most of the restaurants located along the waterfront, it boasts an air of down-to-earth sophistication. A wall of polished whiskey barrels greets customers when they arrive. Everything in S&S is polished mahogany and iron. Crème-colored tabletops and solitary roses sitting prettily in crystal vases bring a sense of romance to an otherwise dark space. No wonder his friend is having his birthday here.

We exit the truck and head toward the entrance. Jim sidles up beside me and takes my hand into his. My eyes widen and when I look up at him, he just faces forward, his spine straight and his muscles tense, as if he's heading into battle. Oh hell, what am I walking into?

My grasp tightens and I mimic his posture, plastering a

smile on my face. I've got this. Once we are inside, we head over to the hostess, Inara, who I met the other day. Her curly, dark-chocolate hair with eyes to match, and a sweetly rounded face, give the woman a cherubic quality that would be hard to forget. But despite her angelic face, Inara's aura dictates she has no problem tearing her dress to put someone into an armbar. And ironically, we'd met before when I came down to the Virginia Search and Rescue Council's conference three years ago.

Inara smiles when she sees me. "Hey, Taya."

"Hi, Inara." I step forward and angle my body sideways as I prepare to make introductions. "This is my husband, Jim."

"Hello," Jim says, extending his hand.

She takes it, giving him a polite smile. "Nice to meet you."

Jim steps back, glances around the place, and then strides off through the row of tables toward Bear, Lucas Craiger, Tony Martinez and three women I don't know. I practically lean past my center of gravity just to stare at Jim's ass before he disappears behind the semi-translucent partition wall.

Inara nudges me with one shoulder. "Oh, Patrick told me to relay that we have training this coming weekend. If the weather holds, we're gonna do some rappelling. You up for it?"

"Hell, yeah."

Bear and a small, redheaded woman talk as everyone takes their seats. They laugh at something with Tony, and she angles her head at Bear for a kiss on the cheek without pausing in her conversation with the other men. My chest aches at the sight. Why couldn't I have been matched with someone who wanted to be in the program?

I smooth my top and walk over to the table, exchanging a nod with Lucas as I turn past the booth on my left. His dark-brown hair is freshly cut. Wearing a light-pink shirt that brings out the olive tones of his skin, he's as well dressed and confident as I've ever seen him. Lucas is a quiet, unassuming man until Tony gets him going, so it's not surprising to see him talking quietly, forehead to forehead, with his own companion.

Jim's lips slacken when I arrive and when he smiles at me, my pulse skyrockets. A small gasp sneaks past my lips when he stands and leans in toward me. Dear God, he's going to kiss me. And I want him to. But he doesn't kiss me. Instead, he hooks his thumbs into the pockets of his jeans and shifts on his feet before placing his hand on the small of my back, ushering me into the seat next to him.

I wave at Bear as I sit, and he lifts his chin in standard man-greeting.

Bear's companion smiles at me. "You must be Taya?"

I nod, and she reaches out to punch Tony in the shoulder.

The larger man winces. "What the hell, Marge?"

She stares him down, her eyes narrowed to slits, and jerks her head in the direction of the other two women in their party. Tony flushes at her censure and ducks his head. He looks like a shamefaced child when he finally turns to me.

"Sorry, Taya." He gestures to the woman he'd walked in with. "This is Candy, and that's her friend, Susan."

We all exchange nods, and Tony mumbles under his breath. "Not like you introduced yourself, *Marge*."

Marge purses her lips, and Tony slumps in his seat. "Dufus over there has a point. I'm Marge, Bear's wife." She stands and reaches out to pat Martinez's shoulder as she passes. "We'll be right back, birthday boy."

He leans back and crosses his arms, a sly grin plastered on his face. "Marge, I know about the cake. Just tell me it's red velvet this year. You know I hate chocolate."

Marge hits Bear in the gut. "Did my hubby open his big mouth again?"

Tony laughs. "Nope. But after a decade, your homemade cake ain't exactly a surprise."

Marge flushes and grabs Bear by the arm. "Whatever. As long as you act surprised when you see it, I don't give a shit."

Tony salutes to Marge and Bear as they make their way out of the restaurant and refocuses his attention on Candy, the raven-haired bombshell at his side. The two of them are talking a mile a minute, his arm slung haphazardly across her shoulders.

Jim clears his throat, and I face him. He's half-smiling at his friends, the soft glow from the lamps above intensifying the sharp angles of his face. "I'm sorry. I should've introduced you the way you did with your coworker."

"It's alright. I know the guys already."

Jim might not have wanted to marry me, but there is no denying he is the husband I need after everything I've been through. Because at the end of the day, he is a steady, infallible presence. Strong, determined, and uncompromising. A port in a storm. And while he may not be operating at one hundred percent, he's determined to get back to it. If only I can convince him I'm the woman he needs. Make him as invested in making this marriage work as I am.

My hand lifts on its own accord and rests on his forearm. His pupils dilate and he shifts in his chair. I smile and turn away, taking a piece of bread from the basket. If I continued to look at him any longer I might have kissed him, and I'm not sure how he would've taken it, especially in front of his friends.

"Long time, no see."

My head jerks toward Jim just as a woman places her pale, delicate hand against the muscular strength of Jim's shoulder. My husband goes so still, it's as if he's made of stone. The woman strokes Jim's arm with exaggerated slowness, leaning in so her breasts practically spill out of her low-cut top. "So, Stephens, this must be that lucky twit of yours?"

Jim shrugs her hand away and shifts in his seat, putting more distance between them as his eyes narrow.

Tony and Lucas stiffen along with their dates. Jim's shoulders are tight, and he's clenching his jaw so hard a muscle jumps beneath the ever-present stubble. He opens his mouth as if to say something, only to clam up with a snarl.

"Hello-o-o?" The woman's long red fingernail taps his head, and I resist the urge to reach out and break her hand. "Are you still all scrambled eggs up there?"

Crimson climbs up his neck and rides his cheekbones, and my patience snaps. He may not trust me enough yet to open up, but she's officially gone too far and I'm over it. "You should keep your damn hands to yourself. And your insults."

Before I can call her all the names currently sitting on the tip of my tongue, Jim whips around to me and gives the smallest shake of his head. So I pick up my glass of water and guzzle it down, then set the empty glass down with enough force to rattle Tony's silverware. Tony leans back, biting the corner of his lower lip, and winks up at me. Goofball. His distraction technique works. Some of my tension eases as I waggle my eyebrows at him.

"And who's your friend there, hmm? She's a little bit of a downgrade, don't you think? Better watch out, though, because she's already making eyes at your buddy there," the mystery woman says.

My gasp is still forming when a low, throaty snarl cuts through the loud chatter, and I whip my head sideways. Jim's expression is thunderous, his brows drawn low over stormy eyes, and his jaw so tight, the muscles look like steel. There's so much anger on his face and in the tight way he holds himself, as if he's going to come out of his chair. Tony places his hand at the small of my back, gently grabbing my shirt when I lean closer to Jim, and Jim's fist crashes down onto the table. "Talk about my wife again and you'll have a problem you won't be able to buy your way out of."

Bear and Marge come back, their arms laden with presents and a cake. The two set everything out on the table and Bear takes his seat. Marge, arms unladen, walks around to pat the woman's shoulder as if she's consoling a grieving friend. "Brittney, why are you here? You stopped being welcome once Jim divorced your sister, so go run along and let us be."

The woman straightens and crosses her arms beneath her breasts. "Soon enough, Jimmy won't be part of the group either. He's on his last leg. I mean, come on, everyone's talking about how Mr. Super SEAL's brain is all fucked up."

That's it. I jump out of my chair with an angry growl and start trying to push my way toward her, but Tony's hand holds me back. Likewise, Bear stands and wraps one big arm around his wife's waist after a small, but evil, chuckle passes her lips. Jim half-rises from his seat, his gaze bouncing between his best friend and the small redhead Bear's holding tight. I get the impression that Marge's calm is only a front. The men are treating her like some undercover ninja with shuriken at the ready.

"You'd better leave now before I tell the manager to throw you out with the rest of the trash. He'd be happy to kick your soldier-hating body right on your ass." Marge drums her well-manicured nails against the table.

"Here, let me show you the way." I make another move to go for the woman, but once again, Tony keeps me in place.

"Easy, girl," he murmurs. "Trust me when I say, she's not worth getting your hands dirty."

I make due with a glare instead. If I had claws, they'd be fully out right now. Brittney had no right to out Jim like that. No right to touch him. She's lucky I'm trapped between the table and my husband; otherwise, she'd be missing teeth already.

With a huff, Brittney makes way toward the front patio doors. Marge salutes her with a glass of whiskey, swirling the amber liquid around so that it dances in its glass container. "Bye, bitch." When Brittney is out of sight, Marge turns to me and lifts an appraising brow. "Well, I do believe we're going to get along just fine."

Bear gives a little chuckle and casts his gaze at the ceiling, before he and everyone else turns to Jim, who's gone silent. I chew on my cheek and swallow hard as the seconds tick by. Jim stares at his glass, unblinking. I sidle closer to him, my body leaning against him the slightest bit to let him know I'm there for him.

But he pulls away and glares at me this time. What the hell did I do? My cheeks, damn them, burn under his scrutiny. Anger mixed with hurt tugs at every muscle in my body, demanding release, but there's nothing, *nothing* I can do to vent the horrible, suffocating mass of it. My chest, neck, and ears boil with the heat of one thousand fires, and I swear smoke must be rising off me. But he's not the cause. Bear and Marge are whispering to each other, so I lower my voice and return his glare. "Don't take what the stupid skank did out on me."

"Drop it." His words hiss out through clenched teeth.

"While you may be fine taking her abuse, I'm not. You're my husband and I'll be damned if anyone is going to talk to you like that."

Jim jerks at my words as if slapped across the face. His hands ball into fists. He closes his eyes and his shoulders lift, then lower. When he opens them again, his expression is more relaxed. "I don't want to make a bigger scene than we already did. I'm tired of people staring at me all the time, for the wrong reasons."

There's a sharp twist beneath my ribs. Jim's a proud and tough man who's probably humiliated at the moment. Which isn't fair. The only person who should feel humiliated right now is Brittney. I sigh, and the last of my anger drains away. "I understand. Thank you for sticking up for me, by the way."

"Thanks for sticking up for me too."

His green eyes soften when they meet mine and I'm trapped, a prisoner to the emotions lurking just beneath the surface. Damn, I can almost imagine that we have a chance to make this marriage work.

An awkward silence falls over the table, until Bear clears his throat and we both turn to look at him. "Hey Jim, did you ever get a chance to finish the comic you borrowed the other day?"

"Comic?" I brighten, looking up at Jim with eager eyes.

"I didn't know you liked comics too. Which one are you reading?"

"The *Halo* one," Bear says, ignoring Jim's stiffly shaken head. "You're into the game, right? Jim's a big fan too. I thought maybe if he was done with the comic, you guys would have something . . . nice to talk about."

"Yeah, I love *Halo*." I tilt my head when Jim shoots Bear a death glare. "You embarrassed to be into comic books?"

The smile slowly slips from my face. Wait a second. How does Bear know about the comics I like?

Shit.

Oh, shit.

I'm practically hyperventilating, my vision going spotty. They were in my bedroom. What if Jim saw the scrapbook? What if they both saw the scrapbook? I could lose everything. My palms are sweating, and I can't catch my breath. Thomas Byrne, the officer killed, was my dad's partner and my godfather. He was the reason my father joined the task force.

Why did I keep those articles?

Oh, that's right. So I don't forget what Santoro has taken away, not just from me but others.

My heart rate spikes, anger replacing anxiety. I slam my hand down onto the table causing glasses filled with whiskey to slosh everywhere, and lean closer to Jim. "You have the nerve to sneak into *my* room and steal *my* things?"

He stands up, the hard edge of his tone full of stubbornness and challenge. "If I need to get something from one of *my* rooms, I will."

I stand as well and poke my goliath husband in the chest. "I know you don't want to be married, that you were forced into the program. But I do want to be here. And we are married. And I'm your damn wife. So, treat me like it. And Brittney shouldn't have been the reason I found out what is going on with you, how sick you are. You should've told me. Should've trusted me. I asked how many times?"

Jim slaps my hand away and shoves his chair back with enough force to send it crashing to the restaurant floor. He pales suddenly and sways. Beads of sweat line his forehead, his breathing becoming rapid and shallow. I reach out to lay a hand on his arm to steady him, but he stumbles out of reach.

Bear scooches his chair back and stands. "Jim, sit."

Jim steps farther away from the table and rakes a hand through his hair. His gaze bounces between all of us, his lips pressed into a tight line. He closes his eyes and takes another backward step, then turns on his heel and storms out of the bar.

CHAPTER ELEVEN

Jim

I'M *SORRY.*

Two words that should be simple enough to say. But putting my business on display for the public isn't my thing. Though, after Brittney's scene two nights ago, people who don't even know a thing about me now know I'm broken. Leave it to my ex's sister to tell the world I'm the emotional equivalent of Humpty Dumpty after his fall from grace. All of my pieces are glued back with such haphazard carelessness that I can't remember what it feels like to be whole. Or what it feels like to go through life without falling apart, without being forced to admit my own weakness.

I drag my hands over my face, my heart in my throat, as I do my best impression of a kicked puppy in the middle of Shaken & Stirred. Taya catches sight of me, slams down her tray, and turns on her heel to stalk off in the opposite direction. My body trembles and I dig my nails into my scalp, wishing for the hundredth time that my stubborn wife had acknowledged me when I'd tapped on her door last night. Or the night before. This whole thing could have been handled in private. Although, shit, guess that cat had gotten out of the bag two days ago. Until then, Bear had been the only one who knew about my TBI, but now everyone knows. Everyone who was within earshot of our table.

But the way Taya leapt to her feet to defend me. She'd been all fiery eyes and blazing cheeks, a hellcat ready to attack on my behalf. Hope bubbles in my chest for a second before I viciously squash the feeling. Taya deserves someone normal, someone who can stand up to the light of her scrutiny without cutting her on all his ragged, imperfect edges. She deserves someone better than me.

But right now, we need to put on a performance for my superiors and any of the committee attending the function later tonight. My jaw aches and I'm grinding my teeth together as I flag down the hostess. "Can you get her? It's important."

Inara crosses her arms, her eyes boring into me. "*Me importa tres pepinos.*"

"Please?"

She turns, flinging her hand at me in a dismissive wave. "Sure."

Inara heads into the back. Despite her snarky claim that she cares more about cucumbers than what I think is important, a minute later, Taya makes her way toward me. I force a smile, but the muscles in my face tighten and twitch. Taya stops in front of me, her forehead a collection of unhappy little wrinkles. With one hip cocked and her arms folded beneath the small swell of her teacup breasts, she's the personification of feisty disapproval in a server's apron and non-slick shoes.

"What do you want?"

"There's a mandatory work party and I need you to come with me." Not the best start, but I'm fully prepared to apologize and grovel for a date rather than show up in front of my commanding officer without Taya on my arm. This is my shot to prove that I'm committed to the IPP program.

"No."

"Please?"

"No."

I want to turn around and leave, but I'm already down to the wire. Maybe I'll just toss her over my shoulder and make a run for it. Taking a deep breath, I try again. "I know you're mad, but I need your help. We don't even have to talk or stand next to one another. We're basically carpooling to an open bar. This is important. If my C.O. doesn't think I'm trying to make the IPP program work, I'm screwed."

Her body slumps, but her eyes remain locked with mine. "When?"

"Tonight."

"Are you serious?" Her voice is high pitched and more than a little accusatory. "You literally waited until the last second?"

"Not exactly." I glance at the time on my phone. "We actually have about three hours."

She swells like a puffer fish and her hands lift, fingers curling into claws. "I get off work at ten. I have to find coverage. And even if I go, I can't stay late. I have plans with Inara and I'm not canceling."

"Fine. We'll leave early. As for coverage . . ." Glancing beyond her, I take in the mostly empty restaurant. There are maybe three occupied tables and a group of servers are at the bar gossiping and watching the overhead television with the captions on. "I think you'll be fine."

A soft growl escapes her as she turns to look at the scene herself. "I don't have anything to wear."

A legitimate concern, if my memory of her closet holds true. A veritable ghost town, the nicest things in there were fancy jeans and some dressy sleeveless shirts. "Most people would have packed more when they move to a new state."

Her bottom lip trembles and her fingers drum against the side of her thigh.

My hand reaches out on its own accord, hungry to touch her, to offer some sort of comfort for once, but she turns away. Sighing heavily, I run my fingers through my hair and edge a little closer, angling my head to one side so I can see her face in profile, if nothing else. "I wasn't trying to be a jerk. When I was in your room the other day, I noticed your lack of clothes."

She hesitates at first but finally shrugs one shoulder in practiced dismissal. She turns to face me, unable or unwilling to make eye contact. "I didn't pack much because there wasn't much to pack."

I reach out slowly, painfully aware I'm treating her like a spooked horse, but unsure of what else I can do. My fingertips brush down the length of her bare arm and it sends electricity crashing through me. "What do you mean?"

"There was a fire." She chokes on the words. "Everything that wasn't reduced to ashes went into my bags."

My stomach coils and the ache in my chest grows claws. Clearing my throat, I motion toward the tables. "See how early you can get out of here. I'll wait for you."

Her eyes narrow and the frustrated wrinkles in her forehead deepen. "Didn't you hear a word I said? I don't have anything to wear."

"I'll take care of it."

She blinks, lips parting. With a small curse, she turns and storms off. I don't know for sure if she'll talk to her supervisor about leaving early, but I'm determined to wait her out either way. When I'd thought she wasn't telling me all of her story, I hadn't expected it to be a fire.

What exactly do I know about her?

I know she hates confrontation. It makes her uncomfortable. More than uncomfortable. Yet, she's more than capable of speaking her mind when she feels strongly about something. I know she's currently struggling with a mission on *Halo 2*, and she enjoys running. There's a bit of a daredevil in her, if the motorcycle is any indication. And she's stubborn like me, especially when it comes to money and what she conceives of as a handout. The woman refuses to use the debit card to our mutual account for anything other than groceries or household goods. She won't even use it to fill her tank with gas.

But when it comes to her reasons for joining the program, all I have are assumptions. Not many people can lose everything, only to turn around and start over somewhere else. What about her friends and family? A lover? She'd asked once if I'd been seeing anyone. Did she leave someone behind in New York?

Maybe I could try explaining the TBI to her. Saying it aloud feels too much like admitting to weakness, but she should've heard about it from me instead of Brittney.

"Now what?"

I jump to my feet at the sound of her voice and spin to face Taya whose hands are wrapped tightly around the straps of her bag. I've been so lost in thought, I didn't hear her approaching. That's a new one for me. "Now, we go shopping."

Her brows furrow, disgust spreading over her face. It's hard to tell whether she hates the idea of shopping or shopping with me. At least we'll be miserable together. "Come on. There's a boutique that isn't far. We'll find you something for the party."

"What about my bike?"

"If you can carpool tomorrow, I'll come by for your bike while you're out."

She adjusts her ponytail, so it sits lower, closer to her neck. I'm tempted to brush my hand through it, but I stop myself.

"I appreciate the offer, but I'll just follow you there." As we exit the restaurant, she mutters under her breath about how I shouldn't have waited until the last damn minute.

It doesn't take long to reach the small boutique. Like most of the shops along the beach, it's a tourist trap. The clothes are high-end and one of a kind, and the price tags are about one hundred dollars more than they would be elsewhere. It's the reason I buy most of my clothes from the outlet mall down the street from my house.

Taya pulls one of the dresses from the rack. Holding it up against the length of her body, she admires the way it sets off the darker undertones in her skin. Then, she catches sight of the price tag and her eyes bulge. "Three hundred dollars for a dress?"

I turn my chuckle into a clearing of the throat. "It's a nice dress."

"It's not that nice." She reracks the dress and searches for something else.

"Doesn't matter what you pick." I comb through the rest of the rack, bowing my head so the brim of my cap can shield my face. "You'll look amazing, regardless of what you wear."

There's a soft inhalation, the smallest of gasps, and she moves away almost immediately. We search in silence for a few minutes before she pulls a long red number made of silk from the rack. I raise a brow at the choice, but don't have any complaints. Considering her usual wardrobe, I wouldn't have pegged her as the dressy, glam type.

"I'm sorry about the other day." It's like popping a dislocated bone back into place. Don't think about it, just dive right in.

Dubious, she readjusts the dress in her arms. "For which part?"

I snort. "How about all of it?"

She shrugs as if she doesn't care as we walk through the shoe aisle, but I can tell by her expression that she does. Everything she's thinking broadcasts on her face. I know the question she wants to ask but doesn't.

"It's not an excuse, but I've been dealing with something. More accurately, refusing to deal with it. I told you what I do, but I guess all the low-level shock waves from breaching entrances took their toll." A massive understatement. "The doctors claim I'm suffering from a traumatic brain injury, and even though it will heal, it sort of screws with my day-to-day life unless I keep up with my meds."

Taya slumps, and the lingering anger on her face disappears like smoke. "You're right. It's not an excuse, but I appreciate you finally telling me. It made me anxious because every time I tried to help, you got angry, so now I'm never sure what to do."

"Never meant to make you anxious. Just didn't want to appear weak in front of you. Or anyone." The urge to brush my thumb across her face, to kiss the curve of her mouth, is overwhelming. "If I had, I wouldn't have needed to break into your room to get my prescription." I chuckle, hoping to lighten the mood.

She gasps. "Oh, my God. Is that why you were . . .?" She groans, rubbing her free hand down her face. "I'm so sorry I yelled at you. I didn't know."

"It's not your fault. I shouldn't have invaded your privacy, and I shouldn't have taken your book. You were well within your right to snap."

Taya waves my words away as she picks up a pair of gold ankle strap heels. "Your medication is more important than my privacy. Just know that next time, you can talk to me. I'm here for you."

"I know." The words are inadequate when it comes to expressing how much her support means, especially when she's offered it all along. If only I hadn't been so stubborn and accepted it sooner.

I head for the front of the boutique and Taya falls into step beside me.

"Hold on a second. Was the prescription for a refill?"

And here we go. I've had this argument with Bear more times than I can count. "No. I refused to take the medication for a while. And please don't lecture me. Bear already has, and he's the one who forced me to go get it. Even went with me to the pharmacy and stood in front of my face to make sure I took the first pill."

"I'm happy someone's been watching out for you, but now you have someone else." She raises a brow. "In fact, Brittney was two seconds away from a WWE-worthy smackdown."

I laugh, imagining Taya beating the shit out of Brittney. I take the dress from her before she can protest and lay it on the counter. The cashier is several feet away and doesn't seem enthused about setting aside his cell phone. "You would've had to wait your turn. Marge already called dibs."

She giggles, and the cashier glances up from his phone, his eyes raking over her body. Taya hasn't noticed, too busy rummaging through her purse in search of her wallet. After a second of my staring into the side of his head, the man's attention shifts from Taya to me. He pales, and my chest swells. I'm one shot of testosterone away from beating my chest like King Kong. Happy to establish dominance the human way, I pull my Mastercard free and start to hand it to the young man.

I blink when Taya's hand on my wrist draws me up short. "What are you doing?"

"What are *you* doing?" she answers back.

"Something nice."

Unable to dispute this, she folds her arms beneath her breasts.

I lift a brow. "What's the problem?"

"You realize this dress is five hundred dollars?"

"And?" I draw out the word for added effect.

"And I don't want your charity. If you feel guilty—"

"This has nothing to do with guilt." I don't sound convincing.

"Good. Because you can't buy my forgiveness, so if you're still trying to make up for the other day, this isn't necessary."

I lean in, close enough to surround myself in her feminine scent. The urge to bury my face against the curve of her neck and drink her in hits me low and hard. Instead of giving in to the urge, I speak so only she can hear my words. "You're my wife and this is a mandated work function for my job, so the particulars are my responsibility."

Taya acquiesces with a defeated little huff that makes me want to drag it from her again, for other, softer, reasons. I smile at the cashier and wiggle the card at him as Taya turns her head in the other direction.

This time, I don't hesitate to brush my hand through the locks of hair at the nape of her neck. Her eyes find mine through her thick lashes as she blushes.

CHAPTER TWELVE

Taya

VIRGINIA BEACH MAY not be New York, but it has its attractions. I've been living here for over a month, and my exposure to the nightlife is made up exclusively of what happens while I'm at work. Or playing video games when I can't sleep at night, especially when Jim's at work and the house is too quiet. Neither calls for nice clothes or full-scale makeup application.

Hell, the last time I went all out like this was for prom.

Feeling my body slip into cool silk and watching the way the deep red sets off the olive tones of my skin makes me feel like expensive chocolate. Rich and decadent. Edible. The dress dips low over my breasts, and I love how plump and round they look. I don't have much to work with, but the double-sided tape holding the décolletage just so draws the eye and gives the illusion of fullness. I'm in love with the way the draping silk hugs every curve and rounds out my thighs and ass. Smokey eyeshadow accents my almond-shaped eyes and a pair of strappy heels give me a few extra inches of height, just enough so Jim isn't towering over me when we step into the renovated theater in the heart of the city.

Jim's eyes trail over me. "You look amazing."

I duck my chin and grab some of the red silk hem as I step onto the carpeted floor. My face heats. "Thanks. But you know, you don't have to keep saying it."

A deep flush creeps up his neck.

God, I love that color on his skin.

He takes my hand and I love the way the calluses on his palm along with the way the neat, surgically cut line of his fingernails plays against the skin across the back of my hand. He's so large, his hand nearly engulfs mine.

The space holds dozens of tables and has plenty of room for a sweeping dance floor. The stage was left intact, and tonight, the curtains are drawn aside so guests can watch the musicians perform. The band is doing a cover of a song I don't recognize, but the beat makes me want to sway my hips, nonetheless. I love dancing. It's the closest thing to freedom on two feet. Dancing and sex, anyway.

Jim looks handsome in his dress uniform. The slim-fitting navy-blue coat with the pins and medals makes me want to sink to my knees before him and let him grip my hair while I take him into my mouth. I've always had a weak spot for men in uniform. Tonight, Jim is pushing all my buttons—the panty-soaking buttons, not the strangle-him-in-his-sleep buttons. He's pretty much worn those down to the nub.

I look away, my fingertips trailing over his ribbons and medals. I remove my hand, walk past him a little and try to gaze at something else. He turns to greet a couple advancing toward us, and a small whimper escapes my lips when my gaze falls to admire the shape of his ass in his dress pants. He doesn't get out any more than I do, if those pants are anything to go by. He must have been a lot less muscular the last time he'd worn his dress blues.

"Taya?" That's my cue. I smile and hold out my hand for yet another handshake. "This is Mrs. Greene."

"You're the general's wife?" Luckily, Jim whispered a five-second backstory into my ear as she sashayed over. "Jim has told me so much about you. You have kids, isn't that right?"

The woman, whose first name has been carried away on the wings of chance, beams at me. "Two boys. They're a handful. And, of course, they want to be just like their father. You'll know what that's like soon enough, I bet."

May God strike me down first.

"Fingers crossed." I force a giggle and chat with her for an indeterminate amount of time that somehow feels like an eternity while Jim speaks with her husband a mere foot away. The longer we spend making the rounds, the less guilty I feel about letting him buy me this dress. My plan had been to return the outrageously priced gown afterward, but to hell with that. Inane chatter has more than covered the cost of my ensemble.

Jim lays his fingers on the small of my back and leads me over to another couple. His touch sizzles with pleasure. The solid maleness of him makes me feel exquisitely soft and female in a way I'd forgotten I could be.

I've been starved for human affection since long before I left New York. Once my dad joined the task force, I'd been preoccupied. He would hardly sleep, eat, or clean. Every spare moment was dedicated to taking down Santoro. Hell, some days I became the parent, demanding he finish his dinner. Or showing up at the precinct with a sandwich and not leaving until every last crumb was swallowed.

Now, I can't remember the last time someone touched me. I enjoy sex. Even the no strings, no expectations, just the satisfaction of touching and being touched kind of sex. But the touch I crave now isn't sexual. I want to lift Jim's hand and press it against the side of my face to rest in his warmth. Being near him makes me feel safe, protected. And makes me feel comfortable.

Jim leans, his lips gently press against my ear. "I'm heading to the restroom. Why don't you take a seat at the table? I'll meet you there."

He pulls away and heads off to the other side of the room, taking the warmth and security of his body with him. I sigh and head over to our table to rest my feet. Tony and Lucas are stationed at a different table for dinner, but Marge and Bear are assigned to sit with me and Jim. However, they are off making rounds of their own. I suppose even the military plays politics to an extent. Charming your superiors and their wives seems to be just as important as being good at what you do. It makes me nervous. I don't want to offend anyone and accidentally get Jim demoted.

"You must be Jim's new wife?" The woman shares a smile with her friend, and crosses one long leg over the other as our table fills.

I don't recognize the woman, but the way she stressed "new" sends bile creeping up my throat.

My eyes widen as another woman sits next to her with a laugh. "Excuse Karen. She's not good at first impressions. What she meant to say was, we all thought Jim outgrew his 'groupie into a housewife' phase after his divorce from Raychel."

Groupie into a housewife? I know these bitches aren't talking about me. Before I can snap at either of them and ruin my resolution to behave, Bear and Marge arrive. As usual, the giant is holding her close and whispering something in her ear. He only softens when she's nearby, and it makes my heart ache.

Marge reads the atmosphere immediately, and her eyes narrow. "Karen. Claudia." She addresses the women with an equal amount of dislike, and I hide a smirk. With Marge here, the two women more closely resemble scolded children than wise-cracking mean girls. I grin up at the two of them, and Bear grins back.

"You mind?" He indicates that he and Marge would like to sit next to me.

I nod.

Marge claims the seat closest to me. "You look lovely tonight, by the way."

I look down at my dress and run my palms over the soft

material. "Thanks."

She smiles and leans in, her next words for the two of us alone. "Ignore these nasty, rank-hungry bitches. They're all bark and no bite. Tell Jim to throw in some jewelry and another outfit for the hostile work environment."

My body goes cold.

He told her. While I'd been thinking about his hands, he'd been gossiping to his friends. I grind my teeth together. I prefer ridicule to pity. And pity is what I suspect has brought Marge and Bear to my rescue.

"Taya, I love your necklace, by the way. I've been staring at it all night."

At Marge's words, I glance down. I don't need to look at the necklace to know what she means, but the sight of it comforts me.

I trace my fingers across the pendant that sits at the hollow of my throat. "It belonged to my grandmother."

Her eyes sparkle, and a smile teases her lips. "So, it's like a family heirloom?"

I can't help but grin back at Marge. "Basically. I'm part Mongolian on my mom's side. *Emee* was an *udgan*, or shaman. The necklace is supposed to protect me."

Jim places a hand on my shoulder as he tries to wiggle between my chair and a waiter, sending tingles of pleasure waltzing down my spine. "Does it work?" The deep, rumbling baritone of his voice sounds like a jaguar purring inside a cello.

I don't talk about my heritage much, but when I do,

people usually misunderstand. They think *Emee* was either a charlatan or a crackpot. I brought the necklace to show and tell one year, shortly after her death. Everyone in class laughed at me and called me the Wicked Witch of the Northside.

My classmates may have given me a hard time, but it could have been worse. My old classmate, Ally, was half Korean and half black. She grew up in a primarily Asian neighborhood and the parents on her block wouldn't let their kids play with her or touch her without making them wash their hands afterward with bleach. Looking at Ally made me feel lucky. It was also a silent reminder to keep the things I considered the most special and interesting about me to myself.

I grip the turquoise stone that hangs on a simple braided leather cord and houses my family's *Ongon*, or ancestral spirit. According to Dad, it held all the spirits of every shaman within our family. It was passed down from mother to daughter, and it's meant to protect me and give me wisdom. But does it work?

I turn the stone around between my fingers. "I'm not sure."

Marge reaches over to squeeze my hand. "Well, it must be working so far, otherwise you wouldn't be here."

Jim says something in that smooth growl of his that vibrates right down into my bones as he pulls out his chair and takes a seat next to me, but I miss the words. Dinner finally arrives but instead of devouring the meal like I want, I pick at it instead. Especially with those evil bitches watching every move I make. And the way their husbands stare at Jim and me, it's as if we're the newest museum exhibit. A spectacle of sorts.

I want to support Jim. But the pressure of worrying about every little thing I do with all these eyes on me is suffocating. Still, I can't fail. It's my duty as his wife to make sure he looks good in front of his superiors, no matter what I feel. The same way my mother put on her game face when she hosted one of the precinct's holiday parties even though she had the flu.

A boom of laughter thunders out of Jim's mouth, and my breath catches in my throat. Wow, I didn't know he even knew how to laugh. But he's good at it. In fact, he's the kind of guy who throws his head back and slaps tabletops when he laughs because the sound is too big for him to hang on to. It's a bright, honest sound. Infectious. It brings a smile to my face, and I sway toward him as if there's physical warmth to be found in his honest mirth.

I start giggling, and he turns to catch my eye. There's a moment of shared silence before we're both laughing at one another. I laugh until I'm red in the face and short of breath.

The band starts to play again and I stand then grab Jim's hand and pull him up from his chair. "Dance with me?"

The corner of his lip quirks up, giving him a lopsided smile, and he nods. We make our way onto the dance floor and Jim pulls me close to him. The violins kick in, then the piano, and finally the slow and sure beating of the drums.

We dance and spin around the floor, my dress billowing out and the lights twinkling with every step. I soak in Jim's scent, his strength, and the pressure of his warm hand on the small of my back. The music twirls around us like thread and I rest my head on his chest.

I think I'm falling for my husband.

The music slows and I lift my head and look into his soft green eyes. Forget think, I absolutely am falling for my husband. I lift up on my toes, inching my lips closer to his. Instead of pulling away, Jim lowers his head, his lips about to meet mine.

"Senior Chief Stephens."

Jim straightens and twists to face the man standing at our side. "Captain Redding."

Redding. I've heard the name before. Crap, this is Jim's commanding officer. I straighten just like Jim did and wrap my arm around his waist.

The older gentleman angles his head to me and smiles. "You must be Taya."

I gently nod. "Yes, sir."

Captain Redding's gaze bounces between the both of us before he shakes his head and laughs. "Appears the program actually works. And to think of all the pushback you gave me, Stephens, for forcing you into the program. Reconsidering only staying in it for a year?"

I glance up at Jim. Then a bright flash blinds me. Then another. And another.

My head jerks sideways as I scan the room. Another flash

goes off and finally I spot the photographers. My muscles tense and the air rushes from my lungs.

Oh, God.

I suck in another sharp breath and close my eyes as my heart beats so hard it threatens to explode. If I end up in the papers, Marco can find me. What if Santoro wants me dead? Another flash goes off and my eyelids snap open.

The photographer is facing us.

Jim pulls me tight into his side. "Sir, it was great seeing you. But I believe our ride is ready to leave. Hope you enjoy the rest of the evening."

Captain Redding nods to the both of us and makes his way into the crowd. Jim ushers me out of the building and into the cold air. When the cool breeze hits my face I take a deep breath. Jim's hand grips my upper arms as if to steady me. "Taya, are you alright?"

I stare at him, unable to speak. Concern etches into his features. I can't tell him. For sure, he'll want to leave me. The man faces enough danger every day. No way he'll want to stay married to me after what happened to my father at the hands of my best friend.

"Is everything okay?"

Jim and I turn our heads to face Marge. Sucking in a breath, I force out an answer before they push any further on the subject. "I didn't eat much, plus it was a lot . . . the worrying about doing the wrong thing. Then the camera flashes did me in for some reason."

Marge places a hand on my shoulder. "Bear just pulled

up with the truck. Let's get you both home."

Jim helps me into the back seat, then climbs in. Marge twists in the passenger seat as she buckles her seat belt and glances back at me. I offer her a weak smile and she only turns back around when Jim sidles up to me.

Bear pulls away from the curb and I can't help but lean into Jim's strength as the truck bounces along. I am safe with him—tethered to him.

Jim lowers his face until his mouth is near my ear. "Are you okay?"

I lean my head against his and close my eyes. "Yes. You're here, so I'll be fine."

The silk of my dress moves in tandem with the sway of the truck, my breasts bouncing without a bra to hinder their movement. It would've been weird for Jim to buy me new underwear and I hadn't wanted any lines interrupting the lay of the dress. Plus, my tits are so small it didn't seem worth it to wear one. I was fine for much of the night, but now I feel exposed.

I look up at him and his eyes are dark, heavy-lidded and hungry. With his cap gone and his hair freshly cut, it's impossible to miss the sharp lines of his face. It's almost criminal for his lips to look so soft, and my gut twists with an answering hunger when he growls softly.

My nipples are hard and aching, and I press them against his arm, hoping the pressure will ease at the touch. Is he hard? I want to see, but I'm afraid to look. If he is, I'll probably moan and end up drawing attention from Marge and Bear.

But the truck lurches to a stop a moment later. Marge turns and smacks her husband's arm. "Easy on the brake there."

I chuckle and Jim shifts to open the door then offers his hand to help me out. I scoot across the seat and place my hand in his as I step down and onto the asphalt. "Thank you both for the ride home."

"Hope ya feel better," Bear says.

"Thank you."

They pull away and Jim places his hand on the small of my back as we walk to the front door. Inside the house is dark, and my heels click against the tile as I step into the kitchen. Aspirin, water and a couple of hours of sleep are needed before I head over to Inara's. Nothing like coming down from an adrenaline dump. I sway and clip my hip on the corner of the island. After the sting subsides, I hold my hands out, searching in the dark until I finally reach the cupboards. "Um, where's the aspirin?"

My skin heats when he reaches past me, his body pressed against mine. His—holy shit—erection presses against my ass. My back arches and I moan, my lips parted and hungry.

He stills.

The spicy cinnamon smell of Jim's cologne fills my nose, the dampness of his hot breath a brand on my neck. His body is taut as if he's afraid to move, but his dick twitches against my backside and I lean into him, picturing the veins running along the length of his dick. I want him inside me so bad it verges on need.

Jim spins me around, then pins me against the counter. "You going to tell me what exactly happened at the party?"

I blink rapidly. This isn't where I thought it was going. "I told you already."

He moves closer, pressing his body to mine. "Yeah, not buying it. Gonna tell me the truth? Or you going to make me drag it out of you?"

A small moan escapes me, and he looks down, making me shiver. I could do with a nice distraction and, considering his dilated pupils and shallow breaths, I may be able to distract him from this line of questioning as well. So, I reach up and grab the back of his head, pulling him down as I crash my lips to his. My teeth sink into his bottom lip before I graze my tongue against his teeth, begging for access.

Jim's massive hands grab at my breasts, kneading them hungrily before traveling to my sides. His fingers claw at my dress, hoisting it over my hips as he parts his lips, allowing me to explore his mouth, his tongue.

He pulls back a little. "Do you want me to stop?"

I reach down and grab the hard bulge between his legs and squeeze hard. "Don't you dare."

His palms pull me into his massive frame as he grinds himself against me, kicking my legs apart with his. My arms press against the granite to steady myself. My body shakes as his hand travels between my legs, his thick fingers stroking the moist skin of my lower lips.

I moan, needing more. "Take me."

Sweeping me up into his massive arms, he carries me across the space to my favorite place in this house, the bay window nook. He places me on the edge of the cushioned seat, my back propped up by the cushions and sprawled before him, dress hiked up around my waist. His fingers dip into my hips, and I raise one leg to give him better access. He steps between my knees, spreading me wide so he can look down at my wet thighs and hungry center. I arch my back and lift my hips, moving back and forth on empty air until his eyes blaze.

Jim practically rips his buttons loose in his rush to undo his pants. I'm not much help. The best I can do is make desperate little noises in the back of my throat while I part my lower lips with my fingertips. Jim's eyes darken to nearly black. As soon as he pulls his heady, throbbing dick free, he's pushing forward.

He sinks deep inside of me in a rush that drags a sharp cry from my lips. I gasp and grip the cushion as my body stretches to accommodate him. He leans over and thrusts again, so tight, so deep, I can feel his balls brush my buttocks. It would be so easy to come from just the feel of him filling me, making me whole. My inner walls spasm around his iron length, and my nails rake his skin.

Jim groans as his teeth graze over my neck and bite my earlobe.

"I saw you," I say, unable to recognize the wanton desire in my own voice.

His eyes dart up, panic flaring across them.

"I saw you," I whimper as he pounds into me in a way that's both raw and possessive. "In the garage."

His fingers clench around my thighs, his pace slowing, his nostrils flaring. Is that vulnerability or just a trick of the light slipping through the shades?

"Did you like it? Watching?"

"Yes," I admit in a groan, growing all the wetter at the memory.

His eyes remain locked with mine and something carnal replaces the control once there. Jim drives into me over and over, the sound of slapping bodies and wild moans filling the room, and I bask in the sharp satisfaction of pushing him over the edge.

I want him to go harder, deeper. I want him so deep inside of me the sensation takes away everything else. I want to forget. I want to forget Santoro, I want to forget the fire, and my dad.

Most of all, I want to forget the fear.

He's close, his shaft growing thicker inside me. My inner muscles quiver around him. I clutch his waist with my knees and dig my heels into the back of his thighs, praying he hears my body's plea to consume me.

His thrusts grow more erratic and desperate. I brush my lips against his ear hoping the words I'm about to speak will cause him to lose complete control. "I know you heard me that day in my room. I was replaying the way you fucked your fist, your shaft growing thicker and harder until you came all over the garage floor to the girls on the video."

The admission causes my orgasm to roll up through my body, warm and all-consuming. I shudder and whimper as Jim continues thrusting into me, drawing the orgasm out longer. I cry out, the pleasure too much as I buck beneath him.

He thrusts deeply one last time, thighs and arms trembling. "You. I came to you."

CHAPTER THIRTEEN

Jim

*W*AS IT WORTH *breaking the one rule I set for myself?*
The question plays in my mind as I lay in bed, arm thrown across my forehead and sheets draped low over my hips, after waking up in a cold sweat and reaching out in the middle of the night from the nightmares, my heart sinking when my hand finds nothing but empty space. Taya was so elegant and supportive at the party. And absolutely breathtaking. I would've kissed her on the dance floor if Redding hadn't interrupted. And God, when we did kiss, then being inside of her . . . I want to break that rule over and over again. When I think about how hard she made me come . . .

I clench my fingers in my hair, only now remembering my fault. "Fuck, fuck, fuck." I hadn't pulled out. At the time, grabbing a condom hadn't occurred to me and neither had pulling free before my orgasm rocked through me.

Shit.

I need to apologize before she leaves in the morning. Would she accept it? Doesn't matter. I should've been more responsible, more in control. God, why do I keep screwing up?

Swinging my legs out of bed, I get to my feet and make my way from the room. We need to talk, and it may as well be now. And my sexual fuck-up isn't the only thing I want to discuss. I still want a truthful answer and I won't be able to sleep without knowing if she's okay.

The house is colder than usual. I check every door and window as I walk down the hall. I check them a second and third time, only to return and check them again. Something's off—something I can't put my finger on.

I reach her door and suck in a deep breath, then tap my knuckles against the door. No reply. My muscles twitch, every nerve firing. I need to hear her voice. I knock a little harder this time.

Maybe she's ignoring me.

Or in a deep sleep. I'm sure playing to the crowd all night tired her out. Ah, hell. If she sleeps in and misses meeting up with her friend, she'll blame me for sure. Pressing my ear to the door, I listen for signs of movement as I knock again.

Nothing.

Pushing open the door, I flick on the light and my lungs seize. The room is empty, the blankets pulled neatly beneath each pillow. My feet carry me into the room. I know I promised not to enter, but I need to know she didn't bail on me.

I scan the rest of the room. Her books are still on the

shelves, the teddy bear on the floor next to the bed. I walk over to her closet and throw open the door. Her clothes are still here. I take in a deep breath as my shoulders slump. She hasn't left me.

Even so, I should've come to apologize sooner. But beyond that, where the hell is she at two in the morning? She wasn't supposed to head out for another couple of hours.

I leave her room and head downstairs to the garage, light-footed and tense. I don't recall hearing the rumble of her bike's muffler. Damn thing is so loud, it'd wake the neighborhood. Not to mention riding a bike exhausted is more dangerous than being behind the wheel in a car.

Of course, her bike is gone.

The emptiness of the house presses in at the sight, and the silence grows deafening. A cacophony of nothingness. If she crashes, she'll . . . No, she's fine. Can't think like that. Sweat breaks out on my forehead. I slam the garage door shut, and the sound ricochets through the house like a gunshot.

What if she's running from something other than me?

The way all the color drained from her face at the party. And when she looked at me, wild-eyed and pupils dilated. The tiny tremble of her bottom lip. Taya's afraid of something. Same reaction our Afghani interpreter had when I pulled my gun on her during our last mission.

My gut clenches when past memories come swarming to the front of my mind.

"What the hell is Aland doing here?" Lux lowers his weapon,

approaching slowly as our interpreter and the boy come into sight.

My stomach churns at the thought of the young boy's name. The boy I killed. Aland had been a regular part of our lives for the better part of our year overseas. Every day, he hauled one of the men and haggled over pricing for his fruit. If he had an errand to run for his uncle, he left his basket on the street corner before scurrying off, only to return for it hours later. Both the boy and his basket had become nonentities, as normal a sight as the sun and the sand.

My head throbs like someone has taken a dull blade to my skull. I pace around the foyer in the dark, unable to sit or relax. My eyes water, my nose runs. A wave of nausea churns my stomach and vomit flies out of my mouth, my knees crashing into the hardwood floor. The muscles of my abdomen lurch again, spewing more vile liquid from my stomach.

I gasp loudly, sucking in air and pushing it out until I feel less dizzy. I sit back and wipe my mouth with my forearm, tears pricking at the corners of my eyes as the high-pitched ringing in my ears grow in intensity. My fingers lace through my hair, pulling at the roots as I scream out.

"I'm not leaving without him." Marwa lost her youngest years ago, and her soft spot for Aland was never more evident.

"You know we can't," Lux snaps back at our interpreter. *"We have to stick to our orders. No natives means no natives."*

The argument was well worn and automatic. Lux and Marwa had been having it out for the past several days.

Though we'd become used to it, I kept my weapon raised. Something felt off, especially since most of the locals had evacuated on their own already, and the building offered no protection from hostile fire. God, I remember the chilling way the hairs on the back of my neck rose and how cold my skin felt.

Squeezing my eyes shut, I will the crushing pain to go away. The same way I did back in Kabul. But just like that day, relief is elusive. What I wouldn't give to be stalking across a stone floor in a bombed-out building on the edge of the city, my men spread out behind me while the acrid aroma of gunpowder, unwashed flesh, and burning buildings floods our noses.

Pipes in the walls creak, triggering another wave of ringing in my ears and blinding throbbing in my head. I stand on shaky legs and make my way to the kitchen, hoping to reach my medicine before I vomit again. Panic rises like smoke in my chest. I hurt all over, my arms ache, and it's hard to tell whether the chills racking me are from the memories or the cold.

Stumbling into kitchen, my hand pats around in the inky darkness. The cold granite of the island offers a landmark. Inching to my left I tentatively step and grasp the countertop on the opposite wall. Grasping my pills, I twist open the cap and pop two bitter-tasting doses into my mouth. They stick to the back of my throat as I force them down, then sink down onto the cool floor.

The low hum of the refrigerator soothes a bit of my anxiety the same way the whirl of chopper blades became my lullaby in the desert. But it's the soft clink that haunts my dreams. The noise no louder than a single drop of water into a pool, but one that may as well have been a bomb going off in the night.

My fingers clench and unclench into fists as I remember the way my bullet hit the wall, spraying concrete into the air and driving Marwa away from Aland. Lux ducked for cover as he pulled his sidearm, so nothing stood between the boy and me as Aland shifted his weight. His hands clasped the edge of his ever-present basket, and his eyes were too wide and round for his young face. As he shifts, I heard it again. The clink.

When he moved, the weight of the objects in his basket slid against one another.

Metal against metal.

My next shot hits him squarely in the chest just as his fingers closed around the detonator. There was no other way to save my men. Anything other than a kill shot would have given Aland the time he needed to detonate the bomb.

But it was the grenade I missed. The grenade the boy hid in his other hand. The one that exploded and sent me flying across the room. Lux had run over to check on me, but I'd insisted everything was fine. I was alive, after all.

Two days later, the piercing ringing in my ears struck, followed by a violent headache that left me helpless and in a cage of agony during a mission. The pain throbbed so violently in my skull I couldn't help wishing my head would just crack open.

That's when Marwa rounded the corner, screaming in a mix of Arabic and English, and I pointed my gun at her. Lux had thrown himself between us red faced and scowling as he tried to talk me down. But the pain was so bad, and the ringing so loud, I couldn't make out the muffled words.

Lux stepped in closer, studying me, and then he pointed at my nose. I wiped it with the back of my hand, only to find a streak of fresh blood covering my glove. There was no hiding the extent of my injury from Lux. He was our team medic.

"Dammit, Lux."

The idiot wasn't supposed to fall for the interpreter, but true to his rebellious nature, Lux didn't give a shit. So, when we returned from our mission, he reported me to the commanding officer of the Forward Operating Base, betraying our team. Our family. We were supposed to watch out for one another, take care of one another.

He betrayed me, his childhood friend.

His brother.

"All for Marwa." I drive my elbow backward, hitting the cabinet with such force, I fear I may have splintered the wood.

Maybe it's my punishment for killing a child. But rage can't drown out the screaming. If I see that small body sinking to the ground every time I close my eyes, then I can only chalk it up to karma. Nightmares are my penance, though no amount of sleepless nights will ever bring redemption for what I've done.

Time to stop dwelling and start scrubbing. Reaching beneath the kitchen sink, I find a treasure trove of cleaning supplies. Grabbing an armful, I cuddle the Clorox and assortment of other cleaning agents against my chest as if they were tiny kittens. The nook catches my eye as I rise to my feet, and my throat relaxes.

The image of Taya sitting there with her book, smiling at me, relieves the tension in my shoulders. I smile back at the emptiness, my grasp on the paper towels lessening. What I wouldn't give to hear her obnoxious singing in the shower right now to pull me out of this spell. The rumble of her motorcycle, or the soft curses she utters after breaking something. She can be such a klutz at times.

My posture relaxes, and I continue thinking about Taya.

Though her absence disrupts an already disturbed system, I'm glad she didn't see me vomiting on the floor. I shudder at the thought of being that helpless and pathetic before anyone, particularly my wife. Taya's been supportive, especially once I told her about my TBI and even has gone as far as to make sure my prescriptions are refilled before they run out, but there is a line. And it's a line I hope I never have to find out about because I know she'll leave and find someone better. Just like Raychel did.

And I can't really say I'd blame her. If only she'd known me before the incident, when I was still whole and unbroken.

Setting the wastebasket to the side, I spray the floor and wipe away the remnants of my unceremonious breakdown. I can't live in solitude again. It's like being stuck in a sensory deprivation tank. I'm floating without an anchor or a port in sight, and I can't scream loud enough to shatter the walls silence has built around me.

There's no telling how long I scrub the floor on my hands and knees. I can still smell the echoes of vomit even though the strength of the bleach stings my eyes as it sits heavy in the air. Shoving away the suspicion that I'll never feel clean enough, I finally put all the cleaning supplies away and dump the garbage. Twenty minutes later, I'm still standing in the middle of the kitchen and wondering why I don't feel any better.

Probably because it's not just the nook and the bedroom anymore. The whole house feels empty without her in it.

I feel empty.

And I'm not so sure this is a hole I'll be able to crawl my way out of. Maybe Redding was right. Maybe it won't be so simple to leave at the end of the year. Maybe it's not Taya's feelings I should be so concerned about, but my own.

CHAPTER FOURTEEN

Taya

I HAVEN'T SNUCK out of a house at one in the morning since I was a teenager. But after waking up to find myself curled against Jim in the window nook, my back pressed against his chest and his dick against my ass, I had to get away. Especially when panic slammed into me like a rogue wave as I recalled the photographers from the party. Jim would certainly ask questions once he woke, questions I'm not ready to answer. Questions that could get me kicked out of the program. But if those photos go public, my problems might come here.

So, I collected my discarded dress and shoes, ran up to my room, and texted Inara to ask if I could spend the remainder of the night at her place. I needed time to think without anyone prying into my past. Inara was more than happy to oblige, and when the door to Jim's room clicked shut, I grabbed my gear bag and snuck out. God, I must've looked like the biggest ass pushing my bike down the street in the dark. But I didn't need Jim running after me, cornering me, and making me confess about what I ran away from back in New York.

"How was the party?"

I glance toward Inara as we step over a log, shrugging halfheartedly and trying to hide my concern. No need for anyone else to know about what little I have. "The whole thing was very cliquey. I mostly kept to myself and ate."

"Sounds like my idea of a good time." She cuts her gaze to me, a thin brow arched. "I just wonder if that was all she wrote. You seemed pretty upset when you called me last night."

Inara hands me her small thermos with coffee in it and I take it willingly. We're high enough above sea level that the cold air still bites through the thermals underneath my cargo pants, shirt and jacket.

I snap a low-hanging branch with my free hand and throw it off to the side. "Eh, I was just a bit stressed. Not used to spending hours putting on some fake facade. This whole thing is still new to me, and I'm not exactly sure how to act. Plus, I wanted to get a head start, so I figured, why not sleep at your place?"

"Uh huh." Inara faces forward and climbs up the hill, her fingers grabbing onto sturdy rocks to help hoist her body upward.

I suck in a breath, debating whether or not to tell Inara about the program and Jim. I need someone to talk to, but things between me and Jim are . . . complicated right now. As much as I want to talk to her about my situation and being Jim's wife, it's not right letting someone I barely know in on our relationship.

My mind wanders back to the party and, most of all, what happened after. I practically groan as I relive latching on to Jim when he came inside of me. Shit balls. No condom. Ah, crap. Jim's gotta be freaking out. I should text him and let him know there's nothing to worry about. I should be getting my period any day.

Come to think of it, now that I have health insurance, I should get back on birth control. Though, not sure if sleeping with my husband again is a good idea. Not if any of those photos are printed for general public access. I won't allow Jim to become a target. Maybe Jim was right after all. Maybe annulling our marriage at the end of the year is for the best.

But I've never had an orgasm like that.

I came to you.

His final words to me make my lady parts clench, and I groan out loud. Inara eyes me questioningly, but I just smile weakly and ignore her curious expression. I could be groaning for a hundred different reasons, like, because this coffee is so freakin' good. I hand the mug back to Inara, and she places it in her pack, continuing ahead of me.

Taking a deep breath, I pull in the familiar scent of pine. Though miles from the ocean, it feels good to be here, breathing in fresh air, putting a pause on life. The woods and ravines of Virginia remind me of the nature reserves back home. If I could shake the strange sense of homesickness that fills me every time I think about Jim, I might even be able to enjoy myself.

"Hey!" Inara calls, and I glance up the hill to where she is. "Stay focused. The air is getting thinner, and if you're not careful, it'll make you scatterbrained and confused."

She isn't telling me anything I don't already know, but the reminder is a welcome one. My fingers tighten around the strap of my new pack. It cost me a pretty penny, but it's worth it to have my own gear once again. When it comes to search and rescue, using the community gear is just as bad as sharing a mouthpiece during band class, so I bought new climbing equipment and rope as soon as I gotten my first paycheck from S&S. The solid weight of them is a comfort against my back, proof that I'm a step closer to putting myself back together.

We're training on hi/lo angling today to practice rappelling off a cliff, and I couldn't be happier. Today will be a training tutorial, a chance to remind myself of the basics after being on hiatus for so long. If I stopped playing video games for a while, I would start back up in training mode to reacquaint myself with the controllers and the combos. This is no different.

As I climb, I make note of the peaks and saddles to keep myself oriented. The rest of the group is up ahead and despite my best intentions, I keep lagging behind as thoughts of Jim play havoc with my focus. Thankfully, not everyone here is a stranger. In fact, I met a few of the men and women while milling about at a SAR conference in New York last year.

My stomach twists. If only I'd known how much my life would change since then.

My phone vibrates, and I pull it from the pocket of my cargo pants. Jim's name flashes across the screen, and my heart skips a beat as I slow my pace. This isn't the time or the place to talk about last night, nor do I want him finding out about where I am. I've had enough of people making judgements about my participation in search and rescue. Hell, Jim would probably make fun of me just like my stepmother used to, especially considering what he does for a living. My finger hovers over the red 'ignore' button.

"You alright back there, Taya?"

I look up to Inara who is about one hundred meters ahead of me. The closer we get to the summit, the more protective she seems to be. It's a relief to know she'll be reliable on a callout, but right now, all I want is for her to go away.

She turns to face me and puts her hands on her hips, breathing heavily. "Hurry up, I want to ask you about Jim. You're avoiding it."

Hell yeah, I'm avoiding it. I'd rather talk to Jim than talk about him to Inara.

I lift my phone, waving it in a universal sign as the phone rings. "I'm going to hang back a bit and take this call."

She nods with annoyance and continues on, giving me some much-needed space and privacy, but slow enough to maintain visual contact.

I bite the bullet and tap the green button. "Hello?" I

don't hear anything. Maybe he butt-dialed me. "Jim? You there?"

"Yeah, sorry. I, um, I don't mean to interrupt, but I can't find a USB drive I need." He sounds irritated, and I can just imagine him ripping his hair out that his thumb drive wasn't in the exact place he had left it.

I smile, even though he can't see it. "It's okay. Where'd you leave it?"

"I thought it was in my bag. I need it to finish a report. Wanted to call and check if you'd seen it, before I took a trip home to look." There's shuffling on the line as if he's lifting every piece of paper known to man to search under them.

"Will you stop making so much noise?"

The rustling stills, and Jim sighs.

Inara looks back at me before she turns left behind a tree. She waves at me, and I wave back with a groan.

"What's wrong, Taya?" His tone is concerned. "What got you so scared at the party?"

Crap.

Think Taya, think.

I shake my head, hoping to jar some explanation, aka, a lie, which might be hiding in my brain. "I just . . . it was what Captain Redding said. I'd forgotten about you being forced into the program. And I've been trying to make this marriage work. Kind of reminded me it's only temporary."

Not exactly a lie, but fuck, I kinda hit below the belt with that one.

The line is silent for a minute. A very long minute.

When Jim continues not to speak, I do. "I'm sorry you can't find your thumb drive. I didn't see anything when I grabbed my keys."

Jim's breath comes in heavy. "I—hope I didn't do anything to make you leave."

"Can we talk about it later?"

"Sure. I just . . . it's your home, too, and I wanted to make sure you knew I'd never do anything to chase you out."

Your home. He had definitely just said that. Do I say thank you? Did he really mean to say that? I want to speak, but the words won't come out.

"See you when you get home."

Home. He did it again.

"See you soon." I disconnect the call and tuck my phone back into my pocket. I brush some burs from my pants and hitch my pack higher on my shoulder before hurrying to catch up to the group.

Near the summit, everyone mills around the team leader, Patrick. When I reach the group, Inara slings a companionable arm across my shoulders. "We're working in pairs today. So, what do you say, partner? Ready to take our relationship to the next level?"

I flutter my lashes and lower my voice to match her whispers. "I thought you'd never ask."

Patrick drones on about the precautions we'll be taking for the climb down. In this exercise, Inara is a victim trapped on the cliff wall, while I lower down with the litter and help her get into it. Inara and I joke about her backstory for falling over the edge of the cliff in the first place as she is strapped in. She waffles between being a high stargazer or a dude bro with a GoPro and a YouTube channel.

Inara wipes a line of sweat from her brow while she is lowered down. As I stand on the ledge of the cliff and mentally prepare myself to scale down the length of it, I'm reminded of something Dad said to me when I first started out.

"If you keep pushing your limits, one day you're going to find them."

He didn't like the idea of me being involved in search and rescue. Not because he thought it was embarrassing, like my stepmom, but because he was convinced I would take unnecessary risks and get myself hurt or killed. I never blamed him. Not after what he'd gone through when my mom died.

But search and rescue is different. Saving someone else is the closest I'll ever be to my Dad again. I just wish I could have found a way to tell him that while he wanted to keep me safe, I wanted to help those who needed someone to save them. That I want to protect other families from going through what we went through.

Shaking my head, I take a deep breath and plant my feet right at the edge, working my butt low until my device and brake hand are near the lip, then I swoop clear in a short bound.

I continue to rappel in one steady flow, slow and calculated, rather than continuing to bound. There's no room for sloppy behavior.

I'm a third of the way down the cliff and almost to Inara when shards of rock and debris rain down as the line hitches, and a sharp crack sends chills down my spine. It happens too quickly to scream. One moment, the ropes are like steel beneath my hands, but the next moment, my heart is in my stomach and I'm falling. The backup Prusik hitch catches, but I slam into the side of the cliff. A second snap cuts through the air accompanied by pain blossoming through my body. I manage to turn in time to vomit down onto the ground below as I swing over the ravine.

What just happened? Did my rigging break? How is that even possible? I'd watched and helped set the entire thing up. It had been solid before my descent. There was no reason for it to give out on me. I turn my head back up to the edge of the cliff. People are yelling instructions as they start to pull me up. I fight, and lose, the battle with my stomach and vomit into the treetops below again.

By the time I'm lowered onto solid ground, I'm light-headed and feverish. I wish my arm would go numb, but agony travels back and forth along my nerve endings and twists around my mind. I can't escape it.

"Can you move?" The steadiness of Inara's voice is soothing. I was right earlier. Her natural competence and that cherub face really are comforting in a crisis. Even if she's a goofball, I'm grateful to know that we'll be working together.

Per instruction and experience, I don't try to sit up. The damage has made itself known, and I fight back another wave of nausea. I have a massive headache, but the agony in my arm is my one and only cause for concern.

I blink rapidly, fighting the urge to cry. "I'm pretty sure I broke my arm."

Though she's careful, there's no getting around the shockwaves even the lightest touch causes. "Let's get this set, and I'll drive you to the hospital."

The pain is my arm is rivaled only by the shame and embarrassment that fills me. And Jim, please God don't let them call him. I don't need him pointing out my failure. I know I messed up. I must have. There's no other explanation for why my rigging snapped apart so easily.

I couldn't save my dad but that doesn't stop me from blaming myself for his death, and today I'd nearly gotten myself killed. If I'd managed to get to Inara before the rigging gave out, things would've been much worse. The tears come but their fall has less to do with the pain in my arm and more to do with the hot mess my life has become.

CHAPTER FIFTEEN

Jim

THE TELEVISION CASTS a comforting glow throughout the living room, and I sink deeper into the couch. It's been at least eighteen hours since Taya left, and I never thought I'd miss being at work so much. Hours of enforced solitude aren't all they're cracked up to be. Bear and Marge are having date night, and only God knows what Craiger and Martinez are up to.

I haven't sunk low enough to call those two knuckle-heads for company, so for the last few hours, I've been binging on '80s and '90s sci-fi. Not that I mind. I fucking love '80s movies. I'd grown up on this shit.

Popcorn sticks in my throat when I swallow too fast, the twin beams of approaching headlights startling me. Who the hell is pulling into my driveway? After coughing the piece up, I straighten on the couch and place the popcorn bowl on the cushion, preparing to hoist myself up. But before I can get up to investigate, keys jingle and the front door clicks open.

Taya.

The hinges on the closet door in the foyer squeak and I tense, heart pounding in my ears. What if she comes in and says she wants to quit the program, that she came back to collect her things? The idea brings something ugly and desperate squirming to life in the center of my chest.

Some of the tension drains away when the car backs out of the driveway. If she plans on leaving, it's not tonight and that gives me time to apologize. Time to make up for being such an asshat.

My chest tightens once again. What if she goes straight to her room, avoiding any further interaction with me?

But a few seconds later, Taya stands in the archway entrance of the living room in an oversized Edmonton Oilers sweatshirt and leggings. Who knew she was a hockey fan? Or maybe it isn't her sweatshirt. The thing could fit me.

She hesitates, like she's waiting for something. When I don't move, she sighs and turns away.

"Wait! Do you want to watch this movie with me?"

Desperate. That's how I sound. A real turn-on. No wonder she ran away.

"A movie sounds great right now." She glances at the TV and her face lights up. "*Ice Pirates*? Nice choice. Do . . ." She clears her throat and tries again. "Mind if I join you on the couch?"

Yes, of course I want her to sit with me. Hell, I want to know if she enjoyed last night as much as I did. I want to ask if she ran because she regrets having sex with me, or if she was afraid of something else. And most of all, I want for her to know she is safe with me.

I also want to ask her if she's on birth control, if she's upset with me. Well, she and I would have that in common, because there's no way I am going to be a father, raising a version 2.0 of my own shitty self. I wouldn't want that for anyone.

"Knock yourself out."

She's stiff in the way she moves around the couch, hesitation where confidence usually resides, an awkwardness replacing her grace. A bright green color peeks out from beneath the sleeve of the sweatshirt when she leans on the armrest to navigate around the coffee table, and I lunge forward, reaching for her when she struggles to sit.

Taya pauses halfway down and shoots me a death glare, complete with puckered lips and narrowed eyes. "I can sit on my own, thank you very much."

My jaw clenches, molars grinding, as I pulverize the popcorn in my hand. I suck in a deep breath, trying to chase away the shadows of fear threatening to engulf me as I lean back onto the couch. "What happened to your arm?"

Taya stares at the television, rolls up her sleeves and reaches over with one hand to steal some of the popcorn from the bowl nestled in my lap as she settles onto the couch.

Our hands brush, and I want to grab her—shake her—anything to get her to look at me and tell me what I know she's hiding. I can read her better than she thinks.

A few pieces of popcorn overflow from her fist, and she

scoops the offending kernels off her cast with her tongue.

My heart is racing, and the taste of copper is heavy on my tongue. She's hurt, and not knowing how or why is pushing my sanity over the edge.

"Taya."

She rolls her eyes, grimacing when she reaches for another handful of popcorn with her uninjured arm. I can't help but notice she doesn't wait until she's done with her first mouthful before shoving in another. Both cheeks expand like a chipmunk's, and I stare her down while she does her best to chew as slowly as possible.

"Mmph pheff."

"What was that?" Maintaining eye contact, I move the bowl out of her immediate reach when she stretches for it once more. Bruises on her skin stretch beyond the cast. My lips tighten. My muscles bunch, straining the seams of my shirt. "Taya?"

Unable to hold my gaze, she turns back to the television. "I fell."

"Elaborate."

Her head whips sideways. "What?"

"Fell *how*? *Where*?"

She doesn't answer at first, and the only thing keeping the silence from growing heavy is the movie. She forces out a self-deprecating chuckle. "Inara and I stopped at a CrossFit gym. I was doing box jumps, and I slipped. My guess is the janitor got a little overzealous with the floor wax."

Liar.

CrossFit gyms don't wax their floors. Most use rubber flooring. I take in a deep breath and count to ten while I plan out what to say next to get her to tell me the truth. But she pales like when we fought over the burnt pancakes.

Pales like the day the arrival of my friends left her shaking and terrified.

"Did someone hurt you?"

Her eyes widen and she sucks in a sharp breath, immediately choking on popcorn. I wait patiently for the coughing fit to pass, content to sit there all night, if need be. When she finally settles, she shakes her head. "Why would you say that?"

"Just the way you freaked out the other night at the party."

"I told you and Marge what happened." Her expression crumbles and she sags in her seat. "Well, maybe not all of it. Some of the wives at the table were being nasty. Marge shut them up, but it got to me. Especially since I couldn't defend myself because I didn't know who their husbands were, and I didn't want to negatively affect your job."

I reach out and press a hand against her thigh. "Wish you would have told me sooner, but glad Marge was there. Dealing with *certain* wives is a skill you'll need to learn. Some can be quite brutal, almost as if they get off on it."

Taya laughs, but it lacks amusement. The lines of strain around her mouth and at the corner of her eyes make my heart ache. I'm not the cause of her pain and I don't intend on adding to it by questioning her further. A broken arm hurts like a bitch. I wedge the popcorn between us, so she can reach it without straining and turn back to the movie, pointing a finger toward the screen. "This is my favorite part."

"The part where they're being castrated? That's a shocker."

My lips quirk. "Pretend castration."

Taya barks out a laugh. "I love the look on their faces, personally."

"Exactly. The whole thing is so nonchalant."

We watch for a beat or two, the sight of the princess issuing her not-so-subtle ultimatum bringing a genuine smile to my face. "I used to have a thing for Mary Crosby. Hell, I still have a thing for Mary Crosby."

"Didn't she play on *Dallas*?"

"She basically made the show."

"Wow. That's quite a claim."

I knock her hand aside when she makes a grab for more popcorn, and one of my brows raise. The woman who shot J.R. made television history.

"And by 'claim,' I mean 'an accurate and astute observation.'" The corner of her mouth lifts in an almost-smile when I release my buttery hostage. "Tell me more about your obsession with Ms. Crosby."

"*Mrs. Brodka*," I correct absently. "And it's not an obsession. I just appreciate the classics."

"Are we talking about the movie or the actress?"

My face heats when she lets loose a bark of laugher. "I

was talking about the movie. It's a good movie. Sue me."

"You're preaching to the choir, sweetheart. They don't make space operas like they used to."

I hesitate before sticking my big toe down the rabbit hole. "Have you ever seen *Firefly*?"

"I'm sorry? I'm alive and breathing, aren't I? When I think about cinematic tragedies, canceling *Firefly* is right up there with the remake of *Total Recall* and the existence of Jurassic sharks."

"*Sharknado* haunts my dreams."

"I saw the movie and it left me feeling personally disrespected. You know there's a movie called *Aliens vs. Avatars*?"

Settling deeper into the couch, Taya leans her head against my shoulder. The remnants of a grin linger around her mouth, and I want to lean in and kiss the vestiges away. My throat tightens. The weekend has not been kind, but for now, everything in my world is good and right. Is it wrong to want the feeling to last?

Dumbass.

Taya spends the next few minutes explaining which sci-fi movies she believes should be classified as acts of terrorism. I don't always agree, but listening to the animated way she shreds plotlines and decimates directors and actors alike makes me wary of disagreeing. Her face lights up and she actively involves her hands the more passionate she becomes, and I can't bring myself to look away. It's as if I've been placed under some sort of spell and the world is moving in molasses around me while my heart races along. Listening to the sound of Taya's voice is more satisfying than any ocean wave I can imagine. Righter than any curve I could master on my bike.

The credits scroll across the screen, darkening the room. Taya angles her body to face me, one knee propped on the couch and her head canted sideways on the cushions. I mimicked her position at some point, and the intimacy of being face to face, separated by only a handful of inches further stirs up emotions that have been building, but that I don't want to examine too closely because they are new and terrifying. They feel like soap bubbles. Swimming in iridescent color and too fragile to live, and that the slightest prod will make them burst.

"Katniss has nothing on my *emee*, though." Taya rolls her eyes, waving a dismissive hand in the air.

"Huh?"

"With the bow and arrow." Taya searches my face, concern etched in her features. "You okay?"

My fingers tug at the extra material around the leg of my Wranglers. Shit. She probably thinks I zoned out from my TBI. "Yeah, fine. So, your grandmother was a professional archer?"

"In a way. Archery and horsemanship are part of Mongolian culture. Did you know many of the warriors in Genghis Khan's army were women? Though, according to my grandfather, I inherited more of my father's side than my mother's. Of course, the comment was made after I accidentally shot him in the foot with an arrow."

I laugh so hard, my head whips backward. "Let me guess, your father's side can't cook, either."

Taya gently kicks me in the thigh, the corners of her lips curling up. I grab hold of her, so she can't pull away, and rest her foot in my lap. When her smile fades around the edges and she clears her throat, I worry I might have screwed things up somehow without even trying.

She tugs her foot away, taking the warmth of her touch with her. "About the other night—" Her face is bright red, and I can't blame her, especially because of how thoroughly I fucked up.

My words shoot out of nowhere. "I should have worn a condom."

Taya sits tall and crosses her arms. "Umm. That's not where I was going, but yeah. An important point."

I take a deep breath. "Sorry. I was just worried because neither of us thought to use protection, and I—"

Couldn't the couch swallow me whole already? I struggle to find an eloquent way to say her pussy was so bomb I forgot to pull out, but nothing comes to mind.

Taya giggles, and I glare at her.

"You're right, we both messed up, but it's nothing to worry about. Got my period," she says, and my shoulders slump almost immediately. "Plus, I was tested before I left New York, and I haven't been with anyone else but you since then."

Why does it feel so good to hear her say that? Taya's no virgin. I get that. But sitting beside her and staring down into those brown eyes makes it impossible to picture her with anyone else.

Taya, clearly uncomfortable by the way she's fidgeting with the drawstring of her sweatshirt, clears her throat. "When you're done reading the book I left you the other day, let me know." She's trying to change the subject on me. When I say nothing, her face flushes a distracting shade of pink. "I have the next one. You can borrow it. Just *ask* first."

Biting back a smile, I nod. "Promise."

Straightening, she extends her uninjured hand. Her fist is closed and her pinkie up. She wiggles it, a flustered mixture of embarrassment and impatience, when all I do is stare.

"What's that for?"

"The promise. It doesn't count unless you swear on it."

I lift a brow in question, and she bites her upper lip, slightly crooked teeth sinking into plump, pink skin. "It's just a thing my dad and I used to do." The pinkie begins to wilt, and I feel like a horse's puckered asshole. "Sorry. It was dumb."

I hook her pinkie with my own before she can lower her hand fully and shake on it. The motion is over and done with in the span of three seconds, but those seconds may as well have been a slice of eternity. Her warmth lingers. My palms itch. I want to touch her again. Longer, bolder caresses across every dip and valley.

Christ on a cracker.

Having deep feelings isn't an option. I'm broken. I work my ass off to forget it, to dispute it, to hide it. But at the end of the day, only I know the truth. She'll want all of me, but I left all the good parts of my soul in the sands of Afghanistan. Even before my last deployment, though, I understood love wasn't in the cards for me. Being away from home over two hundred days a year and barely being able to have any contact because of my job doesn't foster love. A fact Raychel taught me the hard way, along with reminding me I'm no knight in shining armor.

I kill people for a living.

The ghost of every mistake I've made ricochets through my mind in the form of waking phantoms. Even if Taya can get past my TBI, she'd have to put up with the fact that I don't plan on retiring anytime soon.

Unlikely.

Women have tried and failed. The deployments, trainings, injuries, and even deaths take their toll. It's why the divorce rate is so high.

But Taya's smiling at me, and I'm smiling back. Despite my reservations. The moment is unguarded and leaves my skin buzzing.

Taya ducks her head, abruptly shy, and starts talking again. This time I'm not paying attention. I'm too busy listening to the chanting inside my head.

Mine.

Over and over again, the whisper threatens to grow into a shout.

It fills me with horror and dread, but I can't shake it, and I don't really want to.

CHAPTER SIXTEEN

Taya

I RUB THE turquoise stone of my necklace, the braided leather cord draped over my fingers. Jim and I have our first meeting with a marriage counselor in about forty-five minutes. The IPP program wants to ensure success so they mandate those who are part of the program meet with their counselor every other month, sort of a check-in. But truthfully, I have no idea what to expect since this is our first one, and I'm nervous as hell.

My cell rings and I look at the screen from the corner of my eye.

Inara.

I grab my phone from the side table, thankful for the distraction, and hit the green button. My life is finally settling down and I'm finding some stability. I'm not sure I'm ready for things to change just yet.

"Took ya long enough to answer. How are you feeling?"

Glancing down at my arm, I bite my lip. "I wish I hadn't turned down that second bottle of pain killers, but I've had worse."

"That's not exactly a good thing."

"No, but at least it gives me some perspective when I'm bitching about how much it sucks to be in a cast again."

She laughs. "What did your hubby say?"

"Oh, you know, he was a little . . . upset." Talk about an understatement. If Inara's concern surprises me, Jim's overprotectiveness left me speechless. "He can be really intense sometimes."

"As in the 'run out in the middle of the night to sleep over at Inara's' intense, or the 'let's cause a scene at S&S again' intense?"

I flex my quads and spread my toes to get rid of some of the tension in my body. If only she knew about how he's got a crush on the woman from *Dallas* and how he makes his own Spartan-II costumes for Comic-Con each year, maybe she wouldn't be so critical of him.

"So, how'd you two meet anyway?"

The air rushes out of my lungs. Shit. But before I can stop myself, I blurt out the reason Jim and I are together because when it comes to Inara, everything is second nature as if we've been friends for years. "We got married through the military's new Issued Partner Program. We didn't know each other prior. It's kind of like an arranged marriage."

"Are you in love with him?"

The question shouldn't be unexpected, yet my lungs seize anyway. Do I love my husband? Jim's a rock—unbending and unbreakable. He's offered me a safe place to live and makes me feel like nothing can touch me. He's the kind of man who'll fight and die for his own, and I know I can, and will, trust him with my life.

And while my heart senses the answer to the question, the word *yes* just won't come out.

"Come on, Taya, spill. It's just us here." The expectant silence that stretches between us makes me feel vulnerable and exposed. By habit, I reach for my dad's sweater that's folded neatly on top of the nightstand. Luckily, I'd forgotten it in Lyons's car after we left the storage unit one night. I bring the sweater to my face and inhale my father's musky scent, taking comfort in the familiarity. Me pressing my face into the cotton, it feels like home.

"Taya, you okay? You sound like you're huffing glue over there."

"Hang on, I'm thinking." The lingering ghost of cigar smoke and cologne transports me to when I was seven years old and picking my way across an icy sidewalk. I clutch my father's arm with both hands, terrified of falling again. My breath is steam in front of my face, and my nose and ears feel like icebergs. I bury my face against his forearm while he laughs and pats the top of my head. Shuddering, I stick one hand in the pocket of his sweater, where he keeps his wallet, for extra warmth.

My father had worn the same sweater every winter for three decades. I'd finally tossed the old one and bought him a replacement for Christmas last year. After listening to him bitch about the lack of pockets, I'd sewn one to the inside of the coat.

"Come on, girl, how long does it take? It's a simple yes or no question," Inara says.

I lay the sweater in my lap and unfold it while I inhale and prepare to answer. Both Inara, and myself. But my fingers slip into the square of space before I do, and encounter something besides fabric. I withdraw the small piece of paper and stare at information to a cloud account. My heart beats wildly, like it might burst out of my chest. Scrambling to my feet, I hold the sweater tight against my middle with my cast in excitement.

"Hey, Inara? Can I call you back?"

I hang up the phone before she can respond. There's no grace in the way I stumble over to the desk. I grab my laptop and flip it open. It's frustrating to type with one hand, but I manage, and a few minutes later, I'm plugging in the username and password Dad wrote on the slip of paper.

Denied.

I try again, making sure to capitalize the correct letters, but it doesn't work. Fuck. Depending on how long my father had the account, he may have updated the login information. I scroll down and click on the contact page link. Pulling out the phone, I punch in the number for customer service.

After a few moments of frustration navigating through the automated system, I get a living representative on the phone. "Good evening, my name is Thomas. How can I assist you today?"

"My name is Taya Maverick. My father has an account

with you but he passed away. The login information he left must be old, and I cannot access the account. Can you help me?"

"Ms. Maverick, please hold while I transfer you to the Next of Kin department."

Isn't that nice? No condolences, just let me pass you off to someone else. I clutch my fists and my chest rises and falls more aggressively each second that passes. I grab the laptop and head over to the bed. A few seconds later a new representative is on the line denying me access into the account.

"So, what you're telling me is you can't give me the login information?" My teeth grind together. I swear if I could reach through the phone, I'd strangle the woman.

"Ms. Maverick, if you provide us with the information I've requested, we can send you a DVD with all the contents of the account. But I cannot give you access."

"Fine. Send me the email with what you need." I relay my email to her one more time. A minute later a new notification pops up and I confirm receipt of the email.

"Ms. Maverick, is there anything else I can help you with?"

"No." I hang up before my anger gets the best of me and I say something unnecessary to the woman doing her job. If only she knew the account might contain information to put away a murderous crime boss.

Luckily, I have all the information they requested. When I had to close some of my father's other accounts the companies requested the same information. I'd made digital copies of the death certificate, obituary, and all the other standard paperwork, so it only takes me a couple of seconds to fire off the email to the internet service provider.

I slam the laptop closed and fall back against my pillows. I turn my head into one and scream. The jarring motion of screaming and beating my fists on the bed sends spikes of sensation through my broken arm, and I gasp, curling around it until Dad's sweater is near my face, and my knees are drawn up nearly to my stomach.

Maybe the DVD will contain information to finally put away Marco and Santoro. Maybe this nightmare will finally be over and I'll be able to live a normal life without always being scared of the monsters from my past finding me.

A soft knocking on my bedroom door draws my attention. Jim pokes his head in, a gentle smile on his face. "Just got home but we do have to head out so we can make the meeting on time."

I jolt upright. In all of the excitement about finding my dad's secret account, I'd forgotten all about our upcoming counseling session. I'd take that as a good thing.

My heart flutters when I look into his eyes and I want to ask about how his medical checkup went and what the doctor said about how his recovery is coming along. But he's right. We need to get going to make our appointment with the IPP committee marriage therapist for our every-other-month check-in. "Be right down."

Jim nods and ducks out the door. I tuck the slip of paper back into the pocket of my father's sweater, then head downstairs. Jim and I hop into his truck and drive to our meeting. My stomach twists with anxiety from both not knowing what to expect when talking to the therapist and from having to wait to find out what my father had on the cloud drive.

Jim places his hand over mine, which is resting on the console. "How's the arm doing?"

"Better." I spread my fingers so his slip in between mine. "How'd your doctor's appointment go earlier?"

Jim curls his fingers so he's holding my hand. "Doc said I'm progressing well. Should've taken the meds sooner. Might've been back in the field already."

I swallow hard. With the TBI, Jim's been home—at least working at base—so I've never really thought about him going off to war. While I'm happy he's getting better, part of me is worried about what it means. Worried about what happens—what *could* happen—if he's cleared to return to active duty.

Inara's question from earlier races through my mind. Am I in love with brash, take-no-shit, honest-to-a-fault, low-key, geeky, inherently sweet Jim? I stare out the windshield and continue holding his hand. He hasn't changed his mind about the annulment, or at least he hasn't communicated as much to me. But with each day that passes, my connection to him grows and my heart wants more.

I glance back over to my husband and my throat tightens.

Am I ready to bury another man I love?

When Jim parks the car and leads me up to the counselor's office, I know I'm quieter than usual. The stress of the situation crawls under my skin and writhes in my gut. What had I been thinking, marrying a man I'd never met? And worse, developing feelings for him? Jim doesn't want a wife. He wants a way to reclaim his career.

This counseling thing is just an exercise in futility. But we're here now, so I suck in a deep breath and hold my head high as we enter the counselor's office.

"Welcome, Jim. Taya, it's nice to meet you both." The middle-aged man with a thinning hairline, round glasses, and a soothing smile engulfs Jim's hand between both of his, and then turns to me and does the same. He gestures toward a plump blue couch and upholstered chair. "Sit wherever you like."

I sit on the left side of the couch while Jim settles to the right. Our counselor sits in an empty chair across from us, his searching gaze on me. "My name is Dr. Owens. And while I'm planning to start off with a few simple getting-to-know-each-other exercises, I sense a little tension between you, so why don't we start with you both telling me how things are going so far?"

Crap.

Why couldn't I have found the information for the cloud drive after our appointment because this is not the time nor the place to slip up and mention my past? Not with someone who reports directly back to the committee. Not when both Jim and I have so much to lose.

Dr. Owens adjusts his glasses and shoots Jim and me a pointed look. "The only way we're going to make progress is if both of you are open and honest. This is a safe space. There's no assigning blame here. No right or wrong. Only you expressing yourselves and listening to each other, finding better ways of communicating and connecting."

Yeah, right. Withholding information about my father's murder from the committee is definitely wrong.

Dr. Owens pushes his glasses up his nose before targeting me with a warm smile. "Taya, can you tell me how you are feeling?"

Of course I have to be the first to talk. Murphy's Law be damned. Well, maybe there is something I can bring up. One I'm sure won't get either of us in trouble because if I sit here silent, who knows if the committee might view that as a form of insubordination. So, I take a deep breath. "I'm frustrated. Jim was forced to enter the IPP program and this marriage. I thought I was being paired with someone who really wanted to make the marriage work."

Dr. Owens nods and turns his attention to Jim. "Jim, does her statement accurately represent how you feel?"

Jim rakes a hand through his hair and shifts his weight on the couch. Then clears his throat. "My C.O. made it clear I needed to join this program if I wanted to get back to active duty."

"And how did that make you feel at the time?" Dr. Owens asks.

"Trapped," Jim blurts out. "Mad. I have—had—no interest in marriage."

Dr. Owens nods. "Those seem like reasonable reactions to being forced into something as important as marriage. Is there a reason in particular that you had no interest in marriage?"

Jim's hands flex into fists before he releases them again and clasps them in his lap. "Been married already. Didn't go well."

"A bad experience would definitely explain your reluctance." Dr. Owens turns back to me. "Taya, how does this information make you feel?"

I stare at my hands. "Sad, I guess? For Jim, for having such a bad experience. And sad for me because his bad experience means that he's not willing to try again with me." I swallow in an attempt to dislodge the growing ball in my throat. "I came to this marriage hoping to make it real. Hoping for a new start."

Dr. Owens crosses one leg over the other and leans back into his chair. "A new start? Your application said that you came from New York. Do you want to talk about that, about why you're looking for a new start?"

Goddamnit. This whole day I've been blurting out words I shouldn't be speaking. First with Inara. Now with Dr. Owens. And the mention of New York and my past there makes my eyes burn. I shake my head. "No. Not right now."

"That's okay. How about you share a little more about why Jim's resistance to the marriage bothers you?"

Okay. This, I can do. "I guess it hurts to find out your

husband is counting down the days until he can get away from you, like the end of a prison sentence or something."

A small noise escapes Jim's mouth. Dr. Owens's sharp eyes zero in on my husband's face. "Does what Taya's saying not resonate with you?"

I turn to face Jim, who's staring at me with an intense frown etched into his brow. His fingers drum against his thigh as he turns back toward our counselor. "No. It doesn't."

Jim goes silent, leaving Dr. Owens to coax him. "How so, Jim? What did Taya say that you disagree with? Remember, this is a safe place to share whatever you're feeling. Why don't you face Taya and speak directly to her?"

Jim swivels on the couch to face me. "Things started out that way. With me counting down the days." He pauses to clear his throat. "But then, I started to get to know you and it stopped feeling like a punishment. I still have reservations, especially given what happened to my last marriage, but I like you, Taya. You're not at all what I expected. In a good way."

Warmth blossoms in my chest. Not exactly a declaration of undying devotion, but it's a start. Baby steps. We have time. Maybe this could work after all. And because it feels natural in that moment, I reach out and take Jim's hand in mine and squeeze. "I like you too. And I'm glad it doesn't feel like a prison sentence anymore."

"Really good communicating, right there. Remember, the key to any successful partnership or marriage is openness and honesty. Those two things are the only way for true intimacy to grow," Dr. Owens says.

Openness and honesty.

His words ring through my head like an accusation and my stomach twists. I slip my hand out of Jim's and shove it in my lap.

"But don't worry if you're not ready to fully open up yet. Trust takes time to build between two people. Just remember to keep talking and spending time together. That's the very best way for a relationship to grow."

While Dr. Owens guides us through some communication exercise, I make a pact with myself. Once I figure out what's in that cloud drive and get confirmation that my secret won't freak Jim out and get us both kicked out of the program, I'll tell him all about my past.

Until then, I'll work on everything else.

CHAPTER SEVENTEEN

Jim

I F ANY PRESCHOOLER has the potential to break the sound barrier, it's Bear's youngest daughter, Leslie. Two weeks after our counseling session, I'm glaring down at the little girl, but as usual, she remains unimpressed. If a trainee hadn't burst into tears two days before, thanks to this exact glower, I would have worried I was losing my touch. In all fairness, though, with Bear as a father, there's probably not much that scares the kid. In that respect, she's a lot like her older sister.

"Piggyback!" Leslie doesn't ask questions. She demands results. Taya snickers as I crouch dutifully and allow the child to clamber up my back. Her grip is strong as hell. Like an adorable spider money in a pink tutu. The back of my shirt clings to my skin as she smears me with icing, but before I can complain, her small hands wrap around my throat and hook into my windpipe.

Bouncing in excitement, Leslie slams her heels into my sides. If she were three pounds heavier, it would hurt. As it is, her pink slippers do little more than drive home how slow their owner feels I am on the uptake.

"Piggyback, Uncle Jim," Leslie cries, already impatient after 3.2 seconds of stillness. "It's my birthday. Piggyback, please." Only a four-year-old can make "please" sound like an expletive.

God. Dammit.

There's a choking noise beside me, and I glare at Taya. I love the sound of her laughter, but her current lack of loyalty is disconcerting since she's going rogue and teaming up with Leslie.

"Not a word," I warn, trying out the glare again on an equally unimpressed audience. Taya simply lifts an eyebrow in blatant challenge.

She rises up on her toes and plants a soft kiss on my cheek. "My lips are sealed."

"Good."

Leslie's tiny girl talons dig into my trapezius, and I bite back what Marge has dubbed a four-letter no-no.

"Alright, alright, I get it. Piggyback." For a moment, I glance at the broken spine of the piñata and envy its freedom. I'm sure as soon as the kids have tired me out, I'll be tossed to the side with as much disregard. When Leslie tenses in preparation to spur me on once more, I place a kiss against Taya's temple, then take off. Leslie squeals, and the rest of the children give chase. It always amazes me how easily impressed children are. I'm not even running full speed, and Leslie is howling as if I've strapped her to the front of a roller coaster. I dip beneath the candy bleeding carcass of the piñata long enough to scoop up a hanging piece of taffy. Backtracking around the tree loses several pursuers, and I leapfrog a homemade seesaw. Shabby workmanship. Bear may not look it, but the man can't tell the difference between a hacksaw and a hammer. I'll come by in a few days and fix some of those shady screws. Maybe then, the stupid thing will be level.

Jesus.

I sidestep another little girl easily and wonder if the boy currently wrapped around my leg honestly thinks that he can slow me down, or if he's just looking for a place to sit while he catches his breath. Kids are so weird, there's no telling.

When I'm ready to claw my way back into adulthood, Bear has to help me pry Leslie from my back. Luckily, the clown decides to show up at that moment; otherwise, we may not have been able to shake her. As the guest of honor, Leslie has a front-row seat for the performance, though, for a frightening moment, she seems more inclined to lord it over the other kids from the safety of her six-foot-four perch.

"You're getting old." Bear slaps me on the shoulder as we trek back to the grownups.

"Oh yeah?" I swivel my head around the yard in search of Taya, but she's nowhere to be seen. She must've gone inside to help Marge.

"You're slow and breathing hard, Jim."

I toss my head back in exasperation. "You try running with a bowling ball around your ankle, and then get back to me."

Bear exhales, his lips twitching with amusement. "Last year, you could cart at least three of them across the yard and back. I invited you over for one reason, and that was to tucker out my kid. At this rate, I'll need a tranquilizer to put her down for the night."

I arch an eyebrow. "I'm not the fuckwad who thought cupcakes for breakfast and lunch was the way to go."

"Those were more for me than her."

I pat Bear's gut. "Tell me something I don't know. I might be getting old, but you're getting soft."

"Married life will do that to you." Bear purses his lips, and I roll my eyes at the less-than-smooth sequitur. "Speaking of married life," he continues predictably, "how are things going with the missus?"

I shrug. "Fine."

"That's it?" Bear sounds faintly amused. "Just 'fine'?"

Though I had no idea what to expect, our counseling session had gone well. We practiced some communication skills, spoke about the progress we were making, and got to know one another a bit better through some exercises. The marriage counselor appeared quite happy with our progress and I can see why they felt Taya would be a good match for me.

And that scares me shitless.

Taya tensed up at my comment about returning to the field. And while I wanted to bring that up—along with what really happened to her arm—in our session, I didn't want the committee to doubt our success.

Then there was the sad, faraway look on her face when New York was mentioned during one of the exercises. She could be homesick. And that only adds to my concern about her ability to be my wife.

The part at the beginning, though? When she compared herself to a prison sentence, in that uncharacteristically soft voice? That was a stab right to the heart. I hated that I'd made her feel that way. I want to do better.

Even though I'm frustrated at the same time, because, beyond all of my other concerns, I know she's still keeping things from me.

"She's hiding something." Admitting it feels like a betrayal, but I can't shake the suspicion.

Bear pulls off his hat and scratches his head. "Any idea what it might be?"

"I have no idea. She clams up when I ask about anything to do with her life back in New York. It's weird as hell." I rub my fingers against my temple like I'm trying to will some magical answer to appear. "She got really sad when it was brought up in counseling session, like she might cry."

"You know, she came up to me earlier, and after some chitchat, asked me if I thought that people could get booted from the IPP for various reasons, like not filling out their form accurately. Sounded like she was just making conversation, but could be more." He shrugs his broad shoulders.

I run a frustrated hand through my hair. "Do you remember the news articles in that scrapbook?"

Bear nods then puts back on his hat. "What about

them?"

"Do you remember if any of them mentioned the name 'Maverick'?"

"Not really. I didn't really read them, so I can't say for sure one way or another." As always, Bear is quick on the uptake. "Think one of those articles might have been about her old man?"

"Not sure."

The oaf nudges me with his beefy arm, nearly knocking me over. "So, what you're saying is she doesn't trust you enough to open up."

I sigh. "Basically."

Our therapist had talked about the need to be patient, and I'm trying. Patience has never been my strong suit when it comes to someone getting hurt or being in danger. I hated sitting idle when my men were in harm's way. Or when we had to wait for a MEDEVAC helo when someone was wounded. I wanted results right away. And Taya being hurt is the same situation. I want to know what happened so I know if there is something I need to worry about. Some way I need to protect my wife.

Bear whistles in sympathy. "Well, at least you're getting laid again," he says, tone overtly bright.

This has become more than sex, more than duty. Taya is family. My heart gallops while my gaze shifts around the yard, refusing to land on my best friend.

Bear groans beneath his breath and shakes his head. "What the hell are you two doing, then? Holding hands in a circle and singing 'Kumbaya'? You plan on buying her a fucking promise ring next?"

"Shut up." My best friend would have a field day if he found out how often I've been rubbing one out. Between playing imaginary hide the sausage and dreaming about Taya at night, my dick is sore, my balls are blue, and I finished off an entire bottle of lube.

Again.

Bear crosses his arms over his chest. "Maybe it's a good thing. You dodged the baby bullet. You may not be so lucky if you forget to pull out next time."

We're almost to the picnic table set up in the yard. Everyone was asked to bring a dish, so the table is weighed down by foil-wrapped pots and pans. The grill lets loose a steady stream of smoke and sizzling meat weaves its magic around my appetite. Bear isn't done grilling me yet, so instead of heading straight for the food, I pause to allow him the opportunity to get it all out of his system in relative privacy.

Bear places both hands on his hips and surveys the yard. "Has she told you how she broke her arm yet?"

I cock my head in his direction. "You mean you don't believe the gym story, either?"

Bear smirks. "In my professional opinion, it sounds like bullshit."

"Well, when she decides to tell me the truth, you'll be the first to know." I shove my thumbs into the pockets of my jeans, watching as Leslie sneaks off toward the clown's bag of tricks.

Bear's fingers tap against his biceps, eyes focused on the soon-to-be-punished birthday girl. "What did her doctor say?"

"He gives it about five more weeks before she can get the cast off." Five more weeks. It's astounding that so much time has passed already.

"She must be happy to return to waitressing. Swear I don't know whose resting bitch face is worse, yours or Taya's, since she's been stuck being hostess. And you won't need to drive her to work anymore," Bear says, trying to point out a silver lining.

Disappointment briefly darkens my mood. With Taya out of commission, I've been taking on more responsibility to accommodate us both. The extra effort is exhausting, but I chafe at the idea of giving it up. And she's been bringing home food from the restaurant that the cook staff has given to help us out. Wonder if they know she can't cook for shit.

Bear throws his head back, shaking with unbridled laughter, then looks at me, deadpan. "The lucky girl just had to sign some papers to marry you. Imagine if she had to march down the aisle to meet your grumpy ass."

Once when I was younger, I played hide-and-seek with Lux. I dozed off while hiding in a tree in the neighbor's yard and fell to the ground, landing on my back. The impact knocked the air from my lungs, and I laid on the grass struggling to inhale, to exhale, to do anything.

That's how I feel right now, frozen from being stunned and trying to force my body to remember to breathe as

Bear's words bounce around inside my skull. All this time, I'd never thought about a wedding. Was Taya the kind of person who'd dreamed of her wedding day since she was little? Did she want to get married in a church? The program robbed her of that. I groan, rubbing the knot of tension in my stomach.

Bear quirks an eyebrow, tilting his chin in my direction, his eyes studying my face. "You wanna know what I think?"

"Not really." I turn and make my way over to the table, avoiding Bear's scrutiny and scanning the partygoers for signs of Marge. If I'm lucky, I can stack up a plate of burgers and hot dogs and scarf them down on the side of the house in shame before she realizes I've gotten into the food.

"I think you're—"

A scream echoes from the kitchen, drowning out Bear's final words. The sound of broken glass follows soon after, but I'm already on the move. Bear has a hard time keeping pace. Growing old, my ass. I smirk as I slide into the house, with him a split second behind. He stumbles into me, knocking me aside, but I'm too flummoxed by the sight before me to mind.

Taya is crouched near the stove, arms over her head and wild eyes glued to something on the ceiling. Marge is red faced and ranting, slapping a dishrag on each countertop as she stalks back and forth. I follow Taya's gaze to the ceiling and drive my elbow into Bear's side once my brain figures out what it is I'm looking at. "Isn't that the pressure cooker I gave you at your wedding?"

"It's the lid," Bear says, calmly enough.

"I'm so sorry." Taya straightens, color flushing her cheeks.

Marge slaps the counter again, red streaks covering every available surface. It's plastered all over the ceiling as well, dripping onto the hardwood like rain. "It's barbecue sauce. It was premade. All you had to do was defrost it and add the meat. How do you fuck up barbecue sauce?"

"I thought you wanted me to put it in the water," Taya explains weakly. "You know, to thaw it?"

Marge props a hand on her hip. "I'm assuming, by water, you mean the pot of oil I set up for the fries?"

Taya blinks rapidly. "Yes?"

Marge looks like she's about to join her pressure cooker in the ceiling, but a large chunk of still-frozen sauce falls. It lands in Taya's hair, sloughing down the side of her head and leaving a bright red streak along one half of her face. Marge is just as quick to forgive as she is to get angry, and the sight sets her off in a peal of laughter.

"You dolt." Marge grabs Taya and pulls her toward the door. "You're lucky nobody was in here or we'd have burns to deal with. Bear, get the lid out of the ceiling. You and Jim can fix the hole in the morning."

"Why drag me into it?" I mutter, and Bear throws me a dirty look.

Marge waves a dismissive hand in the air. "Probably because your wife is the one who managed to flash-burn cold food."

I haven't seen much of Taya's cooking, but the one time she'd given it a shot, she filled the house with smoke. I'm beginning to think for a badass biker chick, she wouldn't be able to cook her way out of a wet paper bag without setting off a few smoke detectors. "Defrosting can be hard and Taya's not the most experienced cook. Tell Marge to buy the bottled stuff next time. It's easier than homemade, and it's impossible to fuck up."

Bear snorts. "Marge has been on some Martha Stewart bullshit lately. She even made homemade potpourri. Can you smell it?"

I sniff the air and answer honestly. "All I smell is burnt sauce and plaster."

"I can't tell the difference either." Some of the annoyance fades from Bear's face. "Have you told her yet?"

"Told who what?"

Marge strides back into the kitchen, already rolling her eyes. "Taya. That you love her. Duh."

Love. I snort. "What are you two going on about? And where is Taya?"

"I gave her an extra top and pointed her in the direction of the bathroom." She tosses a grin in Bear's direction. "I told you, he hasn't told her. You owe me twenty bucks."

"And I told you, he probably hasn't even realized it yet. So, technically, *you* owe *me*."

"How could he not know?" Marge slaps Bear's hands away when he tries to grab her sauce-covered wallet.

"He's always been more street-smart than emotionally

intelligent," Bear says. "It's not his strong suit. In fact, you can't really quantify it as a suit at all."

"I'm not in love with Taya," I snap, bringing the couple's attention back to me.

Marge is decidedly less friendly, now that money is on the line, and briefly, I regret reminding them that I'm standing here. "Don't mess this up for me, Jim. I have money riding on you not being completely obtuse."

I should've kept my mouth shut.

My best friend, Dr. Fucking Phil, strokes his red beard and winces sympathetically. "Look man, if you're not in love yet, you're headed in that direction."

I'd be lying if I said he was wrong. Not when my damn heart wants nothing more than for the universe to give me a definitive answer that this woman won't leave me because I'm losing this damn battle to keep my feelings in check when it comes to my wife, especially when my feelings are growing stronger for her each day.

But her reaction to the idea of me returning to the field worries me. She might not be able to handle staying married to me. The deployments might be too much, along with the worry about what could happen. Taya may not be strong enough to handle all that.

And I don't want to walk back down that road again.

Bear wiggles his fingers, and Marge shoves a crumbled wad of cash into his hand, lips tight and eyes dark with frustration. The woman is not a fan of losing, and she and Bear bet money on everything, including whether Leslie's next "accident" at preschool will be a number one or a number two. The loser will have to leave work to bring the kid an extra set of clothes. Usually, their bets are funny. Not so much when I'm the topic of conversation and suddenly feeling like a poorly performing racehorse.

"Look," Marge says, her voice stern. "You're falling for her, and she's clearly falling for you. The sooner you accept it, the easier things will be. And from what I've seen so far, Taya's more than capable of being a military wife."

"I'm not . . . there's no . . . she's falling for me?" I can't stop the next words from spilling out of my mouth, even though I know they confirm every suspicion Bear and Marge have. "How do you . . . did she say something?"

Marge shakes her head, and Bear sucks air through his teeth, his face a mask of pity. I hate these games, but can't help but play. "Taya doesn't truly understand what being married to a SEAL encompasses. I've been stuck home so far. What happens when she learns what life would really be like? I'm not quitting, not for her."

"Jim, I don't think she'd ever ask you to quit." Marge's eyes and smile soften abruptly as I visibly scramble. I've seen her calm Leslie with the same expression. It works all too well. "It's okay to love someone, Jim. Nobody survives for long on a diet of one-night stands."

"It's not that bad."

"It's worse." Bear sighs and walks forward to place his hands on my shoulders. "You wrap it, you tap it, and you get the hell on out. It was fine when we were nineteen or twenty, but you're too old for that shit now. You were too old ten years ago. You've always wanted to settle down, and for a while, Raychel was it for you." Bear's hands tighten when I try to pull away at the sound of my ex's name. "You gotta move on, man. Not every woman you meet is going to be a Raychel. This one happens to be a Taya, and the woman is tough. She reminds me of Marge. Look, I know you're not cool with being single for the rest of your life. We both know what dying lonely looks like, and I don't want that for you. So, find your balls and get your shit together before the year is up and you lose her for good."

As far as conversations about love and women go, it's the best I've heard since my old man and 'the talk,' a conversation consisting of him tossing a *Playboy* magazine and roll of thin toilet paper through a crack in my bedroom door and whispering, 'good luck.' When Dad wasn't berating my mother or drinking himself under a table, he was giving me twisted advice on what it meant to be a man. Women are naturally liars. They can't help it. Their weakness is what eventually defiled the Garden. For a man who often indulged in rage, gluttony, and a host of other sins, Dad had been painfully religious.

Bear and Marge are the ones who taught me what it means to treat another person with dignity and respect. Hell, word count alone means Bear has officially given me the best relationship advice I've ever had. I guess that's what best friends are for.

"We're both rooting for you, Jim," Marge says, grabbing

a bottle of Clorox and a set of dish rags. "Now, I'm going to need the two of you to clean my kitchen before the rest of the guests come in."

"You left her unsupervised. You do it."

Marge's smile has a bit of bite to it, and against my better judgment, I take the rag when she offers it to me. "Can't," she says cheerily, likely because Bear has already started wiping down counters. "What's a party without its hostess? Let me know when you're done."

I nod and, all peaches-and-cream now, Marge saunters back outside.

"Marge ever think about signing up? I bet she'd give Redding a run for his money."

I shudder at the thought of Marge backed by the power and influence of the United States Navy. Bear grunts, but doesn't disagree, which speaks volumes all on its own.

CHAPTER EIGHTEEN

Taya

TONIGHT WAS HELL. Someone messed up reservations and it was as if everyone in Virginia Beach decided to come to Shaken & Stirred. Then Jim wasn't answering his phone and after waiting for forty-five minutes for him to pick me up I decided to order an Uber. An uneasy sensation prickles along the back of my neck. It's not like Jim to forget to come pick me up. I blow out a breath and shake my head. Listen to me, sounding exactly like a fretting wife. I'm being silly. He must have gotten stuck at work. Yeah, I'm a little disappointed, because I enjoy our conversations on the ride home. We almost always get into a good-natured argument over comic books or video games, basically because I have superior taste. At least I got some burgers and fries to bring home for dinner.

The road passes by in a blur, the streetlights winking from the corner of my eye. My heart drops at the thought of spending hours in bed, staring at the ceiling thanks to the anxiety that eats at me as I eagerly await the arrival of the DVD. Inara suggested dosing up on melatonin, but there hasn't been time to go to the pharmacy with Jim insisting on driving me everywhere. I don't want to admit to my sleepless nights to him because he'll want me to tell him why.

I sag back into the seat. More than anything, I wish I could share my past with him. But I can't risk putting him in that position. Jim is unflinchingly honest. If I tell him about my family's involvement with Santoro, he'll feel compelled to report it to his C.O., which would put our entire marriage at risk. Plus, I know Jim better now. I know he'd want to protect me, and I won't be the reason he gets hurt. Not after I'm the reason Santoro found out about my father in the first place. I didn't know Marco was working with Santoro, and obviously my father didn't either, or else he would've warned me. But the more my father worked the case, the more I got concerned and I would share those concerns with Marco. What a fool I was.

My chin dips to my chest. I close my eyes, while my lungs fill with lead. I'd been so naïve. So open. So trusting. All of the things that had led to my dad getting killed.

When I open my eyes, a new resolve burns inside me. Until I have all the information, I'm keeping my lips sealed. Whatever it takes to help Jim get what he needs.

Even if what he needs is to ditch me when our year is up.

The Uber driver takes the final turn onto our street and I shift the brown bag in my lap. A tight fist constricts around my heart when the cobalt-blue house comes into view with Jim's truck parked in the driveway. My fingers grip the brown paper bag. Why hadn't he picked up the phone when

I called?

Oh my God, what if the DVD came in? What if he opened it?

When the driver pulls up to the curb, I jump out of the car and race into the house. None of the lights are on and I make my way into the kitchen where a dark shape leans against the far end of the island. I scream, stumbling back against the half-wall. My elbow strikes the corner, and I open my mouth in a gasp with no sound.

Jim straightens to his full height, a luminance from the window at his back. Light reflects off the bottle of bourbon he's clutching. A knot forms in my gut, and I lick dry lips with a suddenly dry tongue. Something's wrong.

"Jim, are you okay?" I place the burgers and fries on the counter and walk over to the edge of the island where he's standing in his boxers, and place the palm of my good hand on the center of his shirtless back.

He slams the bottle down on the corner of the granite countertop and points at me. "You gonna tell me what really happened to your arm?"

My breath seizes. Is he drunk? That's not like Jim. Also, how stupid could I be for thinking he would buy such a weak excuse? But it was the best I could think of and after years of my stepmother torturing me over search and rescue, I just really haven't wanted to listen to what he has to say, especially since I broke my arm. "I told you already."

"Not good enough, Taya." He snorts, bitterness radiating from him like heat, then takes a step backward to move away from me and stumbles. His hand grabs on to the back of a barstool to steady himself.

Something isn't right. "Jim, come on, let's go to bed." I step closer and lay my hand on his shoulder.

"Don't need your help. Stop treating me like I'm fucking broken." He turns, grabs the bourbon bottle, and throws it. The glass bottle crashes against the backsplash above the sink, exploding into dozens of shards that rain down onto dirty dishes. Dirty dishes piled in the sink. Not once since I've been here have there ever been dishes in the sink.

I jump back, my nerves firing like lightning bolts and Pop Rocks. Jim's eyes are like daggers in the darkness of the kitchen, dangerous and glinting. Or—are they wet? He shifts his head just enough for the light to illuminate tears sitting above his lower lids, threatening to overflow.

I reach for his face and stroke gently along his jaw. Nothing more than the softest of caresses, and his anger dissipates, a mass exodus, leaving him deflated and rounding the mountain of his shoulders.

My heart stalls.

"Jim?" I stroke his face again and again, fascinated by the stubble and the way it drags across my palm.

His body presses tightly against mine, encasing me in his warmth. He leans forward until our foreheads touch. Closing his eyes, he shakes his head. He's a ship without a harbor, and I hold him steady when the tears break free and stain my face as well as his. He's always been a rock, something to lean against that never breaks down. For the first time, I'm seeing just how deep his cracks run.

I lay a hand against his breastbone and stay with him in silence, not pressing him but offering my support. I need to show him that I can be his rock too.

Jim walks forward, backing me up toward the sink. "I've known Lux since we were fifteen years old. I kept his ass alive in Afghanistan, put my job on the line to save his neck, only to find out an hour ago that he got taken out by an IED. Ain't that some shit? Asshole wanted to stay back instead of coming home with the rest of us to spite me." He throws back his head and laughs, but it reminds me of broken glass. Painful and jagged, like the pieces that I know are broken inside of him. Just like the pieces that are broken inside of me.

His pain brings tears to my own eyes and this time, the urge to hold him is too strong to resist. I cradle his head into my neck and press my cheek tightly against his, while my other arm wraps around his waist and pulls him close. He goes rigid at first but then, with a shudder, relaxes into me. His strong arms pulse against my back. The wetness from his tears makes the knot in my throat grow bigger, but I can't. I can't lose it. Not when he needs me.

So I stroke his hair and remain silent while he shudders in my arms. How long has it been since someone held him like this and comforted him for once? I'm betting way too long, but I'm determined to change that.

He swallows and looks me in the eyes again. He's a lost little boy, and all I want to do is help him find his way. "Do you think I could have saved him? If I were there, do you think I could have saved him?"

"I don't know." The words come out scratchy and my voice cracks. If Jim had been there and he had saved his friend, would it be Bear knocking on my door this time to tell me my husband wasn't coming home? I push the question from my mind. Jim needs me. He's hurting.

His gaze traces my lips, and for a breathless moment, I think he's going to kiss me. Then, he whirls away, presenting me with his broad back. His posture is rigid as he swipes at his eyes, probably embarrassed by his tears.

He needs something. A distraction. I clench my jaw as I brace my hand on the counter and take a deep breath. I'd rather allow him to ridicule me like my stepmother used to than allow him to suffer. "I'm a search and rescue volunteer. That's how I broke my arm."

Jim straightens to his full height. Then, slowly, he turns to face me. And waits.

"We were training. The rigging snapped, and I fell." Shame twists my stomach into knots as I wait for the laughter to come. But there's only silence where the mockery should have been. I shift, biting my lip.

"You should have told me. Why didn't you tell me?"

The lack of accusation in his voice, or mockery, or anything negative at all unleashes a torrent of warmth through my veins. Suddenly, all I can think about is how close he's standing. How great he smells. How much I want his mouth on me. Anywhere. Everywhere.

"Can we talk about that later?"

He nods and reaches out, his hand hovering just above the side of my face. I lick my dry lips. He tracks the motion with his eyes. A current crackles between us, filling my body with a desperate need. That almost touch is a plea, a question, a silent testament to the need reflected in his eyes.

I lean in and kiss him. He tastes of salt and grief.

He opens his lips to my explorations, and I wrap my arm around the back of his neck, drawing him close while he devours my mouth in a clash of tongue and teeth. Every suckle and every swallowed groan leaves me hungry for more. I've craved his touch, his mouth, his hands ever since our drunken soiree, and when he bites my lower lip, the explosion of hunger is a result of weeks of wanting.

His erection is thick and heavy against my hip, and I step back long enough to reach for it. I massage his massive length through his boxers, arching back against the counter so I can stare at his face while I touch him. His teeth clench, the muscles in his jaw bulging.

I drop to my knees, sliding his boxers down as I go. I admire him for a moment, proud and throbbing, before I open my mouth and take him inside.

His hand fists in my hair, and the other slaps against the stainless-steel door of the refrigerator for balance. I swallow as much of him as I can take, lathering him with my tongue until he's slick against my lips and hand. My fingers wrap around his base while my tongue traces the veins dancing along the underside of his shaft. I bob my head downward while the circle of my fingers rises up to meet my lips. I move faster and faster, pushing farther until the head of his dick brushes the back of my throat. I hold him there, lips, tongue, mouth and throat all wrapping around him until he convulses against me. I hold him within the wet cavern of my mouth until my throat threatens to reject him.

His shaft glistens, and even in my hand, it exudes power and purpose. I drag my tongue across the head, playing with the slit at the top with the tip of my tongue until he gifts me with a salty droplet of precum. My groan matches his when I swallow it. I want him inside of me. I want to touch my own aching slit, but I only have one hand at my disposal, and I need it to hold his dick steady while I bathe it with attention.

The taste of his skin tightens things low in my body, and my mouth waters. His fingers are lost in my hair, his body shuddering and shaking above me. I feel powerful, and I grip his ass, urging him to thrust into my mouth while I writhe before him, hungry for contact of my own.

My hand cups his balls briefly before traveling beyond them. I love playing with a man's prostate. It makes them come so much harder. One partner described it as a deeper kind of release, and that's what I want for Jim tonight. I want the pleasure to take control and overpower everything, even the grief. I want it not just for him, but for myself.

When my wet fingers tease his ass, he stops thrusting. My nails trail along his muscular cheeks, and I suck him deeper. He resumes thrusting, and I explore him again. When just the tip of my finger enters him, I pull free and duck my head, lapping his shaft and balls.

"Taya. Oh, fuck."

He stumbles a little. When I suckle at the delicate skin of his sac, a fine tremor works along his body. I wrap my mouth around his balls and paint them with my tongue. His legs shake, and he rests his forearm against the ledge of the granite for balance.

I duck lower and let the tip of my tongue lap at the tight rose between his ass cheeks, my neck arching with the need to reach. My finger moves in small circles while I work him with my tongue. A deep, rumbling, growl of pleasure explodes from his chest, but the sound breaks the spell, and he pulls me to my feet. His chest rises and falls as if he's been running and he looks . . . scared.

I relax in his grip, allowing emotion to guide my lips to his chest. I kiss him above the heart and rest there until its wild beat morphs from a hummingbird midflight to that of a butterfly. His shoulders relax, and with my chin resting against his breastbone, I look up at him through my lashes. "I'm sorry. I was moving too fast."

He shakes his head. "No. I—" Jim blows out a breath and tries again. "I like it." He trembles with the admission, his eyes wide and vulnerable, as if he expects my ridicule.

Instead, arousal hits me like a one-two punch, and I don't fight it, allowing it to transform my face, so he can see that the need in me matches the need in him. "You can trust me."

He studies me for what feels like an eternity, but in the

end, he nods. The motion is almost imperceptible.

I place my hand against his chest and circle him, pressing a kiss against his shoulder, his arm, the center of his back. His tattoo is a tapestry of color up close, and I spend several moments tracing the graceful black outlines with my tongue. He holds onto my wrist as if he needs the lifeline. I kiss down his spine and over the globes of his ass while my hand trails down his chest and back to his wet cock. I grip it, and in an expulsion of air, he lets my wrist go so I can stroke him while I bite and lick my way closer and closer to his tight entrance. With a cry sounding like defeat, he drops to his knees. My good hand strokes him while I use my casted arm to gently urge him to bend at the waist. When he's finally on his hands and knees before me, I bury my face in the muscled sea of flesh and lap him like a cat with a bowl of cream.

"Oh. Fucking. God." He pumps hard into my fist.

I bathe him with my tongue, teasing the entrance with small, eager licks. He pumps, hard and erratic. I increase the pressure of my tongue and circle the tight entrance.

"Taya, I'm gonna. Oh, fuck. Squeeze me harder." He convulses, clenching against my tongue.

I pull us both upright and press my tits against his back, milking the remaining cum from him until it coats my hand. He arches in my arms, and I hold him against me, unwilling to back away from his warmth after the last of the shudders subside and he's struggling to breathe.

He relaxes into me bit by bit. Jim let himself go and gave me control, not only of his pain but of his pleasure. The tough-as-nails Navy SEAL is so dedicated to the role of the alpha male, I never thought he'd allow himself to be vulnerable.

Especially with me.

CHAPTER NINETEEN

Jim

M Y EYES DRIFT open, consciousness making itself known by slow degrees. The digital clock flashes two a.m., and I throw my arm above my head. An unfamiliar, although not unwelcome, weight shifts at my side.

Taya.

Christ.

The woman had me on all fours, moaning her name. And the moment she stepped out from the bathroom, I lifted her in my arms and carried her to my bedroom like a love-struck teenager.

My jaw tenses, and my breath hitches painfully.

Raychel was the only other woman to play with my ass, and she mocked me for it every chance she got. Nothing had been about my needs, only the power trip she got from my submission to the physical pleasure. But it wasn't enough for her.

The day our divorce was final, I'd been out celebrating with a bunch of SEALs. She stormed into the bar, spilling our private business to the public. Many snickered while others were too uncomfortable to make a sound about how she screwed so many guys right under my nose. It's why I hate dealing with anyone besides Bear and occasionally, Martinez and Craiger.

Lux was a different story. I called Lux "brother" long before the military taught me to think that way. Raychel and her betrayal had enraged him, but he'd been overseas at the time. I hadn't seen him again until after the divorce had gone through, and then the horrors of war briefly distracted us both from our lives back home.

Taya makes a small sound. Vulnerable, soft and wholly satisfied. When she shifts, a hint of cool air hits my skin, and I shiver as I glance down at her. I study her features and commit each bold line to memory.

I can't afford another scandal. The only reason I haven't been completely discredited, in the eyes of both my superiors and my subordinates, is because I've proven myself time and again in the field. If I showed the slightest hesitation, if I slipped up, made a wrong decision, or fucked up in the slightest way, my career and everything I'd worked for over the years would go up in smoke.

If things with Taya go belly up, my personal issues would label me as an ineffective team lead. I'll be written off as disruptive and incompetent, and assuming I'm not laughed off the base entirely, I'll be lucky to get a desk job in human resources.

From Navy SEAL to civilian desk lackey. My life reduced to a punchline of a joke I always stumble over.

But the promise of her warmth is a heady thing, and I reach out to pull Taya closer. The line of puckered skin along her shoulder makes me pause. The roughened skin travels down beneath her light pink camisole out of my sight, so I follow it with my fingertips. It's soft with age and feeds into another scar along her spine.

These aren't scratches.

She would've needed stitches for the scar tissue under my fingertips. And now she lies against my side with her arm in a cast. My stomach twists in on itself at the idea of my wife hurt and bleeding. My fingers clench into tight fists as if there's some enemy I can fight to keep it from ever happening again.

Taya shifts in my arms, eyes opening to slits. "You okay?"

There's no easy answer. Before I can speak, her eyes snap wide open, and she sits up and brisk air replaces the warmth she'd given. I pull her back, the idea of letting her leave abhorrent. One arm tightens around her and fingers from my free hand trace down the length of her spine.

Her body relaxes into me.

How have I lasted so long without the taste of her?

The sentiment grips every cell as our lips meld. I've never shared breath with another person, never breathed in bits of their soul and shared my own in a single motion. Our chests rise in tandem and even our heartbeats, in that moment, are synced. She is softness and silk. Her tongue is apple pie, warm against mine and just as sweet. I swallow her down, angling my head so I can devour more of her. Taya whimpers into my mouth and the thrill of power, the thrill of being exactly where I belong, leaves me light-headed and shaking. The kiss grows in intensity, and our tongues crash and retreat like waves, over and over again until I feel as if I'm going to burst out of my skin.

The sensation is almost too much, and Taya must agree because she pulls away with a soft, whimpering cry. Her lips are swollen and red.

I stop myself from pulling her back for another kiss. "I'm so fucking sorry."

She blinks up at me, dazed. "For what?"

"For never kissing you like you deserve to be kissed."

She shudders, her nipples puckering against my skin.

I'm painfully aware of the fact that only my needs have been met so far, and now that I have her in bed, I'm eager to rectify that. The urge to watch her unravel is snarling and alive within me. My arm tightens around her and there's a thrill when she glances up in surprise.

Her almond-shaped eyes are a deep brown, with hints of amber that peek out when the light hits them just right. They remind me of a rich brandy, a dark liquor I'm all too willing to grow drunk on.

They dilate as I slip my hand beneath the band of her boy shorts and between the plump folds of her sex. Sucking in a deep breath at how wet she is, I stare into her eyes while my index finger circles her clit. My other finger travels a little lower, until I can slip inside of the tight, wet, heart of her.

Taya's mouth parts on a soundless cry, and I capture her lips with mine. I stroke her with short shallow thrusts until she's panting into my mouth, her body arching against mine.

"Tell me what you like," I whisper.

"What?" Her face flushes, her eyes a little wild.

"Tell me what gets you off."

"Oh." Her breath hitches. She stays silent for a long beat as color blooms across her cheeks. She bites her lower lip, breathing quickly. "Watching you jerk off."

I draw back, searching her face for signs of dishonesty or deflection. But only eagerness, with a pinch of shyness, is found in her eyes. "This is supposed to be about making *you* feel good."

"Jim." She places a hand against my abdomen, and my nerves fire off. "Nothing makes me wetter than watching the way you get off when you're with me."

I lean in, kissing her hard and gripping the edge of her panties. I slide them down her legs and toss them aside. Pulling her flat on the bed, I place a knee on either side of her head. She wraps eager fingers around my length. I grip her by the chin so she has to meet my eyes. "No touching."

She grins and lays back against the pillows. I'm so hard, I ache, my balls high, tight and ready to blow. She grabs my wrist long enough to drag her tongue across the palm of my hand. Knowing my skin is wet from her tongue, even by proxy, makes my veins thrum with lust. While my intent was to go slow, her watching me has me jerking off hard and fast. My fist tightens and a bead of clear liquid rises along the head.

Her tongue flickers out, licking at random moments. The muscles in my arms and thighs bulge with the urge to thrust forward. She works her tongue and teeth over my length, making my toes curl. A groan builds up from the depths of my chest.

The pads of her finger press against my ass, and I grit my teeth together, afraid I'm going to come. Her touch circles and teases, as if asking permission. I found peace in her touch last night when grief was all the world had left to offer. I want her to make me feel good again. So, with a crisp nod, I sink myself onto her digit and breathe through the pressure.

Intense arousal washes over me, heating my skin, when she slips a second finger inside, stretching the ring of muscle until it burns. Sweet fuck, the sensation shakes me to the bone, electricity slipping through every vein.

I rock back and forth, reaching a hand up to place against the wall to steady myself. My ears ring, the skin around my dick stretched too tight. Taya's smile is bright with mischief and she twists her fingers inside me, stroking my nerve endings until my mind lights up. I draw in a sharp breath when she pops me out of her mouth, only to nip at the flesh of my inner thigh.

Her chest rises and falls a little faster as she squirms on the pillow, biting her upper lip and twisting her fist into the sheets while she watches my hand blur around my dick. Goddamn, I'd go anywhere, do anything, to keep that bright, wild-eyed look on her face.

A low, rumbling growl erupts from deep in my chest as I pull away, ignoring her mewl of protest. Scooting lower on the bed, I grab her beneath the thighs and spread her wide. Her clit is a gem hidden within a pocket of flesh, and when I tease it free, licking it in slow, heavy strokes, Taya shivers and lifts her hips, pressing her heat tighter against my mouth.

Sandalwood fills my nostrils until my world is nothing but the taste and scent of Taya. Her hips rock as my tongue continues to explore, dipping deeper into her sex. Her moans are hoarse and shaky, a continuous song as she climbs closer and closer to release. The muscles in her thighs shake and a fine tremor wracks her.

"Oh, God," she cries, clawing at the bed, body tightening as she loses herself in orgasm.

My hands grip her knees, and I track the way the sweat on her breasts trails down her sides. I lick it away, following it back to its source and slipping her nipple into my mouth. Her mouth parts on a gasp that morphs into a smoky moan that incites something raw and possessive in me.

"Jim." The raspy, low tone of her voice sounds like an orgasm as it leaves her swollen lips.

Oh, how I love when she says my name like that.

My lips travel up her body, caressing the length of her throat, nipping at the sensitive skin. I pull away and grab a condom from my nightstand, unwrap it and roll it on. My breath catches at the sight of Taya sprawled out before me. "I want you."

Her eyes flutter, color seeping into her cheeks. "Yes. More. Please."

Her panting makes me lose control, and I thrust forward.

"Jim," she cries out sharply, throwing her head back as her body clenches around mine like a fist.

I pump into her faster and faster, our bodies moving in time with one another, milking me with each roll of her hips.

My balls tighten, fire shooting up my shaft when it violently explodes. My orgasm encourages her own, and with a long, muffled groan, her body seizes up as waves of pleasure rock through her body. I hold her close, not wanting to let her go. But it isn't enough.

I need more.

I need her, forever and always.

There's no gentle withdrawal from pleasure. It settles in close and deep and urges me to sleep. Taya is a rag doll on top of me, and it's easy to maneuver her lax limbs until she's back in my arms, head against my chest. I press a kiss against her sweat-soaked hair and breathe in the smell of sex and warm skin.

Before I give in completely to sleep, I squeeze her to me. "In the morning, you're going to tell me exactly how you broke your arm. No more lies."

She nods weakly, and I kiss her again.

"We're moving your stuff too. You're sleeping in here from now on."

CHAPTER TWENTY

Taya

THE KITCHEN SMELLS like freshly made coffee and baked bread. I never thought such little things could represent happiness, but the feeling warming the center of my chest is a familiar one, one I haven't felt in a long time. I didn't think I could. But there it is, a bright ball of warmth.

Moving easily through the kitchen, I cast another anxious glance toward Jim. He's been quiet since we woke up this morning, and that silence tempers some of my glow. He hasn't mentioned Lux, but shadows linger in his eyes. He's moving more stiffly than usual, and there's a heaviness to his shoulders I want to smooth away.

I take another step toward him. "What are you making?"

The muscles in his arms bunch as he kneads another ball of dough on top of his wooden cutting board, his back still to me. "Told you. It's a secret."

I perch on the edge of the kitchen counter and take another sip of coffee. "Do you want to talk about it?"

"Talk about what?" His voice is hoarse, and my own throat tightens. Jim woke up before me, and the house is spotless. Even more so than usual.

"You're not a very good liar." The words escape as a whisper.

"I'm an excellent liar."

I shake my head. "Nope. The cleaning is a pretty major tell."

He pauses but still doesn't turn. "Oh, really?"

"Yup." I swallow, telling myself to be brave. Things between Jim and I are better than they've ever been. Even so, my heart races at the thought of rejection. "What was he like?"

I don't have to speak his name. Jim's sagging shoulders say it for me.

Lux.

"He is . . . *was* a dick."

"Like all your other friends?" I quip.

He laughs. It's abrupt and strained, but it's a start. "Pretty much. Birds of a feather, I guess."

As he speaks, he begins working again. "We've known each other for a long time." I don't bother pointing out his use of present tense. I never knew sentence structure could make my chest ache. "I was fifteen when he moved into the house across the street. My dad was a drunk, and when he got out of hand, Ma would send me running for cover."

He walks over to the stove, and his Adam's apple bobs. "I was too old for running. I told Ma, but she said she needed me out of the house for her sake more than mine. She didn't want me and the old man getting into it. She was afraid we would kill each other. So, I stayed with Lux while he screamed at her. His mother worked as a chef at the nearby hotel. Lux wasn't interested, but sometimes I'd get bored with playing video games and wander into the kitchen. I'd watch her cook, and one day, she started to teach me."

"She sounds like a lovely woman."

"She was—*is*. We thought the cancer would take her, but it wasn't fast enough." He turns his head over his shoulder toward me, his expression stark. It's a blade through the very center of my being. "She won't even be able to put her son in the ground. There isn't enough of him to send home."

I can't stand the distance. Sliding from the counter, I go to him, setting my coffee aside so I can wrap my arms around his waist from behind and bury my face against the curve of his spine. My arms tighten as he works to find an easy breath that doesn't shake on the exhale. I pray my heart close to his will give him strength.

After a moment, he nods and pats the back of my hand. "It's almost ready. Can you grab some plates and pour me some coffee?"

Placing a kiss against his back, I comply.

We work in silence for a few minutes. I make my way to the front door to grab his paper off the porch. I'm scanning the pages, looking for the comic section, when the smell hits me. One moment, I'm padding barefoot into the kitchen and the next, I'm nine years old and *Emee* is pressing a kiss to my cheek.

Alagh is with the ancestors now. Peace, child.

I drop the paper on the tabletop with a muffled sob. When Jim hands me a plate of *gambir*, his face warring between grief and nervousness, my knees give out, and I fold into the nook seat. The plate warm in my hands and confectionary comfort kisses all my demons to sleep.

"You made Mongolian pancakes." I'm staring down at the fried dough stuffed with sugar and shiny with melted butter. It's home wrapped in a flaky crust. Jim placed sliced bananas and blueberries on top. Drizzled over that is melted chocolate and a fine layer of powdered sugar. Tears prick my eyes.

"I heard you mention your grandmother at the ball." He shrugs as if that small confession explains everything.

"I stayed with her for a while, after my mom died." Glancing up, I smile slightly at the tentative pride that begins to creep over him. "Dad . . ." I swallow the tears and try again. "Dad was having a hard time, and he needed a break. She made these for me every morning for a week. I never got to watch her make them. I just woke up, and they were there, like magic."

Jim would have had to research this and buy the ingredients. All because of a passing comment. No one has ever done something like this for me. He paid attention, not only to what I said but what I didn't say. I'm supposed to be comforting him, but this . . .

Something irrevocable blossoms fully within me, and my world shifts on its axis.

"How is it?" There's nervousness in his voice, and I want

to wrap him in my arms and protect him from the world. Is this really the same man that terrorized me upon my arrival? It can't be.

I take a bite. "Just like *Emee* used to make."

I meet his eyes, and the grin he levels on me is like the sun coming out from behind a thick veil of clouds. The corners of his eyes crinkle, and he's transformed from dour Jim into someone ten times more alluring, more . . . perfect.

We eat in relative silence, and after the plates have been licked clean and set aside, I get up to get us both more coffee. I make two trips because of the cast, but it's a fair exchange for Jim's cooking.

Sunshine streams through the windows of the kitchen. It's a montage of warmth across the tile, and I sag against the windows of the nook, luxuriating in the view and the warmth of the coffee cup in my hands. Jim sits across from me.

I take another sip of coffee and try not to bite my lower lip. Invisible ants crawl along my skin, and I fail to stifle a wracking shudder.

"Cold?" A few months ago, he would've ignored me. Now there's genuine interest in his voice. I smile, shifting amongst the cushions so I can throw my legs over his. He pulls me close, rubbing my bare outer thigh.

"Not anymore." His T-shirt, soft and defeated after years of use, slips down one shoulder. Ducking my head, I take a deep breath of sandalwood and ocean breezes.

Jim and I are intertwined in more ways than one.

"You should go green." I smooth the paper in my lap and smile at one of the panels in comic section. "The internet has made newspapers obsolete."

"I like something tangible." Before I can protest, he reaches across me to pull several pages free. Handing me the rest, he settles back on his side.

"I was reading that." I furrow my brows and pout.

"No." He shakes the page straight so he can read the headline. "You were hiding behind it."

"Hiding from what?"

"Hiding from the fact that you still owe me more information on the whole search and rescue thing." He folds the paper and sets it down on the table. "Let's get back to where we left off. Why didn't you tell me?"

The answer doesn't come easily but in for a penny, in for a pound. He's bound to discover what a mess I am soon enough. I lay my half of the paper on top of his discarded section, so he isn't tempted to pursue his curiosity about the article featuring Santoro.

"I was ashamed." The words bringing tears to my eyes. "My stepmother used to make fun of me for it. Not many people get it. I'm a volunteer, so I don't get paid or anything." I shrug as if it doesn't bother me. "If it weren't for the people I've saved . . ." The sentence hangs there, unfinished. Honestly, I'm not sure how to finish it. I love being a part of search and rescue. It's fulfilling in a way I can't put a name to.

"You're something else, you know that?"

"It's a hobby." God, I must look so lame staring into my coffee as if it holds all the secrets to the universe.

"Hobbies don't usually break your arm."

"Granted, it's not scrapbooking. But it also doesn't pay, so it's not a real job, either. Which means, technically, it's a hobby. If you have a better word for it, I'm all ears."

I'm ready for all the words I've heard before, for his mockery, his dismissal, and his laughter. I'm ready for almost anything except for what actually comes out of his mouth.

"Amazing."

His eyes are bright with pride, his shoulders square with it. Dad gazed at me like that when he thought I wasn't paying attention. After he died, I never expected to see it again. More importantly, I never thought I wanted to.

He slips his thumb beneath the bend of my knee and strokes the delicate skin there. "I wish you had told me."

"I didn't want to argue about it, in case . . . in case you felt differently. It made more sense to keep to myself."

"Just for the record, you never had anything to be ashamed of. It's brave as hell."

I clear my throat but trying to control the tremor in my voice only makes the tears more imminent. "Thanks."

"Just promise me something."

"Anything."

"Be careful." His fingers begin to travel and excite unexplored nerves. Goose bumps decorate my skin in waves as my body memorizes the sensation of each callus. "I couldn't stand if anything else happened to you." He traces a scar stretching from my hip to my upper thigh.

"I was trying to pop a wheelie. It didn't end well."

His head jerks up and he lets loose an explosion of air through his nose. "I'm not asking you to stop, just be careful. You may be able to handle another broken bone, but I can't."

Warmth fills my insides like a bonfire, and Jim's every word only stokes it to greater strength. I'm light-headed and a tad giddy, and while I'm not sure if I'm doing a great job hiding it, I still try. I take another sip of my coffee to hide my obvious pleasure. "I promise."

He nods in approval, and I squeal when he grabs me beneath the knees and pulls me more fully into his lap. My coffee is stolen and unceremoniously set aside. "Thank you."

I giggle. I've never been a giggler, but Jim brings it out in me. Being this close to him, staring up into his eyes and remembering the way his lips feel is enough to bring on more than a giggling fit. "You're very welcome. By the way, did you ever find your missing flash drive?"

"No." Jim leans in, gently nipping at the tendon where my neck meets my shoulder. "Probably should've written notes instead of recording them. Or gotten a bigger voice recorder."

"The military has flash drives that record voices? Like some new sci-fi tech?" I tilt my head, giving his soft lips better access to the side of my neck.

Jim laughs, showering my skin with his hot breath. "I wish. They are just recording devices in the shape of USB drives. Martinez ordered a couple online. I won't even tell you what he uses them for. He gave me one, and I figured I'd use it."

"I'll continue to keep an eye out for it." I lean in and kiss him. His lips are too soft, like rose petals. I sink against his chest, careful not to put too much pressure on my arm. I can't imagine a day without him in it.

I bite my lip. I know I need to tell him the truth about my past, at some point. Even though Bear's responses to my questions about getting kicked out of the IPP weren't especially reassuring. But Jim's my husband. He deserves to know. No matter where the chips fall. Look at the way he'd reacted when I'd confessed what really happened with my arm. No freak-outs. Nothing but support. Maybe together we can figure out what to do in terms of the IPP program.

But, I still worry. Am I willing to put his life and his happiness on the line with Santoro still free, still a threat? And what happens when he gets deployed, when one day my real world might no longer include him in it? I press a hand against the side of his stubbled jaw and deepen our kiss. There is no easy answer, and I'm not ready for a hard one. At the very least, I'm going to wait to see what my dad kept hidden. If I'm lucky, maybe it's a way to put Santoro behind bars for good. Then, that worry magically disappears.

I'd waited this long to tell him. I could wait a little longer.

And then, I quit thinking as I let him take control of our kiss.

Jim's hands and mouth leave me drowning, all my thoughts and worries disappearing beneath the onslaught.

CHAPTER TWENTY-ONE

Jim

THE OPEN BACK road is a familiar streak of gray beneath the tires of my bike. The ocean on my left adds a slight chill to the air. It's been a while since I took my GXSR 750 for a ride, but what better way to celebrate the doctor's report coming in today clearing me for duty. No more meds, no more worrying about being left behind as the rest of my team is sent off. Plus, with Taya speeding along at my side, I honestly can't think of anywhere I'd rather be.

I downshift, another curve coming up. Of course, Taya speeds up. Not much, but enough to make me tense in preparation for a fall. I forced her to tell me the origin of the rest of her scars. Most are the result of a fall from her bike. So, I set a few ground rules after announcing our plans for the day. The biggest one was no wheelies. And what was the first thing she did the moment we pulled out of the driveway?

Popped a fucking wheelie.

My little daredevil.

The woman is too flippant when it comes to her own

safety, and the more I witness it for myself, the higher my blood pressure rises. The search and rescue factor makes things worse. I'm proud of my wife. But things happen and having her dangling over a mountain unsettles me. Mountain bikers, hikers and tourists are all thick in this part of the country. If she's called in, she could get hurt again. Even die. Bile rises in the back of my throat.

What if something happens to her when I get deployed again? Maybe I should have brought it up in our counseling session earlier today. Will it destroy what we have . . . the way it did in the past? I smack my lips together, my mouth dry, and my stomach flops in an unfriendly way as my stupid brain fires off a million other unhelpful thoughts.

Speaking of deployment. I have some news I need to share with her. I'm just not sure how to broach the subject. Maybe I'm wrong to wait and tell her after we spend this day together?

I shake my head to chase away my doubt and race to catch up with her. She's going too fast again. I don't think she can help herself, which worries me. Taya turns in her seat long enough to wave wildly back at me, and I grin. Her daredevil streak will age me early, but without it, she wouldn't be Taya.

I signal for Taya to let me take lead and take the next turn. The mountain road allows us to put on a burst of speed, and Taya whoops as she takes off. Her excitement is contagious, and the engine purrs beneath me as I match her pace. I pull even with her at a dip in the road, and she shoots me the bird. Returning the favor, I slip past her, and we race the rest of the way to Lake Lawson.

The lot that we pull into is so small that most of the people who visit have no idea that it exists. We're able to park our bikes in the shade, and I grab Taya's hand as we make our way along the trail to the heart of the park.

We find refuge at the base of a large oak tree heavy with Spanish moss a couple of meters away from the water. Taya smiles wide as she takes in the view of the lake, a few strands of her hair blowing in a gentle breeze. God himself couldn't have created a better scene for a proposal. Although, knowing Taya, she'd probably prefer a skydiving proposal.

My feet stall, frozen in place, while my cheeks radiate enough heat you could fry eggs on them. Why am I thinking about marriage proposals, of all things?

Except, now that the idea is in my head, I can't seem to make it go away. What if I did propose to Tara? Offered to marry her of my own free will this time? A true commitment, not one with an expiration date built in?

Rolling the idea over in my mind, I meander over to Taya. Thankfully, I'm soon caught up in picnic prep, which pushes any lingering proposal ideas from my mind. At least for the moment. I pull a blanket from my pack, and once we lay it out, I place the containers of food I prepared that morning on top of it, hoping I'm no longer blushing. We spend the next ten minutes or so eating in an easy silence and watching the water lap the shore. Taya pauses suddenly, a portion of sliced fruit halfway to her mouth. Cocking her head to one side, she studies me with a partially bitten strawberry dripping juice down her wrist.

"I've never seen you smile so much." She licks the juice away.

Shit.

I've been grinning like a moron. I scowl instead, trying to chase it away.

Taya laughs and hits me on the arm. "That doesn't mean stop, you dummy. I like seeing you smile."

"Sorry." I reach out and squeeze her hand where it rests on the blanket. "I'm not used to compliments."

Her eyes widen. "You're serious?"

"Is that so hard to believe?"

"Yes." Finishing off the strawberry, she points her fork at me in accusation. "You're practically perfect."

"Perfect?" My eyebrow quirks up. "Can I get that in writing?"

"Hell, no." She tucks a stray lock of hair behind her ear. "And just so we're clear, by 'perfect,' I meant you're a hottie with an attitude problem."

I throw back my head and laugh, and Taya flushes. "Hottie. That's new. Bear's gonna lose his shit."

"Oh, come on. I doubt you've been around for thirty-six years without one of your many admirers telling you how attractive you are."

"You'd be surprised. Those 'admirers' didn't care about how I looked or who I am. It wasn't me they were attracted to but the uniform. I liked keeping it that way."

"Past tense?"

Taya's made it impossible to settle for the vapid women who once occupied my bed. The pain in my chest is proof she's cracked whatever walls may have kept her out. I'm unwilling, or perhaps unable, to build more. If she decides to leave the program—leave me—after the year is up, I'll be truly alone. "Definitely. What about you?"

She glances away and picks at the remaining fruit in the plastic cup. "Not really. I've kept things casual, for the most part."

I should let it go while I'm ahead, but it's like picking at a scab. "Why?"

"What?" Her tone is too casual, and I latch on to the hesitation.

"Why no serious relationships? Any guy would be lucky to have you."

Including me.

"Too busy. Between college, work, searches and training, I barely had time to ride or hang out with friends. Dating took a back seat."

Sounds familiar. Once I decided to join the military, any hope of a social life went out the window. I wasn't interested in the trivial bullshit all my friends couldn't seem to live without. I had a goal in mind, and I was going to achieve it. Lux was the only one who understood, and it was my interest in the armed forces that eventually stoked his own.

Thinking of Lux sends a fresh wave of grief through me, and I have to clear my throat before I can try and change the subject. "What about family?"

There's an air of sadness to the way she lifts the corner of her mouth. "What about them?"

I take a bite of my sandwich to hide my wince. The question was intended to lighten my mood, not darken hers.

I swallow the bite that was just shy of too large. "You've told me about your mom, but you never talk about your dad. We've been living together for almost six months, and I don't think I even know his name."

Her lips twist, and her fingers clench so tightly around her plastic fork that it snaps in two. "I don't know anything about your parents." The words are a challenge, and I lean back against the trunk of the tree we're stationed beside.

This is an old wound, and it only hurts a little when I say, "They're both dead."

She gasps, and I regret my automatic bluntness.

"I'm sorry."

She reaches for me, and I squeeze her hand, my voice softening. "Don't be. They died when I was fifteen." It happened not long after Lux and I met, actually. Dad was driving drunk, again, and Ma just happened to be in the car. As had become the norm, I was with Lux and his mother the night it happened. I thought losing Dad would hurt, but it was a relief, not sadness, that greeted me at the news of his death. I saved all my tears for Ma. Thinking about it now makes my throat ache, and I box the sadness away in the dark where it lays beside my hurt over Lux. "I was raised on base by my uncle. He's the reason I decided to join the military."

She leaned forward eagerly. "What's he like?"

When had I seen the old man last? I can't remember. "Strict. No nonsense. He's too old to fight, so he goes from state to state, lecturing at colleges and preaching to kids in ROTC about the virtues of listening to authority."

"He sounds precious."

A picture of Uncle James comes to mind. With his cigar and his penchant for telling dirty jokes. Like Martinez. Maybe that's why I've put up with the moron for so long. Nudging her foot with my own, I lift my chin. "Your turn."

"My father's name is Phil." She begins, and my heart twists as I catch sight of her fingers digging into the blanket as if searching for comfort. "He remarried after my mother died and eventually divorced the evil bitch."

My eyes narrow. Taya is so bold and fierce that it's hard to imagine her growing up with a woman who did nothing but talk down to her. Glad she's not part of Taya's life anymore because I'm convinced that the two of us wouldn't have gotten along. "Any siblings?"

"No. Janice couldn't have any kids, and by the time they found out, the marriage was already falling apart." She chuckles, more bitterness than mirth to the sound. "It was for the best though. There was no one else to screw up but me."

"You don't seem all that screwed up to me."

"Maybe you aren't looking hard enough."

There's a bleakness in her eyes that hurts me deep inside.

I want to dispel it but don't know how. I hook my leg with hers and drag her closer. "Believe me, I'm looking plenty." The vein in her neck flutters, and I want to calm it with my tongue. My fingers itch with the urge to smooth the frown lines between her eyebrows.

"What happened?" Her voice is unbearably sweet, considering the bomb she's laying at my feet. "Why did you have to join the program?"

My mouth snaps shut and all the warmth in my chest turns to ice. I pull away and squint into the bright blue sky, avoiding her eyes. The sudden shift from affection to withdrawal is so pronounced that I'm shaking with it. "We should go." I'm like a child, too flustered to think straight. "It looks like the weather is about to take a turn."

Taya glances up, but I don't need to look to know what she sees. A sky so blue it hurts and not a cloud in sight. "No, it doesn't." Her voice cracks with hurt. For once, I'm glad for the tell, and I don't dare look to see if her expression matches. "Why won't you share what happened?"

It's agony to ignore her as I pack up the remaining food and sling the backpack over my shoulder. I'd rather Taya be angry with me than to know that I shot and killed a child. Somehow, I manage it without expression, though I sound gruffer than usual when I finally decide to speak. "Hurry up. I want to be back in town before it gets too bad out."

I'm proud of my cool outer shell. I'm the only one who will ever know the chaos it hides. My phone vibrates wildly in my pocket, which doesn't aide in calming Taya down.

"Fine." Taya scrambles to her feet. "And for crying out loud, answer your phone."

She bends over to snatch up the blanket and winces.

Her arm is still bothering her and I lunge forward to help when my phone flops onto the grass. Before I can reach for it, she grabs it.

She taps at the screen, her face scrunching tight and turning red. "Tell me what?"

My head flinches back slightly.

She holds the phone out to me. "Bear wants to know if you told me yet."

No, no, no.

I reach for the phone, but it dings, and she pulls it back, tapping at the screen again.

Her face twists into a scowl, her eyes shooting up to meet mine. There's a slight tremble in her chin. "When were you going to tell me you got cleared?"

"I planned on telling you after we ate."

Taya hurls the phone at me and makes a beeline for the trail. I snatch my phone from the ground and tap the screen. Fucking Bear. Why can't he just keep his mouth shut? With a snarl, I race down the path. My feet pound on the loose dirt until I make it to the bikes. "Taya, wait."

Taya pulls her helmet on, then spins toward me. "I'm your wife and this is the second time I'm the last to know what is going on. That's not right. I shouldn't be finding out what is happening in your life, especially when it affects me as well, from other people."

I clench my jaw. She's not wrong, damn it, but also, where does she get off giving me shit about hiding things? "Just like I shouldn't have to wait weeks to find out about how you really broke your damn arm! And what about that scrapbook in your closet, Taya? Is it right that you keep something that's obviously so important to you hidden away?"

She flinches, and something flickers across her face. Guilt? Sorrow? I can't tell, but I feel like an ass. She's still hiding things from me but, Christ, it's not like I've been completely on the up and up with her, either. Clearly we both have more work to do. I shove my hand into my hair and sigh. "Look, why don't we both take a deep breath and—"

The revving of her engine drowns out the rest of my sentence, and with a squeal of her tires, she's headed back toward the main road.

Fuck.

I kick the dirt, sending a slew of pebbles flying. And her words, goddammit, her words ripped my heart in two. Besides the deployments and the stress that comes with the risk that one day I might not come home, Taya will have to deal with the fact she won't be privy to a lot about my life in the military, information my teammates will know.

I grind my molars and snatch my own helmet from my bike. I'm not leaving the military and that one decision could very well upend everything Taya and I have built this far. Christ, when will I ever learn that my life is meant to be lived alone?

CHAPTER TWENTY-TWO

Taya

THE DISHWASHER DOOR slams shut with a resounding *thunk*. Jim's been gone for a week, one full week, and the house is so empty without him. Regret sits awkwardly in my chest, putting pressure on tender places inside of me. I readjust my shoulders to ease the ache, but it doesn't help. If only we'd had a chance to talk before he left.

Why did I let my anger get the best of me and take off on my bike like that? We're married. We're supposed to work things out. But no, I'd bailed, and being the stubborn ass that I am, came home hours later only to find a note on the kitchen counter my husband, saying that he got put on a training assignment and would be gone.

If only I could talk to him for a few minutes and apologize. But no. Radio silence so far. Which leaves me with far too much time to beat myself up over the things I said back at the park . . . and didn't say.

My cell phone rings and I curl my hand around the device, praying Marge isn't about to cancel her plan to stop by briefly before picking up her youngest daughter. I really could use a friendly, yet stern, shoulder to lean on. I accept the call without bothering to check the caller ID. "Hello?"

"Taya?"

I close my eyes and squeeze the phone. Oh, thank God. Jim's voice is nirvana to my ears. "Jim? Is everything okay?'

"All's good. How about you?"

"Great, I'm doing great!" I cringe. I sound like I'm fifteen, and I doubt I'm fooling anyone with my forced cheerfulness. This is stupid. I need to start being honest. "Look, it's been tough, but also, I really am okay. I have work and Marge and Inara . . . it's just . . ."

"It's just . . ." Jim prods.

Oh, screw it. "I miss you and I hate the way we left things."

Jim clears his throat. "Don't get long to talk, but I want to apologize. You were right, and I'm sorry. You should have been the first person I told about being cleared to return to active duty."

I grip the phone tightly in my hand and curl up in the window seat and close my eyes. "I'm sorry too. I shouldn't have flown off the handle like that, or run away. We can hash it out when you get home? Come up with a plan to do better next time?"

"Yeah. I'd like that. And I miss you too."

My heart warms and hope unfurls inside me. Right up until I hear Tony's voice in the background.

"Oh baby, I miss you too," he yells, in a high falsetto. "Why don't you tell her the little souvenir you've got planned for her . . . that'll really make her—"

He's cut off by some loud crashing sound. "Jim?" No response. "Jim?"

"I'm here."

My eyes narrow as my husband returns to the line, sounding a little out of breath. "What's going on over there?"

"The usual. Trying to beat some sense into Martinez."

"Hey, I heard that!" Tony yells in the background.

I roll my eyes and smile at their antics. "So, what's this about a souvenir?"

There's a deeper muffled voice in the background now. "Uh, hang on a sec." About five seconds pass before Jim returns to the line. "Sorry, but gotta go now."

Disappointment dulls my smile, but I swallow it, knowing better than to burden Jim with the negative emotion. He'd called. That's what matters. I'm grateful for what I can get. "See you when you get back."

"Bye, Taya."

The line goes dead, so I set my phone down and stare out the window. I don't move again until the doorbell rings. I spring up and head to the front door, sighing with relief at the sight of Marge. She gives me a quick hug before following me into the kitchen.

I plop down into the chair next to Marge and let out a heartfelt sigh. Marge rests her hand on top of mine. "I understand how you feel. Nothing is worse for me than when Papa Bear is out of the house, and it doesn't get any easier."

"You call him Papa Bear?" The moniker fits, but it's jarring to hear someone as imposing as Bear being referred to like a character from a children's book.

Marge grins. "Only behind his back."

I laugh, and it is much needed. Jim's schedule is crazy. He can be gone at base for hours or days at a time with no consistency. But I wasn't prepared for him to be gone in the blink of an eye without warning, and not know where he was going. Between the ride home from the park to Jim walking into the house, he'd gotten orders to leave for training. He barely had time to get ready. He couldn't tell me exactly when he'd be back, only that it would be roughly two weeks, but could be extended.

And we had no time to discuss what happened. No processing what it all meant.

Marge takes a sip of her tea, then places it back down on the counter of the island. "I must say the house looks more homey than the last time I was in it. Jim has always asked me to stop by and check on things when the team is deployed."

My toes curl and uncurl in my sneakers as if rubbing them against the inner soles would provide me with comfort. "Is it always going to be like this? Them taking off without warning?"

Marge sighs, her silence speaking volumes.

At least I'm not alone in this. While I have Inara, she doesn't really understand what I'm going through. Thank God for Marge. Having someone who's gone through this and is still going through it makes the scenario a bit more bearable. But I can't even imagine how it must be for her daughter. "How's Leslie?"

Marge leans back in her chair. "She's with Lucas's ex-wife. Leslie and their son are friends. Plus, she got bored at home without her usual targets to play with. Thank God, Lucas remained friendly with his ex-wife; otherwise, I have no idea what I'd do with Leslie sometimes."

I chuckle. "No piggybacks from Mommy?"

Marge sips her tea. "Are you kidding? My piggybacks are the preschooler's equivalent of a declaration of war. I'm too slow, too short, and too out of shape. Last time I offered, she fell to the ground and played dead until I went away."

I have to cover my mouth to stifle my bark of laughter. "That's one way of getting out of social obligations. Maybe I'll give it a try."

"It figures you'd approve. After all, your husband is the one who taught her how to play possum."

Imagining Jim, large and expressionless, teaching four-year-old Leslie to drop dead to avoid confrontation has me doubling over. He was so good with her that day at Bear and Marge's barbecue. He'd probably make an amazing father one day. My cheeks heat at the thought.

Marge cocks her head to the side, her gaze sharpens and her smile dims around the edges. "How are you really doing with all of this?"

"Better, now that he called."

Marge brightens at this bit of news. "He did? When?"

"Just before you came over. I can't believe how great it

was to hear his voice. Even if the call only lasted a few minutes . . . and I had to share him with freaking Tony."

Marge rolls her eyes. "I've never known anyone who needs a wife to whip their ass into shape more than that idiot."

"It's still hard though. Harder than I thought it would be."

Taking another sip of her tea, Marge sits back and stirs the amber liquid with her straw. "Jim has a good heart. Wants the best for those he cares about."

"I know." My pulse is pounding in my ears.

Placing her hand on my forearm, she squeezes lightly. "The trainings and deployments can be hard, so if you need anything, anything at all, I'm here. You don't have to figure it out alone."

"Thank you, I appreciate that. Maybe next time, he can tell me about it sooner." My voice is weak, my hands twisting the material of my sweatshirt.

Marge shrugs matter-of-factly. "They can't always tell us what goes on, where they go, or even when they'll be back. It's part of their lives we have to accept."

I sigh. "Basically, you're telling me to suck it up and quit being such a wimp."

Over a sip of tea, Marge's eyes twinkle. "Honey, cut yourself some slack. The first time is always tough, and you guys didn't have the most conventional start, either."

I should cut myself some slack. I mean, there's no doubt in my mind that I can do this. I'm the daughter of a cop. I've dealt with some pretty harsh stuff.

It's just nice to know I'm not alone in my struggle.

Marge's phone vibrates and she glances at the screen. "Time to go pick up Leslie."

We stand and I walk Marge over to the door. I'm thankful for her visit and her friendship. While I had some inkling of what to expect being married to someone in the military, there are aspects of it I wasn't prepared for, at least not emotionally.

I steel my shoulders. I might not have been prepared, but I can learn. If Jim needs me to be a rock, then dammit, I'll be the most solid, indestructible stone I know how to be. There's just a little bit of a learning curve while I toughen up my soft spots.

As she pulls away and I head back up the driveway, my eyes catch sight of mail sitting in the bed of Jim's truck. Odd. Though maybe in his haste, he put it down to get something from the cab and forgot to grab it afterward. Reaching in, I collect the myriad of envelopes and circulars, then go inside.

Flinging the mail onto the coffee table, I drop down onto the couch. My hands drag down my face, a frustrated whimper echoing through the room. I miss Jim and I hate not being able to talk to him—another *lovely* aspect of his job. This sucks.

I rummage through the stack of mail, most of which is junk advertisements with the occasional bill for things that aren't set up on autopay, like our landscaping account. I snort. Jim pays for the weekly service, yet gripes about what they do wrong every time they leave. The lines on the lawn aren't straight. The guys moved one of the stones out of place. Blades of grass weren't completely swept up from the walkway. My husband is definitely a person I would not want to have as a client.

A square manila envelope catches my eye and I pull it from the pile. The yellow is dirty and the paper wrinkled. How long has this been sitting in Jim's truck? The name on the return address belongs to the ISP company. Finally!

My breath catches and my pulse races like a Formula One car.

Did Jim find this? Did he try to open it?

And while I worry about the answers to those questions, the information contained on the DVD is what I crave. So, I leap up off the couch, tearing into the envelope and head upstairs to my room. This is it. Please, oh please, let there be something to put Santoro behind bars. Let me be able to put this whole thing behind me once and for all. Surely if the criminal responsible for my dad's death is in jail, my omission on the IPP form will no longer matter.

I drop down into the chair at the desk in my room, flip open my laptop and insert the disc into the external drive. Clicking on the folder, I draw back in horror at the images on the screen. I've been around death. I've seen violence. But this is different. It's casual, cruel, and without rhyme or reason. I swallow bile and work my way through each file.

There are dozens of jpegs, some just as gruesome as the

first. The others are of Santoro. I click onto another image. It's a receipt, dated back to Christmas last year, for a motorcycle plastics kit. While I'd gotten Dad a new coat for the holidays, he'd bought me new plastics, even insisted on putting them on for me. But why would he save a digital copy of the receipt amongst files for his case?

The last jpeg is grainy and blurred, almost as if someone took a picture of a picture. In it, Santoro is standing between two men, arms thrown over their shoulders and a large smile on his face.

One of the other men has his hands jammed into the pockets of his leather jacket, his lips pressed into a tight line. My throat tightens as bile claws its way up my throat. Marco. There's no denying he's one of the other two men.

I check the date, only to realize it was taken the day before Dad's death. I squint and try to make out the third man's face and my heart nearly stops. My body tenses, my eyes unblinking.

The third man in the photo is the random robber responsible for my father's death.

Except it wasn't random. And my former best friend was more involved than I first thought.

Now I have potential proof that could put them all away.

I'm so close to closing the door on my past so that I can fully open the door on my new life here in Virginia Beach.

A life I pray will include Jim.

CHAPTER TWENTY-THREE

Jim

I NEVER EXPECTED to be proposing again. Hell, I didn't think it would be happening now. Not after the argument Taya and I had before I left. The entire training, I just kept replaying the beginning of our day at Lake Lawson and those proposal ideas kept swarming my mind, and then during dinner one night, I mentioned to the guys how a part of me thought Taya would prefer a new motorcycle over an engagement ring. Craiger had to use the Heimlich on Bear, who choked on his food.

Of course, Martinez almost gave everything away two weeks ago when I had finally gotten the opportunity to speak with Taya. I give the ring one last look before snapping the black box shut and nod at Terry. "It's perfect. Thanks for doing this under such a tight schedule. You're a lifesaver."

The thick-necked jeweler in a blue shirt and matching tie is built like a brick house. Not surprising, since he's an ex-SEAL. A friend of a friend, who was more than happy to help me out on short notice by designing a ring from my vague notes I sent over a few days after my call with Taya. I'd worried right up until a few moments ago when I saw the end result. The diamond catches the light and sparkles like magic.

"She'll love it," he says with a wink.

I think he's right. Now the only thing I have to worry about is whether or not she'll love *me*.

I shake Terry's hand, exit the shop and head to my car. It's a nice day, so pedestrians dot the sidewalks while they enjoy leisurely afternoon strolls. I wish I had half the calm that they're exuding.

Once I unlock the door, I check my cell phone. Some of the tension eases from my neck. Okay, still on target to go pick up Taya and get to the restaurant on time. Being late for our first date since I returned home this morning is no way to kick off the new relationship I hope to establish with my wife.

Less than forty-five minutes later, Taya's in the car and we're headed to dinner. A muscle twitches involuntarily at the corner of my right eye, my fingers tapping the steering wheel furiously as I stare out the windshield.

God, I missed her. Two and a half weeks away from her and only getting to talk to her once for barely two minutes and once for a bit longer had been a special kind of hell I didn't know existed. Especially when she monopolized the entire conversation trying to convince me that she can handle my life, that she spent time with Marge learning about what it's like now that I can return to the field. But something's still wrong.

Of course, all three men are sworn to secrecy in case the night goes belly up and Taya turns me down. I don't need Marge meddling. The darn woman might actually stalk the restaurant—with Bear—and record the entire event.

Another quick glance at Taya only knots my stomach more. She is staring out the window, lips tight, hands folded in her lap. Like we aren't heading to dinner but to prison. Even when I came home, something felt off. The way she hugged me, too tight with a small tremble in her body, made my gut shift.

Bile creeps up my throat. Maybe asking her to marry me isn't such a good idea. What if she agrees, then bails? The easiest time to leave—the time most realize this life really isn't for them—would be while I'm deployed. But coming home to an empty house . . . it'd be better than finding her with another guy in my bed.

I shake my head.

Sheldon's comes into view, and I pull up to the valet parking before I drive myself crazy. The restaurant is the epitome of class and beachfront snobbery, but their pier is the perfect location for a proposal. I want this to be special for her, to show her that she deserves way more than getting "married" by signing a document. Luckily, the moon is shining through the partly cloudy sky. The universe is working with me tonight, holding off the storm that's supposed to roll in tonight.

The maître d' leads us to a table in the secluded part of the restaurant. We pass the table by the veranda, and my stomach shifts uneasily. My hands clasp and unclasp each other as if in constant need of touch and reassurance. We take our seats at the table, and I reach across to take her hand into mine, hoping that touching her will calm my nerves. "Get into any trouble while I was gone?"

"What are you, my dad?" She pulls away from me and grabs a piece of bread. The muscles in her shoulders go rigid, and her skin flushes a few shades darker as blood suffuses her cheeks. "I'm sorry. I don't know why I said that."

I capture her wrist between my fingers. The cast is gone, and her arm is pale from the elbow down, a reverse tan. My thumb grazes across the delicate skin, the vein running along her forearm fluttering a little faster.

"Do you want to talk about it?" Knowing she's fully recovered from her fall eases the anxious beast in me, but I still check her arm for any lingering weakness before kissing the delicate skin just below her wrist. The sharp intake of her breath is like music.

"I do." The sadness in her eyes has eased somewhat, color returning to her pale complexion. "But let me ease my way into it by way of carb overload—these rolls look amazing."

I grin. Partly because, at last, Taya is going to open up to me, but also because she looks like she needs the encouragement. And maybe just a teensy bit because her talking first means I get a temporary reprieve from my nerves. I reach for the box in my pocket, touching the square to reassure myself it's still there and then try not to snort out loud. Look at the big, brave SEAL about to piss himself over asking a simple question. Good thing Bear can't see me now. "Sure thing."

I let her go and lean back in my seat and scarf down half of the dinner rolls. They're delicious. Or maybe they aren't. Where the hell is the waiter? I force down the last mouthful of bread and want to kick myself. Engaging in a one-man carb eating contest is not romantic.

Taya finishes off her last bite of roll and wipes her mouth on her napkin, before clasping her hands together on the table. When she looks up at me, her expression evokes a different type of stress. My gut clenches. I have no idea what she's going to say next, but I can tell it's serious.

"So, I haven't been completely honest with you. About my past," she says, dropping her gaze to the table.

I hesitate, and then reach across and curl my hand over hers once again. I honestly have no idea where this is going, but I want her to know that she can trust me. "Take your time, we're in no rush. I'm here for you."

Her fingers tremble beneath mine, but the small smile she flashes me is all the proof I need to know that she appreciates my support. She closes her eyes. When she reopens them, all of the words tumble out in a rush. "My dad is dead, murdered by someone I considered one of my best friends."

She sags into the booth, like a burden's been lifted off her back. Meanwhile, I'm frozen in place while an icy finger trails down my spine. "I'm sorry, did you just say that your dad was murdered? By a friend? I don't understand, I thought he was still alive."

She hangs her head. "I know, and I'm sorry. I was too scared to tell you. I didn't update my IPP application, and I was worried they'd kick me out of the program. Plus, you needed this program and well . . . I needed a fresh start. I'm so sorry, Jim." She looks up at me with glistening eyes. "I should have told you sooner, I just panicked. I didn't want to drag you into my mess if I didn't have to."

My shock wears off, chased away by adrenaline. My body switches into high-alert mode. I squeeze her hand one more time before leaning onto my elbows while my mind whirls. "Is the person, this former friend of yours, who murdered your dad, in jail?"

Taya shakes her head. "No. They didn't have any proof." When she looks at me this time, her eyes blaze. "But I know for sure that Marco did it. And I'm partly to blame. I told him about Dad's investigation into Santoro. That's the only way they would have known Dad was coming for them." A tear slips down her cheek. "If I'd just kept my mouth shut, he might still be here today."

My heart cracks at the raw pain in her voice. I might only have a fraction of the story and no clue who any of these people are yet, but it's enough to understand the guilt has been eating away at Taya for a while now. Guilt that is entirely misplaced. She looks so small, huddling in the booth. Maybe I should be upset that she lied, but all I want to do right now is comfort her.

This time, I reach out with both hands and take hers in mine. "Taya—"

I never get to finish my sentence, because a small hand curls around my shoulder. Taya's looking behind me, confusion etched on her face. I turn, expecting to find the waiter with our appetizers. But what I get is a slap in the face.

Spoiler alert: I did not, in fact, order a slap in the face.

"It's good to see you, Jimmy."

Apparently this is a night full of surprises. The face and voice of the woman whose red nails are wrapped over my arm is a blast from the past. A terrible one. My muscles tighten in anticipation and I grip the edge of the table, preparing my body for the overwhelming onslaught of emotions that usually accompany my ex-wife—stabbing pain or fiery rage, or some combination of the two. But to my surprise, there's nothing beyond a few twinges. Transient reminders that this woman was bad news.

The main thing I'm feeling? Impatience over the interruption. "Raychel, we're a little busy here . . . ,"

Tactical error. Raychel's claws dig into my shoulder. She never did like being dismissed. Her eyes narrow and home in on Taya. "Well, who do we have here? Come on, Jimmy, aren't you going to introduce me to your little . . . *friend?*"

"I'm his *wife.*" Taya is stiff-lipped. Her face is flushed, fists clenched on top of the table while she zeroes in on my former wife's nails on my shirt.

I pluck ex's hand off my shoulder and grimace. A social visit from my ex is about the last thing Taya needs right now. Raychel's expression twists further when the light from a nearby wall sconce reflects off of Taya's wedding ring. "Bummer. I didn't get my wedding invitation in the mail."

Before I can process that yes, my ex is really going there, my former wife scoots into the booth beside me. "Isn't this cozy?"

She's squished up against my side, her leg pressed to mine. Once again, I wait for the emotions to flood me. Hatred. Desire. Loss.

Once again, there's none of that. Nothing except a warm rush of gratitude, that the woman in my life now is the one sitting across the table from me, and not the mess beside me. The sensation is new, and I take a few moments to revel in the relief sweeping through my veins.

"You swore you'd never marry again, and yet, here you are." Raychel focuses on Taya's ring again and a malicious smile spreads across her face. "I guess that means you know all about Jim's past. How he's all messed up because of that kid he shot, and how his buddy Lux hated the sight of him so much afterward, that he volunteered to stay behind just to avoid him."

The air leaves my lungs in a rush at the memory. Taya blanches, while Raychel's smile widens before she lifts a hand to her mouth. "Oh no, did I let the cat out of the bag?"

I can only stare at Taya and absorb the shock and pain on her face. Dammit. This is the worst possible way for her to find out. "Taya, please, I can—"

Raychel makes a *tsking* sound that frays my nerves. "Explain how you gunned down a kid in cold blood? Oh sweetie, I don't think there's any way to explain your actions. That's the reason you're such a disaster. Because you know you're guilty."

The pain stabs now, slicing right through my chest. Raychel knows exactly how to wield the blade. I can't even defend myself, because what she's saying is true.

But apparently Taya can. "Shut up. Shut your lying, trouble-making mouth before I shut it for you. An opportunity I clearly missed out on when I met your sister. Anyone with half a brain knows that Jim is one of the good ones, which I guess doesn't say much for your intelligence."

"I'd do as she says. My *wife*," I emphasize the word on purpose as the corner of my mouth quirks up into a lopsided smile, "has quite a right hook."

I scour the restaurant until I find who I'm searching for: a familiar face. The face of the Marine who I'd found Raychel screwing in my bed. "And besides, your date looks restless." I offer him a smile and a wave and try not to laugh when the man grabs the menu and ducks behind it. The last time we'd met, I hadn't been nearly so cordial. The sight of him used to send me into a rage. Now? I'm happy that my ex is his problem.

Raychel stiffens and turns to me and traces a finger down my chest, batting her eyes up into my face. "Well, if you ever want to meet up . . . for old times' sake, you know where to find me."

Taya starts to rise from her seat, but I wave her back down. Raychel is my problem. Gently but firmly, I push

Raychel's hand away from my chest. "Let me be very clear. I'll never want to meet up with you, in any context. I thought I loved you once, but as it turns out, I didn't even know you. You're my past. I've moved on, and I'm happy now. I hope you find whatever makes you happy, but that person never was, and never will, be me."

Raychel's eyes go wide and her mouth opens, but no words come out. Still, I brace myself for another outpouring of nastiness. Instead, she stands up and tosses her hair. "Whatever. Enjoy your boring little lives together."

Taya continues to glare at my ex-wife but no further exchanges occur, and Raychel walks off. As I watch her saunter back to her lover, some heavy, old knot inside me loosens and slips away. What I told her was true. She's my past.

My future sits right across the table.

My wife, who looks more than a little shaken by all of this. Shit. Not exactly the romantic evening I had planned. "I'm so sorry, Taya, I had no idea she'd be here. What can I do to make it up to you?"

Her eyes are soft, kind, compassionate. "It's okay."

I reach for the water and gulp the cool liquid down, hoping it settles the snakes writhing in my gut. Because even though I'm over Raychel, that doesn't make what she said any less true. Taya has a right to know the stuff I've been keeping from her. Has a right to decide if she wants someone like me in her life at all. "None of this is what I wanted tonight for you. For us."

Taya squeezes my hand and sits back. She takes a remaining scrap of bread from the basket and picks at it. Her face is drawn, her eyes sad. How do I make this right? How do I show her what she means to me, what I want us to be?

On a mission, I do whatever is needed. As the leader of my team, whatever move or decisions I make in the heat of the moment have to be the right ones because there is no going back. I learned through war to act without regret. Marriage to Raychel taught me a different lesson entirely. I know how to say sorry, but I don't know how to make amends and get back on the right track.

Now it's my turn to put all my chips on the table. To open up and let Taya decide if she feels I'm worth being with. I know Taya still has details to tell me about her past, but we'll have time for that, after. Hopefully. Unless Taya walks away.

I take a deep breath. Before I lose my nerve. "Raychel and I were never good together. She was always mean, and I don't say that lightly, either. My C.O. during basic could chew on nails and shit out bullets, but Raychel is a different kind of mean. She needed my constant attention and when she didn't get it, she was cruel for the sake of being cruel. She'd do little things to break me down, then laugh about it behind my back. I used to admire her for her drive. She had ambition, and I saw it as passion, at first. When I think about it, I see now that her 'ambition' was nothing but opportunism and manipulation. I think something inside her is broken, but it's not my responsibility anymore to figure out what."

Taya lifts her head, her eyes searching my face.

I pause, because this next part is humiliating to admit. "I caught her fucking two guys from base in our bed. Talk about a welcome home after a nine-month deployment. We were having problems, but I couldn't wait to see her. There was no apology after. She told me it was my fault. I was gone all the time, I never gave her enough attention, I demanded too much. She said I was too hard to love, that being married to me was a burden. She hadn't been cheating on me. She'd been trying to save herself." It still baffles me how someone could be so flippant about infidelity. During my resulting explosion, Raychel had been all too eager to tell me about her dalliances.

"That's bullshit." Taya's words are stern with conviction.

"Maybe. But it didn't matter. I believed her."

"You're an idiot." Her gaze drops, chin tucking in. "Why were you forced into the program?"

My stomach twists into a knot. There's no way around the truth. "My actions while deployed . . . are . . . *were* under investigation. My commanding officer went to bat for me and saved my career. In return, I had to join the program with no issues and at least make it through the one year that the annulment clause covers."

Taya straightens in her seat, her gaze unblinking and focused on me.

I'm picking my way through landmines, and the more I talk, the more mines there are. "There was a boy who sold fruit in Kabul. I don't know when or how, but somehow, the hostiles got to him. Planted a bomb in his basket on the day we were clearing the city in preparation for an airstrike."

I pause again when the images flood me. Everything was such a blur, but the expression of surprise on the boy's face when he sees my gun will haunt me until my dying days. A tight lump clogs my throat. I shake my head. "Sorry, need a second."

"It's okay, Jim. I'm not going anywhere." Taya's voice is soft. Warm. Strong. I lean into the support her calm presence offers and somehow find the strength to utter those last, devastating words.

"I made the boy and took him out before he could blow my team to hell."

Am I trying to justify what I did to Taya or myself? Probably both. It's not like I haven't spoken the words to myself before. I stare into her eyes because their brown depths make the world a little softer, a little sweeter and just the right amount of forgiving.

But she pales. And a second later, she is out of her chair and heads toward the front door. My heart constricts, my deepest fear punching me in the gut. Maybe she just needs a second. Or maybe she finds me deplorable.

Either way, I opened up, and she left me.

I bend my head and close my eyes, attempting to breathe with constricted lungs and a shattered heart. A cynical voice whispers to me. What had I expected, after all? After Raychel?

Except, that voice is full of shit. Taya is nothing like my

ex-wife. So why am I sitting here, letting the best thing that's happened to me in a long time walk out the door without a fight?

I toss some money on the table and jump to my feet. I rush through the restaurant and when I push outside the door, brisk salty air slaps me in the face while I look right and then left. Relief swells when I finally spot her, over by the public beach bathroom.

But Taya's not alone.

There's a man with her.

My hands tighten into fists as I break into a run.

CHAPTER TWENTY-FOUR

Taya

EVEN THOUGH I'D prepared myself for the worst, Jim's words had still come as a shock.

I made the boy and took him out before he could blow my team to hell.

And then, I'd looked up into Jim's face, and my heart had cracked even more. I didn't have to imagine the kind of guilt he'd feel over causing someone else's death because I'd lived it. But in his case, it was so clear that he wasn't at fault. And yet, he'd carried that weight ever since.

In that moments after his confession, all I'd wanted to do was pull him into my arms and comfort him because I love him.

But before I could tell him, I'd spotted a familiar face lurking in the front of the restaurant. Without stopping to think, I'd raced outside to catch him. And now here we are.

The two of us, all alone on this deserted stretch of beach, under a night sky heavy with an impending storm. The air is still and thick clouds blot out the stars, leaving behind a vast expanse of jet-black. The faint wind brushes against the water's surface, the ripples ruffling the stillness of the surface.

My fingers curl into the fringes of my shawl.

A wave of different emotions washed over me. Lyons couldn't have arrived at a more inopportune time. Jim was opening up, finally trusting me. But fear won out. Fear that Lyons is here because of something bad. Fear that if Lyons found me, maybe Santoro did, too. Fear Jim could be put in danger.

I squeeze my eyelids closer together, huffing. "What are you doing here?"

Lyons shoves his hands into the pockets of his jacket, his hazel eyes a mixture of sad and angry. "Really? That's all you have to say?"

I pull my shawl tight, chilled by a sudden cool breeze. His disapproval makes me tense and uncomfortable. "How'd you find me?"

"Taya, you did tell me about that stupid bet. But I didn't remember right away." Lyons runs a hand through his thick, blond hair, his jaw tightening imperceptibly. "When you disappeared, I thought Santoro had gotten to you. Killed you too."

I bite the inside of my cheek as I stare out over the water. I thought leaving without a trace would keep my friends safe, would keep Lyons safe, since he was in the police force. But it never occurred to me he'd think Santoro killed me. I glance over at him, at the wrinkles etched into his skin. Maybe I should've told him. "I'm sorry."

Lyons clears his throat and shifts his feet. "How's married life?"

I snort. "Really?"

He levels me with a glare.

"It's fine."

Lyons quirks an eyebrow.

"What?"

His eyes narrow.

I watch Jim's ex leave with her date.

I throw up my hands. "It's nothing. Just . . . I don't understand men's taste in women sometimes. Jim's ex is . . ." I make a face and shudder.

Lyons laughs and bumps me with his shoulder. I missed my friend. He's like the brother I never had, the same way Bear and Jim are brothers. His arms come around me, and their weight is like slipping into a familiar coat. I rest my head against his shoulder and we both stand in silence for a bit, gazing out over the ocean.

"I found a picture linking Marco and Santoro to my father's murder." The admission is like a weight off my shoulders, but also cuts deep into my soul. "They were both with the supposed random robber. Fucking Marco was directly involved. I have it on a DVD."

Lyons snarls and opens his mouth to respond, but his attention is captured by something over my shoulder. He goes rigid.

I whirl to find Jim, standing only a few feet away. His lowered brows and angry curl to his upper lip make my breath hitch in my chest. His body language reads as barely restrained violence. Shit! "Jim, this isn't what it looks like."

Jim steps forward, pulls me to his chest, and squeezes. When he leans back, he tips my chin up with one finger, and his expression softens a fraction. "You ran out like you saw a ghost. I thought at first it was my story, but when I went to find you, I saw *him*." His eyes narrow on Lyons.

I pull back a smidge and turn toward my friend. "This is Lyons, a friend of mine from back home."

Jim wraps his arm tightly around my waist. "Which friend?"

Oh. I probably should have clarified, seeing as I just dropped my lurid past on him no more than twenty minutes ago. "Not the one who killed my father."

Lyons extends his hand. Jim eyes it for a moment before reaching out with his own. The two men size each other up and exchange a brief handshake while my pulse returns to normal.

Jim turns back to me. "So, what's that you were saying when I walked up? You found a picture?"

Quickly, I fill Jim in on the cloud, the DVD, and the photo that I found, linking Marco and Santoro to the man who'd supposedly randomly killed my dad.

At the end, Lyons's eyes are wide and dark. Shaking his head, he lowers his voice. "I still don't understand. Why the fuck would Marco do this? To us? To your dad?"

His shoulders slump and I reach out and squeeze his arm, understanding the need for comfort. "I don't know. Has anyone else gotten hurt?"

Lyons shakes his head. "Marco's been quiet. No one's been visiting the bakery. Actually, Marco disappeared for a couple of days a little while back. Thought maybe he got what he deserved. But then he popped up again."

My eyes narrow. "You're not still trailing him personally, are you?"

Lyons turns and straightens to his full height. "Hell, yeah, I am. He betrayed us. We were his family. I'm not letting him get away with it."

Before I can protest, Jim nods approvingly. "Best to keep track of your enemies, so that they can't sneak up on you."

My mouth hangs open. Why do the men in my life have to be so damn stubborn?

Lyons exhales, dragging his hand down his face. "I'm sorry. I know today of all days isn't one to go through all of this."

Understatement of the year. Though I should never have to go through any of this on any day, but on my birthday—the first one since my father passed—is just a cruel twist of fate. Somehow though, having Jim by my side, makes me feel better. Stronger.

Jim frowns. "What day is it?"

Lyons shuffles his feet in the sand and slides me a sideways glance as if to say "sorry."

I sigh. "It's no big deal, just my birthday."

Jim touches my cheek. "Why didn't you tell me?"

I shrug and duck my head. "I don't know. Because it's really not all that important? And because it reminds me of my dad."

"It's important to me," he says, his voice soft.

A short silence follows until Lyons breaks it with a brisk clap of his hands. "Why don't we continue this conversation somewhere a little less open? I can make my world-famous hot chocolate as a birthday treat and you can tell me all about newlywed life."

I glance around the deserted beach and wrap my arms around my waist. Lyons is right. Our house would be a lot more comfortable—not to mention, safer—place to talk about Santoro.

"You got a ride?" Jim asks Lyons, who nods. "All set then. Follow us."

The ride back home is short and mostly silent. Until Jim reaches over and squeezes my thigh. "Please, don't ever run out on me like that again. Especially now that I know the truth about your dad."

"I promise."

The rest of our conversation waits until the three of us are safely tucked away inside Jim's kitchen. Once Lyons finishes making hot chocolate, we all carry our steaming mugs into the living room. I curl up on the sofa next to Jim, leaving Lyons with the love seat.

Jim takes a sip, and then lifts his mug at Lyons. "You weren't joking about world famous. Shit's damned good."

Lyons brushes his knuckles on his chest and grins. "We all have our things we're good at."

"And modesty isn't one of Lyons's things," I say.

"Just like cooking isn't one of yours. Speaking of which, strong work not burning down the kitchen . . . yet."

Jim snorts. "Oh, don't worry, she tried that the first morning she was here. Her attempt to make microwave pancakes. May they rest in peace."

I grab a throw pillow and swat my husband in the head with it as Lyons snickers. Jim grabs the pillow and pulls it from me, resting it on the other side of the couch. Then his gaze bounces between myself and Lyons. "I want every detail about what went down."

Lyons and I take turns filling my husband in about how Marco, Lyons and I used to be inseparable. About what a great man my dad was. About the investigation my dad did into Santoro, and how we were all clueless that Marco was working for him until it was too late. How there was no way my dad's shooting was random, and how we're both convinced Marco started the fire that burned down my house. Every last painful detail, until there was nothing left inside me. All of it, out in the open.

Jim gets up and paces. "So, you're saying you don't think Santoro or this Marco fucker will come after Taya? How can either of you be sure?"

Lyons leans forward, resting his elbows on his knees and clasps his hands together. "At the end of the day, we can't be sure. That's why I've been trying to keep tabs on him."

I sit up straight and jump in to attempt to relieve some of the worry my husband is obviously feeling, judging by the wrinkles in his forehead. "There's really no reason to believe they would. They have no idea I found my dad's cloud storage and was able to retrieve info about Santoro and Marco from it. All they know is I turned whatever I'd found prior over to Lyons, then disappeared."

Jim stops pacing and sits back down next to me, pulling my head onto his shoulder when I yawn. "Maybe we should continue this tomorrow night? I could bring the team in on this too."

I jerk my head up and frown. "I thought we would go over the DVD tonight."

Once again, Jim and Lyons perform some of that silent guy communication over my head before Lyons rises to his feet. "I don't see what one more day can hurt. Plus, I'm all in favor of any reinforcements we can get."

Jim nods. "Need a place to crash tonight?"

Lyons shakes his head. "Appreciate the offer, but I'm good. Already paid up on a hotel down by the water. I'm looking forward to opening my windows and sleeping to the sound of waves."

I stand up and Lyons hugs me tight. "Happy birthday."

"Thank you. So good to see you."

I sink back onto the couch and twist sideways while Jim walks Lyons to the door, where they exchange numbers. Jim tucks the phone back into his pocket and opens the front door. "I'll text you tomorrow once I've got a time that works for everyone."

"Sounds good. Oh and, Taya?" Lyons says.

"Yes?"

"I know you didn't ask, but I think you did good here." He motions his head to Jim, flips me a thumbs-up, and then strolls outside.

When the door clicks shut, Jim turns to me with his head cocked. "Am I missing something, or did your friend just give me his stamp of approval?"

"I don't think you're missing anything." Lyons has always been a little overprotective, so him taking to Jim so easily is completely unexpected. I'm thrilled that my best friend and my husband seem to have an instant affinity for one another.

Jim collapses onto the couch next to me and his hand snakes down to reach for mine. "There's a lot to process, but that's not a bad thing."

The uncertain waver in his usually deep baritone tugs at my heart. In all of the excitement about seeing Lyons and recounting my story, I'd never had a chance to comment on his. I wrap my arm around his waist and snuggle up next to him, burying my nose in his shirt and inhaling his warm, spicy scent. "Definitely a good thing. No more secrets, deal?"

His big body shudders before he squeezes me tight. "Deal."

We cuddle like that for a few minutes, with his arms wrapped around me and my ear pressed to his chest, rising and lowering with each of his breaths.

He shifts his weight. Coughs. Clears his throat. "So, um, exactly how tired are you?"

With that one sentence, my body zings to life. "Not as

tired, now that you asked me that question." I press my lips to his warm neck and nip his sun-kissed skin gently.

He shivers before pushing me a foot or so away. "Hold that thought—please—but I actually wanted to ask you something else. Something important."

CHAPTER TWENTY-FIVE

Jim

TAYA STARES UP at me with a combination of anticipation and trepidation. Feelings echo inside of me. I twirl around the small, velvet box in my pocket until my fingers clench around the case, squeezing the life out of it.

My wife tilts her head. "What?"

In truth, she deserves better than me, someone who makes her feel safe and cherished. Someone whom she can be proud of. I want to be that person in the worst way.

I stare into her trusting brown eyes and make a vow. I *will* be that person. Especially now. Knowing how much my wife needs protection.

That trust, shining up at me, almost brings me to my knees.

No secrets, I remind myself, giving the box one last squeeze.

"No secrets," I repeat aloud. More to bolster my courage than anything else, but Taya sits up straighter.

"Is something wrong?" She bites her lip and her brows furrow.

Here goes everything.

I pull the box from my pocket and slide to one knee. Before Taya understands what's happening, I flip the box open. I had a long speech planned out, but fuck it. We've done so much talking already.

"Will you be my wife?" My voice barely registers above a whisper. "Will you marry me, the traditional way?"

Never has one question made me more nervous. More like my entire life hangs in the balance. My heart beats so hard and fast in my chest, I'm afraid my ribs are going to have bruises.

Taya's brown eyes go wide when they fall on the diamond, sparkling against the black velvet backdrop. Every second that ticks by is an eternity of both hope and agony. My hand is this close to trembling on the box when she flings her arms around my neck and burrows her face into my neck. "I'd love to."

Her response unleashes something in my chest. I want to whoop but instead, I burst into a stunned smile. Though, I'm not above begging for a little extra affirmation. Not from this woman. "You would?"

She pulls back and her matching smile makes her entire face glow. "Yes. I would."

Under her encouragement, I slide the ring onto her finger. The sight of the diamond, sparkling against her skin, rouses some primal feelings. *Mine.* Finally.

Taya's eyes search my face. She leans back against the cushions in slow degrees and places her narrow feet across my lap. I grip one, marveling in silence at how my hand dwarfs even this part of her. Oftentimes, Taya feels like a Valkyrie, unafraid and all-encompassing. Then something will happen. It could be a large moment like when she came home after her fall or a small insignificant touch like my hand on her foot. It drives home just how fragile she is, how human. She's a warrior, and I'm a shield that's a shade too small. I feel ill-equipped to protect all of her precious, vulnerable pieces.

Her gaze drops, chin tucking in. "I'm sorry again about how I ran out of the restaurant. It wasn't the right thing to do. Not after you trusted me to open up."

My stomach twists into a knot as my fingers trail along her smooth legs. "Yeah, well, can't say I blame you. And you didn't even get to hear the rest of it."

She starts to protest but I shush her. "No. You need to hear it all. Especially if you're agreeing to be my wife for longer than the year."

Taya quiets down and slides fully into my lap instead, wrapping her arms around my neck. I clutch her instinctively as the darkness that had begun to edge my vision recedes like low tide. Taking a deep breath, I finally admit to what the psych eval had been insinuating all along. "I missed the grenade the boy hid in his other hand and it went off. I hid the fact I was hurt from my team, even from Lux, who was our medic. But he figured out two days later when we went out on a mission and I nearly shot our interpreter. He reported me and I retaliated, confronting him and hitting him with the butt end of my gun. Bear dragged me away, but the damage was done."

Taya draws in a sharp breath through her teeth and there's worry for me in her wrinkled brow. "Did you ever get a chance to apologize?"

"To Lux? No, I didn't. After he outed me to command, the team turned their back on him. So when it was time to come home, he swapped out with a SEAL from another team who'd gotten injured to stay in Kabul. Maybe even to get away from me. Now he's dead, and there's no more time for apologies."

"I'm so sorry, Jim. That has to be so tough. But I bet Lux understood in the end. He wasn't just a SEAL but your best friend, after all."

Her simple words give me hope for the first time. I bury my face in her neck. She smells amazing, like sweetness and sandalwood. "I'm sorry again about your birthday. I should've known, especially since the information was on the paperwork we were given at the beginning of the program. What about a present? I'll get you anything you want."

Taya lays her head against my shoulder and wiggles her finger in front of us. "You already gave me the most amazing gift."

"That wasn't for your birthday. So, tell me what you want."

"A kiss will be just fine."

I press my lips against the column of her throat before trailing more kisses lower, nipping and biting my way down her body She still has on her dress from dinner, and I slip her free of it. By the time she's naked before me, she's stationed on the edge of the couch, and I'm crouched between her legs. I toss the last of my clothes off and grip her beneath the knees. Taya squeals when I pull the lower half of her body off the couch so she's flat on her back, ass hanging in midair, and her legs hooked over my shoulders.

"I said a kiss." She sounds breathless, and I smile, pleased.

"You didn't say where."

I don't give her a chance to retort. I want her on my mouth. I give her a combination of tongue and teeth, savoring the flavors of her skin and committing each sound she makes to memory so I can replay them later. She arches against my mouth, helpless to back away or bring me closer. She rides my tongue and when she shatters, I let her slide, boneless, down the front of my body.

"I don't—" I know she's on the pill, but I should still wear a condom. My body trembles, taut and unwilling to pull away from her warmth as my hand reaches over to my discarded pants.

Taya grips my bare length for one sweet, torturous moment. "I want to feel you."

I slip inside of her, and as her inner walls clamp hungrily around my width, we groan in unison. Moving with her is like a dance, one smooth stroke after another until the sound of flesh against flesh is the only sound in the room.

I lose bits and pieces of myself with each stroke. When

she clutches me close, and our bodies move as one, it's impossible to tell where one of us ends and the other begins. It's all sweat, tongues, skin and an ever-growing need for more. I push deep one last time, and her legs, wrapped around my waist, spasm. She bucks as my orgasm sets off her own, her muscles clenching and releasing while she rides out the waves until every drop of my cum is milked away. I hold her still so I can feel the way her walls spasm.

Our heavy breaths calm by slow degrees, and the sweat cools on our skin. It's warm enough, luckily, that we don't need a blanket. Skin on skin is more than enough. I pull her into my arms on the couch, and she nuzzles her body tight against mine, her eyes shut.

I mouth "happy birthday, Taya" against her shoulder and press a kiss there.

Tomorrow morning, I'll run out and get her some flowers and balloons, maybe a small cake. God, I want to see the surprised happiness I'm hoping will light up her face.

She sighs heavily, as if fighting a losing battle against falling asleep. "I love you."

My chest swells as if my heart just grew three sizes. A wide Grinch-sized grin plasters on my face. More than anything, I want her words to be true, not some feeling mumbled as part of a dream, because being with Taya is like finding my place in the world. I belong here, wrapped around her and growing drunk off the smell of sandalwood. I want her completely. Forever and always.

And I want to be hers.

CHAPTER TWENTY-SIX

Taya

THE NEXT MORNING, I awake to a wonderful, liquid feeling in my limbs and a note from Jim.

Stay in bed, birthday girl. Ran out to do a few errands but I'll be back soon for round two.

My inner thighs clench together and tingle at the promise. Round two and if I'm lucky, round three and four later.

The world seems brighter and there's a warmth within me that leaves me light on my feet. Peace has always been hard to come by, but my soul is quiet for the first time in my life. Love was always that thing in movies that made people sing in the rain and climb castle towers. Love was a knight in shining armor and a picket fence.

Yet, I have something better.

Something real and unconditional. Something I'm willing to fight for. I roll onto my side and a sparkle catches my eye. My engagement ring. As I study the gemstone Jim picked out, optimism buoys me into sitting up. After the day we had yesterday, I expected to be exhausted today. Instead, my body hums with newfound energy. Like speaking our truths last night had cut away the dead weight dragging me down, leaving me fresh and ready to embrace a brand-new day. A brand-new start of my life.

And the first thing I want to do with this new life? Make Lyons and Jim eat their words by cooking my husband an edible breakfast.

I slip into a comfortable pair of leggings and an old T-shirt of Jim's, and then head downstairs. A quick perusal of "easy, quick breakfast recipes" on my phone pulls up a few likely options. I scroll until I find one that I'm convinced even I can't screw up: microwave omelets in mugs. Yeah, okay, so I burned the microwave pancakes, but that really was a fluke. I'm pretty confident I can mix together eggs, cheese and ham in a cup, press *start*, and not cause a major explosion.

I hum while I crack the eggs, pleased when I don't get even a single piece of shell into the mix. This is going to turn out perfect.

I tidy as I go, and by the time the mugs come out of the microwave, the kitchen is almost as spotless as when I started. I remove them and take a hopeful look inside. Yup. They look omelet-esque. Next I sniff and when that pans out, I bite the bullet and fork a tiny bit of yellow egg concoction into my mouth.

The texture is firm without being dry, flavored with the bite of sharp cheddar and the sweetness of ham.

I swallow. Holy shit. It's actually *good*.

"Yes!" I shout to no one in particular, and then pump my fist before doing a little dance around the kitchen.

The front door opens and the grin splitting my face is probably more appropriate for someone who just won a *Chopped* final than a grown woman who cooked some eggs that don't suck, but I don't care. I grab a mug and a fork and hurry out of the kitchen to greet my husband as he walks in.

"Wait until you taste this, you won't be able to make any burning-down-the-kitchen jokes any—"

The cup slips from my grasp and shatters on the floor, the loud noise drowning out my gasp. My nerves fire off as if they've been doused in gasoline and lit by a match, and my feet root to the spot. "Marco?"

Marco locks the door behind him. His head swivels a little too slowly, as if he's taking in the surroundings. Then he grins—the kind that's so wide it was more as if he wanted to eat everyone rather than say hello—causing the fine hairs along the length of my arms to rise and the temperature of the room to fall a little. "Hello, Taya."

I take an involuntary step back and stumble slightly when something sharp pierces the skin of my heel.

"Careful, there. Looks like you got yourself a nasty cut."

Blood freezes in my veins while my pulse ricochets in my ears, but I manage to lift my chin. "My husband will be home any second and then you're fucking dead."

Marco moves like a snake. One moment, he's several feet away, and the next he's grabbing my wrist as he stalks past me. His eyes become dark and hollow as he yanks me farther into the house. Pure disdain is etched into every one of his features. "Yeah, yeah. If poor Lyons couldn't keep himself safe, what makes you think your SEAL will fare any better?"

My heart slams against my chest. No! Oh, God, not him. Please, not him. I swallow and straighten my shoulders. "What did you do?"

"Lyons got T-boned earlier this morning. He'll survive, and hopefully he got the message to stay the fuck out of Santoro's way." Marco looks down at me, his pupils dilated. Shaking his head, Marco lowers his voice. "The lengths I have to go to in order to keep you two morons alive."

His words push a button in my brain and release me from the fear that's trapped me up to now. Rage laces through me and crawls up my spine like an uncontrolled forest fire, its heat burning my skin until all I can feel is the desire to hate. The acidity of the emotion waits to be spat out of my mouth in foul and vulgar words, but all I can do is screech out one question with every ounce of breath dwelling in my lungs. My eyes lock right on his, jaw clenching, and heart smacking against its bony cage with each thunderous beat. "Protect us? You betrayed us. Betrayed my father. Betrayed me!"

He lets go of my arm and I step closer, ready to beat the shit out of him, but he backhands me across the side of the head. The blow stuns me, sending me to the ground. I fight to breathe past the ringing in my ears. One side of my face feels numb and throbbing all at once, and when I pat my lip with shaking hands, I come away with blood.

Marco crouches before me. He looks confident, unruf-fled, and for the first time, I take stock of just how large he is. How imposing. Reaching out, he grabs me by the chin, holding me still while he cleans up the blood on my lip with the pad of his thumb. "If you don't want any harm to come to that husband of yours you like to fuck raw, I suggest you get me that disc of information."

The first spark of anger tries to ignite within me, but fear is poor kindling. His words sink in slowly. He's been watch-ing me? And how did he know about the DVD? My stomach heaves and bile sits heavy on my tongue. "You've known where I was this whole time?"

His nose wrinkles, brows furrowing. "Don't look at me like that. All I had to do was let Lyons believe Santoro got to you. Didn't take long to figure it out, and not like you'd stay away from search and rescue for long."

My breath seizes. Oh, God. That last search and rescue outing and my terrifying equipment failure. "You tampered with my rigging?"

"I barely clipped your rigging. Santoro didn't think I'd be able to kill you if it came down to it. Figured I'd show him there was nothing to worry about."

My bottom lip trembles, and I bite it, using the pain from the broken skin to steady me. "Why'd you kill my dad? You were family to us."

His grip on my chin tightens until I whimper at his nails digging into my skin. "I didn't kill your dad. The task force was closing in and Santoro wanted to use you to get your father to back off. I chose to save you and dropped the information you trusted me with to save your life."

My mind, my heart, my everything goes very quiet and cold. "Why work for Santoro in the first place? The bakery was doing well."

"Not well enough. I needed the money." His tone is sardonic.

"Your father must be rolling in his grave." This can't be happening. I close my eyes and pray to wake up, but Marco strikes me across the cheek. The strength of the blow rocks me back.

Marco drags me to my feet, gripping my face. "Shut up. Do you know how much debt we had from the funeral after my father and sister were killed? My grandmother has cancer and I can't afford to take care of her. And let's not forget how the cops did nothing to catch the person. But you know who did find him? Santoro, and he killed the gunman, avenging my father and sister."

My breath hitches, and I squeeze my eyes closed. "Marco, we would've helped you."

"You don't understand—can't understand." The words hiss out through his clenched teeth. "My grandmother's not in this country legally. I had no choice."

"You always have a choice." My breathing picks up, harsh and painful in my chest, and the ceiling and floor threaten to switch position. "I considered you my brother! Now, you're nothing more than a mere sliver of worthlessness. You're nothing to me anymore."

Marco snarls as he invades my space. "Good to know. Now get me that damn disc. Those pictures and audio files will never see the light of day."

My eyes flick to the messenger bag sitting on the floor by the closet. While Jim promised not to go into my room, I couldn't take any chances, so I kept the disc tucked away in my bag.

"You are so easy to read." Marco snorts, then twists my arm behind my back and starts to lead us toward the bag.

Every fiber of my being screams at me to do something, anything, to keep him from taking that DVD. I need to stall until Jim gets here. And then what? Hope that Jim can overtake Marco? But what if he can't? Marco has the element of surprise and for all I know, a gun.

No.

I need to get rid of Marco before my past has a chance to ruin Jim's life too.

When my pace slows, Marco leans closer so his mouth is up against my ear. "Even if you think your husband can take me, it won't matter. Santoro will just send someone else to finish the job. Plus, you wouldn't want anything to happen to your friend, Marge's, sweet little girl, would you? What is she? Four? If you play along, she might make it to five."

Leslie.

"No." I'm begging now, and there's nothing I can do to stop. "Marco, don't. Jim doesn't know anything. I haven't told him about what happened or why I really came here."

"What happens to them isn't up to me, T. It's up to you." His voice is cold.

I'm frozen. Ripped apart by indecision. If I give Marco the DVD, my dad's killer will walk free. But I have to protect Jim. And Leslie. My old life, or my new one. I have to choose, and choose fast.

In the end, there's no contest. Jim's safety comes first. And I only know one way to protect him.

By giving Marco what he wants.

When we reach the messenger bag, Marco shoves me forward until I stumble. "Get me that disc. Now."

With trembling hands, I search through the bag, going straight for the zipper pocket where I tucked the DVD away.

Empty.

The disc is gone.

"No, no, no." Frantic, I dig through the other compartments, but come up short. I sink back onto my heels. "It's not there."

With a snarl, Marco shoves me aside and searches the bag himself. "Where is it, Taya? I'm not fucking around here." He wraps a calloused hand my throat and slams me into the wall. "You'd better find that disc right now."

"I don't know where it is. I left it in my bag."

Marco squeezes my throat even tighter, replacing my fear with determination and anger. I slam my head forward, driving my forehead up and into his nose and mouth. He curses viciously and releases me. "Fuck . . . you," I gasp, while my throat spasms.

Stumbling back, I dart past him, ceramic from the shattered mug embedding itself into the soles of my feet. I barely make it into the kitchen before his hands are on me again. I turn on him like a dervish, pushing in close before he can use his longer reach to do more serious damage, and I drive a fist into his solar plexus. The air is driven from him, and when he doubles over, I shove his face onto my knee, hitting him so hard and fast, I shriek with it. Once, twice, three times. He goes down but hooks my legs with his arms and brings me with him.

I land on the kitchen floor and cry out, but the sound is choked off when Marco slams his fist into my face. The metallic taste of blood fills my mouth, and my eyes roll into the back of my head. The world darkens for a brief, terrifying instant.

Marco drives his elbow into my side and a rib cracks. I scream, nausea an instant and vicious companion. I vomit onto the tile, and bright spots of red decorate the mess on the floor. Marco rolls off of me, and I lay there for precious seconds, trying to breathe past the pain. Terror is leaching the strength from my limbs, and an overload of adrenaline has me shaking so hard, my body jerks with it.

Get up. Get up and fight.

As I slowly push my way to my hands and knees, Marco lets out a sound of excitement. "What's this?"

The room spins while I lift my head, black dots piercing my vision as Marco reaches for Jim's laptop sitting on the kitchen table. I'd been so excited to cook him breakfast that I hadn't noticed the external disc drive sitting next to it. Then I recall my husband whispering in my ear last night, asking me about the disc so he could look through the information while I slept.

A faint whirring sound fills the room and then Marco clasps the DVD in his hand. Seconds later his boots thud against the floor just as I sit back onto my knees. The shrill clang of metal fills the room and makes me curl in on myself. Once again, I try and get to my feet. Once again, my vision goes white with agony, and I collapse back down to the floor.

The next moment, Marco's hands are in my hair. He holds me down, breathing hard against the shell of my ear, his body a crushing weight that drives my broken rib into places it shouldn't go. "I really didn't want to do this, but you left me no other option. I'm not going to jail for assault. Luckily, I found my scapegoat. 'Emotionally unstable SEAL murders cheating wife.' Works for me. How 'bout you? But first, I'll take this."

Before I know what's happening, he's yanking Jim's engagement ring over my knuckle.

His calloused palm covers my mouth and he punches me.

Once.

Twice. Where he strikes, my muscles go cold and numb. It doesn't hurt. It just feels strange, invasive in a way I have no words for. It isn't until the butcher knife clatters against the tile that I realize what's happened.

My breath sounds ragged, my heartbeat loud. I try to

crawl again, but my body weighs a ton. My cheek presses into an ever-growing pool of blood. Briefly, I see Marco's boots disappear through the garage door, but I don't wonder where he's going. I don't especially care anymore. I'm too tired to care.

But I can see the sky through the panes of my window nook. The scene is overpowering, even from where I lay. The clouds rise up like mountaintops into the sky, the sun a heavy disc of warmth filtering through the trees. Everything dances, even the leaves.

Especially the leaves.

I wish Jim was here to see it.

It would have been nice not to die alone.

CHAPTER TWENTY-SEVEN

Jim

T HE DOZEN GIANT helium balloons enter the house before me, jockeying for position and filling my view with their reflective surfaces. My other hand holds a huge bouquet of colorful flowers, and I have a pink pastry box nestled to my chest. I push the balloons and take a few steps into the foyer, sniffing the air. "Hey, is that food I smell? Unburned food, even?"

The next step I take, something crunches under my shoe. I glance down, and that's when every cell in my body turns to ice. Broken ceramic punctuated by bright red blood. Both droplets and a trail.

The balloons slip from one hand and float up to the ceiling. The pastry box and flowers crash to the floor. My body kicks into fight mode.

My heartbeat is anything but gentle, my pulse drumming away in my ears. "Taya!"

The tips of painted toes peek around the corner into the kitchen. Taya's toes, but with the angle all off. Like she's lying on the floor. Not moving.

A hard body slams into my legs the second I round the corner into the kitchen. I fall backward, twist and roll while kicking out with my foot, breaking my fall and connecting with something solid.

I scramble to my feet while my attacker does the same. We face off in the foyer, circling one another. I recognize the dark-haired man from the picture on the disc and too many thoughts pulse through my head, accompanied by the taste of fear. "Marco."

"Sorry it had to be like this. It's just business." He smiles and then rushes me, something silver flashing in his hand. I whirl away just in time while bile fills my mouth. The end of the blade glistens red with blood.

Taya's blood.

Fury on a scale I've never experienced before erupts beneath my skin, spewing like an active volcano. So intense, that I'm half waiting for lava to explode from my pores. I want to explode so badly, but I know I can't. One wrong move and Taya is dead for sure.

So I dig somewhere deep down and tap into every bit of training I possess, until a cool detached calm clears my head. *If you don't see an opportunity at first, that's okay. Bide your time until you can make one. Be brave, but smart. Brave men die all the time. Smart men live to be brave another day.*

All I need is for him to make one mistake. Just one. Then I'll have that knife out of his hand. I search the area for anything I can use, and my gaze lands on the disc in Marco's other hand. "So you found it. Good for you. Too bad I made copies."

The other man's nostrils flare before his eyes narrow. "Liar."

I shrug like I don't have a care in the world. Meanwhile, another piece of my heart dies, every second I can't reach Taya. When Marco hesitates, I try a different tactic. "Why don't I make you a deal? Let me go make sure Taya is okay, and then I'll call my friends and have them all dump the discs at a location of your choosing, no questions asked. Either that, or you can take another run at me."

When Marco's hands dip the slightest bit, I stomp on the piece of shattered glass next to my right foot. The sharp crunch causes his gaze to drop down toward my feet, and that's all the advantage I need. I feign to the right and lunge, grabbing the wrist of the arm holding the knife and ducking beneath him while using my other hand to brace his shoulder so that I can crank his wrist until he screams. A bone cracks and the knife clatters to the floor.

I kick the cutlery away and punch him in the kidney. Again. And again. And again.

Then I use my legs to tangle with his and flip us both to the ground.

Marco surprises me by twisting free. Panting, he crawls for the knife, his left wrist bent at an unnatural angle. My hand curls around a thick, jagged piece of the broken mug just as he grabs his own weapon and starts to roll over. I'm on top of him, pinning him across the throat with my forearm. He struggles, and the knife flies toward me. The blade grazes my skin and I hiss just as I jam the thick chunk of ceramic into the side of his throat, bisecting the carotid. Blood spurts everywhere. "Go straight to hell."

His eyes bulge, and gradually he goes limp. When his chest stops moving, I'm on my feet and running the last few steps into the kitchen and round the corner of the island.

Taya is sprawled on her stomach on the floor. There's so much blood, it brings me to my knees. Her clothes are soaked with it, and when I pull her into my lap, cradling her against my chest, I'm both relieved and heartbroken her body is still warm.

I break through the nightmare haze and pull my cell out of my pocket, and pick out the three numbers.

"Nine one one, what's your emergency?"

"My wife has been stabbed. She's not moving. Please. Send an ambulance. Hurry."

I barely remember giving my address. Or hanging up and calling Bear afterward. I barely remember anything at all but the contrast of the pale, cold flesh of Taya's face against the red blood pooled on the floor.

I thought when I finally snapped, it would be in stages. Instead, I'm torn down all at once, decimated in a single breath. She doesn't stir at first, but when I shift her in my arms, pain brings her eyes open with a suddenness that damn near stops my heart.

"Please don't die." Is that my voice? It doesn't sound like me. I've never begged for anything. Not even my life. I'm begging now. "Hold on for me, baby. Please. I need you to hold on."

Her eyes flutter, and it's hard to tell if she can hear me. I keep talking anyway. It's not like I can stop. Desperation won't let me. "Taya, keep your eyes open," I snap when her next blink lasts a second too long.

"I'm sorry." I'm starting to hate those words, but I say them anyway. "I'm so, so sorry I left you. Fuck the balloons. I shouldn't have left you all alone. I'll never leave you again, just please keep your eyes open."

Tears fall from me to strike her cheeks like raindrops. Her eyes gaze dreamily at something above my head. "You got me balloons."

I glance up and sure enough, there are the balloons I brought home. Bobbing against the ceiling like a crowd of voyeurs. I'm going to pop every one of those bastards the second I know Taya is okay.

I swallow as pain claws through me. "I love you." A part of me thinks if I whisper it, it will reach her wherever she's drifting off to. The look on her face says it's a soft kind of place. "I'm sorry it took me so long to say."

"Marco." She chokes, and it's a painful sound. I try to quiet her, but she shakes her head, refusing to be silenced. "He's got a DVD with evidence. Find it. Please, Jim, we have to . . . make things right."

It's a chore for her to breathe, and she gives in to unconsciousness just as abruptly as she tried to fight her way from it. A frown tugs at her lips. "Your arm . . . hurt."

I glance at my arm. There's a vicious looking cut halfway

down my forearm that's leeching a steady stream of blood. It's nothing, though. Shit, I'd cut the damn thing off if I thought it would guarantee that she'd be okay.

"Hold on," I whisper urgently, when Taya drifts off. "Dammit, Taya, hold on!"

I don't know how long I'm holding her like that, urging her to fight, before the wail of a siren fills my ears. Somehow, Bear gets there just before the ambulance. He squats down in front of me, his hand reaching across to lay on my shoulder. "Jim, the paramedics are here."

I rock, clutching her close, but Bear pries her limp body from me, gently placing her on the floor. Two men dash in and begin working on her as my best friend wraps his arm around my waist, dragging me backward.

I resist, thrusting my weight against his arm, but he wrestles me to the floor, pinning me against the cold, ceramic tile. "It's my fault. God is taking my Taya to punish me for Aland."

Bear adjusts his body on top of mine when I start clawing at the floor to drag myself over to Taya. Bear shakes me, and my head bobbles, pain shooting through my eyebrow as my face slaps the floor. "Stop! The bomb in that basket would've killed everyone in a mile radius. You are a hero. I get to hug my little girl because of you."

Sobs wrack through my body. "I never should have left her alone."

Bear's grip loosens. "You can't blame yourself for all the evil in the world, Jim."

I can't help her. I can't save her. Tears spill from my helpless eyes as I shake uncontrollably under Bear. "I can't lose her."

"I know." His words are just right and yet, not nearly enough.

CHAPTER TWENTY-EIGHT

Taya

I T FEELS LIKE a long time before I open my eyes again. The room I'm in smells like medicine and sickness. It's a familiar smell, and my nose wrinkles in distaste. There's an IV in my arm and a stiffness to my limbs that makes me think of bandages.

Makes sense.

My lips purse at the memory of Marco's duplicity, and someone laughs.

"Not even awake a full minute, and she's already irritated."

The voice is only vaguely familiar, and I finally glance around the room in search of the culprit. Tony slouches in a chair by the window. Lucas, standing next to him, waves in greeting. On the other side of my bed is Bear with Marge asleep in his lap, and Leslie curled up napping in hers. A tiered cake of a family.

I find Jim last, though I suspect that I was aware of him the entire time and only waiting for the moment I was ready to face him. He's sitting next to me, studying my face as if he can't bear to look away. He's drawn and tired. Defeat is in the slump of his shoulders and the cant of his mouth.

"Where's Marco?" As much as I want to touch him, I can't rest without knowing the fate of the man who tried to kill me and murdered my father. "The disc!"

Jim smooths a big hand over my hair, soothing me. "Marco's dead. We still have the disc."

There are holes in his usual baritone and his eyes are red. My husband has been crying.

"Are you okay?" I say, searching him for a sign of an injury. All I find is a bandage, wrapped around his forearm.

"Now that you're awake, yes."

A feeling I can only describe as awe drifts over me. Or maybe it's the pain meds. Or a combination of both. All I know is, despite my discomfort, that I'm touched, deep in my heart, over the knowledge that this strong man cried over me. That, and he doesn't look remotely embarrassed to show it.

"Lyons?" I rasp out.

"He's fine," Jim reassures me. "He's here at the hospital too, on a different floor. Stable condition with a few broken bones. Local police officers are assigned to him to make sure he's safe. Plus, some of our off-duty friends."

I try to speak again and end up clearing my throat, which feels as dry as ash. "Water?"

Jim hands me a pink plastic cup with a bendy straw. I take a grateful sip before attempting to speak again. "Marco's dead?"

"As a doornail," Bear says. "He made the fatal mistake of trying to keep Jim away from you."

The relief his words provide is so strong. The pinch of sadness is unwelcome but not entirely unexpected. I meet Jim's eyes, while emotion claws around in my chest. My face crumbles. "I tried to get him to leave before you got there. I didn't want him to hurt you. I'm sorry."

"Don't you dare apologize. I will always, *always*, come to save you. I'm just sorry that I was almost too late." Our fingers entangle above the sheets while he chokes up.

"No, it's my fault." My breath saws in and out. "Should've told you sooner. Should've updated the committee. Then we could have had a plan."

Tony groans. "Alright, alright, enough with this crap already. We get it. You're both to blame, now kiss and get over it before we all vomit from the sweetness."

Jim's head jerks up. His eyes blaze and I'm convinced he's going to lose his shit. Then a reluctant smile tugs at his mouth. He shakes his head. "How about this? I promise if your wife ends up in the hospital, I won't give you half as much shit, because I'm not an asshole."

Tony gasps. "Wife? Bite your tongue. That's just mean."

I laugh, instantly regretting the impulse when the motion floods me with pain. Jim's smile turns into a frown. "What is it?"

I nod while the pain recedes. "Just try not to say anything funny for the next, oh, month or so."

"Mr. Sour Pants here? Should be a piece of cake," Tony

says, only for the oxygen to release from his lungs in a loud whoosh when Jim elbows him hard in the ribs.

I have to bite my lip to keep from laughing again. Oh, how I love these people.

Jim hooks his pinkie with mine, and the expression in his eyes when he gazes down at me makes my heart swell. "I love you, Taya."

My heart swells and tears clog my throat. I sob, warmth suffusing once-cold limbs. "I've been waiting for you to say that."

Marge shifts in Bear's lap. "*We've* been waiting for like six weeks. I had money riding on it."

Her words bring a weak smile to Jim's face and an outright laugh from Bear. My pinkie squeezes Jim's, locking in our promise. "I love you too."

I never want Jim to doubt my feelings for him again. If I have to tell him every day, several times a day, I'll do so gladly. Why wouldn't I, when he smiles so much brighter when he hears it?

"It sounds much better when you're awake."

My eyes widen.

He smirks. "You talk in your sleep."

I flush, a little light-headed at the rush of blood to my head. Apparently, I'm too hurt to handle embarrassment just yet.

"And no one is ever going to hurt you again." Jim's brows pull together, happiness leaving his eyes. His posture is rigid, and a vein in his neck pulsates.

"You got that right," Bear interjects, and I glance at him in surprise.

Marge nods, viciously determined. "You're family."

Lucas and Tony step up to my hospital bed, solemn for the first time since I've met them. "No one messes with family."

Family.

These people are my family. I may not be as close to Tony and Lucas, but I know in my heart, they wouldn't hesitate to risk their lives for me. And that they'll watch over me and take care of me if ever Jim can't.

Marge's lips contort into a Cheshire grin of sorts, so wide her gums are exposed. She folds her arms, gaze turning to Jim. "Bear told me you guys were done repainting your guest bedroom, so when are you planning on moving Leslie's old crib over? You know, I want my garage cleaned out before y'all are deployed again."

My head whips to my husband, who's growing paler by the second. Kids? He's thinking about kids? My earlobes are on fire, showcasing my embarrassment, as usual. I slap at his forearm, but Jim continues to avoid my gaze, his cheeks a deep red. Yup, he's definitely considering it. Who am I kidding? The man probably has a detailed mission plan on it already.

Tony snickers. "Pre-deployment baby?"

Before either of us can answer, the hospital door bursts inward.

The men tense, but the woman striding up to my hospital bed isn't a threat to anything but my ribs. She's the last member of my new tribe, a fact Inara demonstrates as she throws herself into my arms. Inara hugs me much too tightly for a woman reacquainting herself with consciousness. I groan, and my friend pulls back with a tearful chuckle.

"Sorry, chica." She fans her still-tearing eyes with one hand as if she can will the water away. "I get really handsy when I'm nervous."

I grin. Inara is a bond I formed all on my own, and it feels good to have her there with the rest of the people who are dear to me. "Well, almost dying can be worrisome."

She perches daintily on the edge of my hospital bed, near Tony and Lucas. "It's the absolute worst. You have to give a bitch a head's up about this kind of thing. I feel like I would be more emotionally prepared for all of this if I'd known ahead of time that people were trying to kill you. Ya dig?"

I bite back a smile.

"I dig." Tony angles a little closer, a grin on his face, and his eyes assessing.

Inara looks at him from the corner of her eye, and her upper lip curls in prim disapproval. "*¡Escucha!* Take two steps back, or you'll be ending that sentence with 'my own grave.'"

"I like you," Marge says.

Bear shakes his head. "Of course, you do."

Inara stands up and walks over toward Tony, her gaze dancing between Jim and me. "How much damage did he do?"

Jim's face tightens as he pales. He takes a second to clear

his throat before he speaks. "He stabbed her three times in the back. She lost a lot of blood. She also has some broken ribs, a concussion, cuts on her feet, and a fractured eye socket."

"God, chica, you must be in a lot of pain."

My lips turn up into a lopsided smile. "Only when I laugh. I think they must have me on some really good drugs."

I turn to Jim and rest my hand on the side of his face, swiping away a stray tear that has fallen. I didn't realize how severe my situation was, but the anguish on my husband's face tells me there's more he isn't saying—that he can't say right now.

He nuzzles into my palm and squeezes my hand. "Taya?"

The rest of the room seems to fade away, my focus shifting from my husband's green irises to the slight tremble of his lips. "Yes?"

"You lost something, but I got it back for you." He reaches into his pocket and withdraws my engagement ring. The one that Marco ripped off my finger.

I frown when an old anxiety wiggles its way into my head.

Jim pales. "Did you change your mind?"

"No. It's just . . . what about the committee? What happens when they find out about all this?" I gesture to my bedridden body. "And that I didn't tell them about Santoro and Marco?"

Jim's already shaking his head. "You just focus on healing. I'm taking care of the rest."

I lean back against the pillow, allowing his reassurance to wash away the bulk of my concern. "Then, yes, I'll still marry you. Nothing would make me happier."

EPILOGUE

Taya

"THANKS FOR ALL of this, Taya." Lyons smiles as he grips a copy of the DVD. "This should help."

"Will it put him away?" I want to hope but don't dare. I won't feel truly safe until Santoro is behind bars.

He pats my arm, one of the few uninjured places on my body. There's a warning grunt, and I glance along the length of the bar at Shaken & Stirred to frown at Tony. Lucas is sitting next to him, talking to the bartender. Bear, Tony, and Lucas have been working in shifts to keep an eye on me when I'm not with Jim. I'm grateful for the precaution. Until Santoro's organization is dismantled, there's still a chance the crime boss may try to retaliate.

Seeing the look on Tony's face, Lyons pulls away.

Fiddling with my hands, I glance up at Lyons. "I'm just glad you're okay. I couldn't bear to lose you too." I grip the hard wood of the table. "I can't believe my father didn't warn me."

Lyons's expression softens. "Your dad looked out for all of us. He protected us even when we screwed up. Like the time I got busted hacking into the school server to change my grade."

"Yeah, but he also made you paint the entire house over the summer."

Lyons's expression grows solemn. "Your dad probably thought he could help Marco, get him out of whatever trouble he'd gotten caught up in."

I slump in my seat and my injuries twinge, a clear sign I'll need more painkillers soon. "I just wish we still had those recordings."

Inara slides onto the stool next to me, lips red with a fresh coat of lipstick from her run to the ladies' room. "What recordings?"

"Marco mentioned some audio files. My father recorded him and Santoro, but no one knows where they are."

Lyons places his hand on the top of mine. "When I get back to the precinct, we'll go through the flash drive. If your dad knew how to use a cloud account, I'm sure he knew how to hide computer files."

I jerk back slightly, my mouth opening and closing like a goldfish with no sound coming out as I process his words.

Inara rolls her eyes. "You can hide files on a flash drive by left clicking and changing the properties. It's kind of like a magic trick. My ex-boyfriend did it with his porn. It fucked up my computer, and I couldn't figure out how I kept getting viruses. Turns out, Big Booty Bitches is just another name for malware. Who knew?"

I stifle a laugh. Only Inara.

Lyons fights back a smile. "We'll also check the images. Your father could've imbedded the files on one of the pictures." Lyons pushes back his chair and stands, leaning on his cane for support. "Reach out if you need anything."

I stand and walk over to Lyons, wrapping my arms around him and momentarily forgetting my broken ribs. "Thank you. Tell everyone when it's safe, I'll come up and say hello. Let them know I miss them."

"Should I be jealous?"

I loosen my hug and turn my head just in time to catch the kiss Jim presses against my lips upon his arrival. He pulls away long enough to shake Lyons's hand. "Make sure to keep us updated."

"Will do." Lyons nods at the rest of the group and makes his way out the door.

Bear and Marge swoop past Jim to offer their own greetings. Bear's hug is gentleness itself, his large frame dwarfing me in a way that would have been alarming if I hadn't known what a softie he is. Marge gives me a kiss against the cheek and squeezes my hand for the briefest of moments. Tony and Lucas leave their seats to come join us. As the two of them greet Inara, I spot the customized helmet tucked beneath Jim's arm for the first time.

I laugh, quirking a brow. "Are you seriously getting your cosplay costume ready for the San Diego Comic-Con? It's months from now."

"Maybe. Thought it would go well with the Yamaha YZF-R1 outside."

I glance between the three bodies. "You bought yourself a new bike?"

Jim shrugs, his casual air ruined by the pride and amusement in his smile. "The Ninja has a bunch of miles on it and I figured it's time for an upgrade. Think of it as your belated birthday gift."

I bounce on my toes, ignoring the way my excited motions make me sway. But when I reach for the key, Jim pulls his hand back and tucks it into his pocket. I pout. Of course I can't ride in my condition, but I desperately want to. With a huff I nod toward the helmet. "So, you're gonna ride around on my new bike with your costume helmet?"

"Last time I checked, you have a thing for Master Chief."

"Oh yeah?" The corner of my lip curls up. "If you wear your milnjor armor, you might get lucky tonight."

"I'm already lucky."

Bear and Marge roll their eyes in unison.

"I told you they were geeks." Bear holds out a hand, and grumbling, his wife pulls a ten from her purse and shoves it into his open palm. Smiling, he leans down and puckers up for a kiss, but Marge scowls at him and stalks off.

Inara laughs, nudging me with her shoulder before leaning in. "You guys actually manage to make this marriage thing look like fun. Maybe I'll give the program a shot next."

As if summoned, Tony sidles over and grins down at her. "Why do that when perfection is right in front of you?"

Inara's sigh is all of her lost patience rolled into a single sound. "You're worse than an STD."

If anything, Tony's chest swells with pride. "If by 'STD,' you mean resilient, adaptable and sticks around after sex unless heavily medicated, then call me herpes."

"Jesus Christ." Inara can't help but laugh, and Tony shoots me a look of triumph.

I shake my head. If she isn't careful, he's going to wear her down sooner rather than later.

Jim closes the distance between us, and I lean into his warmth. "Speaking of the program, I have some more good news. I pled our case to the IPP committee and they agreed that no terms were violated since when you filled out the application, everything was valid. They're going to tweak some protocols going forward, but we're in the clear."

"Oh, thank God. Thank you for taking care of that." One of my last two stresses, gone for good. Now Jim and I can truly focus on each other.

Pressing a kiss against my shoulder, he murmurs, "My pleasure. So, excited about tomorrow?"

I look up at him, and one brow raises in question. "Duh. Marge is baking, and Inara is bringing the alcohol along with sparkling cider just for me." I lean in and whisper seductively, "We're having a tea party with Leslie, and we're pretty sure Fisher-Price is the perfect size for shots."

"Sounds like one hell of a bachelorette party." He chuckles as if he and the boys aren't going to be nearby, keeping an eye out.

I nod solemnly. "You have no idea. Marge says Leslie can have extra marshmallows in her hot chocolate. Shit's going to get real. We may even stay up past ten."

"You wild woman." He leans in, and I lose myself in the power of his kiss.

"Only for you," I purr against his lips and pull him down for more. In that moment of bliss, the world, both the good and the bad, takes a back seat to something so much sweeter, and completely of our own making.

THE END

If you enjoyed *Issued*, please take the time to leave a review!

Sign up for Tule's newsletter for more great reads and weekly deals!

If you enjoyed *Issued*, you'll love the next book in….

THE NAVY SEALS OF LITTLE CREEK SERIES

Book 1: *Issued*

Book 2: *Matched*

Available now at your favorite online retailer!

ABOUT THE AUTHOR

Paris Wynters is an adult romance author repped by Tricia Skinner at Fuse Literary. She lives on Long Island (in New York) with her family, which includes two psychotic working dogs. Paris is a graduate of Loyola University Chicago.

Paris and her son are nationally certified Search and Rescue personnel (she is a canine handler). She is a huge supporter of the military/veteran community. When not writing, Paris enjoys playing XBOX (she is a huge HALO fanatic and enjoys FORTNITE), watching hockey (Go Islanders), and trying new things like flying planes and taking trapeze classes.

Thank you for reading

ISSUED

If you enjoyed this book, you can find more from all our great authors at TulePublishing.com, or from your favorite online retailer.

TULE
PUBLISHING